THE GOLDEN FLEECE

Borgo Press Books by BRIAN STABLEFORD

*Alien Abduction: The Wiltshire Revelations * Balance of Power* (Daedalus Mission #5) * *The Best of Both Worlds and Other Ambiguous Tales * Beyond the Colors of Darkness and Other Exotica * Changelings and Other Metaphoric Tales * The City of the Sun* (Daedalus Mission #4) * *Complications and Other Science Fiction Stories * The Cosmic Perspective and Other Black Comedies Critical Threshold* (Daedalus Mission #2) * *The Cthulhu Encryption: A Romance of Piracy * The Cure for Love and Other Tales of the Biotech Revolution * The Dragon Man: A Novel of the Future * The Eleventh Hour * The Fenris Device* (Hooded Swan #5) * *Firefly: A Novel of the Far Future * Les Fleurs du Mal: A Tale of the Biotech Revolution * The Florians* (Daedalus Mission #1) * *The Gardens of Tantalus and Other Delusions * The Gates of Eden: A Science Fiction Novel * The Golden Fleece and Other Tales of the Biotech Revolution * The Great Chain of Being and Other Tales of the Biotech Revolution * Halycon Drift* (Hooded Swan #1) * *The Haunted Bookshop and Other Apparitions * In the Flesh and Other Tales of the Biotech Revolution * The Innsmouth Heritage and Other Sequels * Journey to the Core of Creation: A Romance of Evolution * Kiss the Goat: A Twenty-First-Century Ghost Story * Luscinia: A Romance of Nightingales and Roses * The Mad Trist: A Romance of Bibliomania * The Mind-Riders: A Science Fiction Novel * The Moment of Truth: A Novel of the Future * Nature's Shift: A Tale of the Biotech Revolution * An Oasis of Horror: Decadent Tales and Contes Cruels * The Paradise Game* (Hooded Swan #4) * *The Paradox of the Sets* (Daedalus Mission #6) * *The Plurality of Worlds: A Sixteenth-Century Space Opera * Prelude to Eternity: A Romance of the First Time Machine * Promised Land* (Hooded Swan #3) * *The Quintessence of August: A Romance of Possession * The Return of the Djinn and Other Black Melodramas * Rhapsody in Black* (Hooded Swan #2) * *Salome and Other Decadent Fantasies * Streaking: A Novel of Probability * Swan Song* (Hooded Swan #6) * *The Tree of Life and Other Tales of the Biotech Revolution * The Undead: A Tale of the Biotech Revolution * Valdemar's Daughter: A Romance of Mesmerism * War Games: A Science Fiction Novel * Wildeblood's Empire* (Daedalus Mission #3) * *The World Beyond: A Sequel to S. Fowler Wright's The World Below * Writing Fantasy and Science Fiction * Xeno's Paradox: A Tale of the Biotech Revolution * Zombies Don't Cry: A Tale of the Biotech Revolution*

THE GOLDEN FLEECE

AND OTHER TALES OF THE BIOTECH REVOLUTION

BRIAN STABLEFORD

THE BORGO PRESS

MMXII

THE GOLDEN FLEECE

FIRST EDITION

Published by Wildside Press LLC

www.wildsidebooks.com

THE GOLDEN FLEECE

CONTENTS

INTRODUCTION

This is the seventh collection of shorter "Tales of the Bio-tech Revolution" that I have published, the others being: *Sexual Chemistry* (Simon & Schuster UK, 1991), *Designer Genes* (Five Star, 2004), *The Cure for Love* (Borgo Press, 2007), *The Tree of Life* (Borgo Press, 2007), *In the Flesh* (Borgo Press, 2009) and *The Great Chain of Being* (Borgo Press, 2010). There have also been eleven novels of the same ilk: *Inherit the Earth* (Tor, 1998), *Architects of Emortality* (Tor, 1999), *The Fountains of Youth* (Tor, 2000), *The Cassandra Complex* (Tor, 2001), *Dark Ararat* (Tor, 2002), *The Omega Expedition* (Tor, 2002), *The Dragon Man* (Borgo Press, 2009), *The Undead* (Borgo Press, 2010; in a double volume with the novella *Les Fleurs du Mal*), *Xeno's Paradox* (Borgo Press, 2011), *Zombies Don't Cry* (Borgo Press, 2011) and *Nature's Shift* (Borgo Press, 2011). Many, but by no means all, of the stories in the series share a common future-historical background, an early version of which was first sketched out in a futurology book, *The Third Millennium: A History of the World 2000-3000*, written in collaboration with David Langford in 1983 and published by Knopf and Sidgwick & Jackson in 1985.

The train of thought transporting the stories has, therefore, now been running for more than a quarter of a century, and the dates attached to some of the earlier stories have already elapsed without any sign of the possibilities sketched therein materializing (the one obvious exception being the advent of Viagra, anticipated, although not under that brand name, in the story variously known as "Sexual Chemistry" and "A Career in Sexual Chemistry"). Although such dates are, in essence, arbitrary, progress in practical biotechnology has, indeed, been a trifle slower than I anticipated in 1985, and it now seems highly unlikely that its products will be able to make the kind of impact on the current phase of the unfolding ecocatastrophe that I once hoped it might. It is, of course, the general fate of possibilities that only a tiny minority ever come to fruition, but there are still grounds for hope (no matter how slim) that constructive biotechnology might eventually have a role to play in recovery from the Crash whose inevitability all the stories in the series anticipate, so I am not yet ready to consign the entre sequence to the rubbish heap of optimistic moonshine.

This collection includes the story that maps out the first revised version of the *Third Millennium* future history in the greatest detail, "Mortimer Gray's History of Death," the first version of which was drafted in April 1987. That version did not sell, and I revised it in 1994, increasing the wordage from 19,000 to 26,000, mostly by fleshing out the first and last chapters, which thus became a frame narrative of sorts. The revised version was published in the April 1995 issue of *Asimov's Science Fiction Magazine*. I subsequently expanded the story again in 1999, into the novel *The Fountains of Youth*, fleshing out all the chapters concerning the protagonist's own biography, thus altering the balance of the story very markedly, obliterating what little remained of the careful symmetry of the original version. Had the original version survived I might have been tempted to reprint it here instead of the published novella, but I no longer have a copy of it. The *Asimov's* version is probably the most widely-read of the stories in the series, being included in Gardner Dozois' *Best of the Year* collection and then in his *Best of the Best* sampler, but I thought it worth reprinting anyway, if only for the sake of completeness.

"Alfonso the Wise" was first published under the pseudonym Francis Amery in *Interzone* 105 (March 1996); it was one of two ultra-short stories that the editor asked me to produce in order to pad out the contents list of the issue in question, which was dominated by a very long novella (much longer than the various novellas of mine that the editor in question had previous rejected on the grounds that they were too long). It is admittedly trivial, but, again, I thought it worth reprinting on the grounds of completeness.

An abridged version of "Next to Godliness" was published in an anthology edited by Ian Whates, entitled *Celebration* (2008) and published by Newcon Press. As all regular sf readers will have noticed by now, the standard requested length for contributions to anthologies of original stories is 6,000 words, but I routinely exceed that, usually hoping to get away with 8,000 or even more. In this instance, alas, the editor demanded that I cut the product down to the required size, which I obligingly did, consoling myself with the thought that, one day, I would be able to reprint the unabridged version in a collection like this one.

"Some Like it Hot" was written in January 2008 in response to a request from an editor who was trying to assemble a collection of stories on the theme of global warming (which had been a constant feature of my vague future history since *The Third Millennium*, although I claim no credit for the anticipation, which was blatantly obvious even in the early 1980s to anyone but an idiot or a professional liar). The anthology was never published, probably because of the controversy deliberately stirred up by professional liars, and the story eventually appeared in *Asimov's* in the December 2009 issue.

The most recent story in the collection, "The Golden Fleece," written in the last days of 2011 and the early days of 2012, is original to this volume, largely because it overshot the initial target length of 6,000 words by such a ludicrously vast margin that there seemed to be no point in even trying to submit it to the market that I originally had in mind for it. Even as I realized that fact while being carried away during the white heat of the composition process, I consoled myself with the thought that I would at least be able to include it in a collection like this one.

I do not know whether there will be any further volumes in

the series, but as it is proverbially unwise ever to say never, I shall refrain from negative prognostication.

THE GOLDEN FLEECE

When Adrian told his Ph.D. supervisor, Professor Clark, that he'd been invited to the Savoy to meet Jason Jarndyke, the professor sighed.

"It wasn't me," the old man said.

Adrian knew what he meant. You couldn't apply for a job at Jarndyke Industries; you had to be recommended, or spotted by a professional headhunter. Professor Clark was denying that he'd been the one to put the bloodhounds on Adrian's trail.

"It's okay," Adrian assured him. "In fact, it's the perfect opportunity for me. I only hope I can impress him."

The professor took on the expression of a man who had just found half a caterpillar in his apple, but he controlled it swiftly. "If you think so," he said, implying that no sane man would. "But you have real talent. You could do *anything*."

He meant real talent as a genetic reverse engineer—the kind of talent you could take into the pharmaceutical industry, or retain in the upper echelons of Academe; the professor had never understood Adrian's *real* real talent. Few people did—but there was just a possibility that Jason Jarndyke might appreciate its potential results, even though he was reputed to be a crass businessman and an epitome of Yorkshire bluntness, with no talent at all but a genius for making money.

Adrian was pretty sure that he could make Jason Jarndyke money—*lots* of money—by means of his talent as a reverse engineer, but his real objectives lay far beyond that. They were vague, as yet, but he was sure that they would become clearer in time. The first step was to get a good and secure job, working in the field of the genetics of pigmentation. Once that base was secure, other possibilities would become visible, with the all the myriad blues of the sky to tempt and guide him. The future would be limitless.

Adrian figured that if the industrialist could only be persuaded to glimpse the prospect of the future bottom line that innate coloration would add to his products, Jarndyke would forgive him, not only for being a effete southerner and a confirmed esthete, but even, perhaps, for having ambitions beyond the confines of the textile industry—although he hoped to keep those further ambitions under wraps to begin with, and only to confess them, as and when necessary, by degrees.

"Well," said Professor Clark, sighing again. "I suppose the only advice I can give you is to watch out for Medea."

"Who's Medea?" Adrian asked.

Professor Clark raised his eyes to the heavens. All serious scientists cultivated some area of humanistic interest in order to deflect of suspicion of terminal dullness. Clark was fond of mythological references. "Jason's wife," he said, wearily.

Even Adrian could get the gist of that, although he knew that he would have to use a search engine to find out exactly what crimes the mythical Medea was supposed to have committed, if he could ever be bothered—but he couldn't help putting on an ingenuous expression and replying: "I believe that Mrs. Jarndyke's name is Angelica." He had no definite knowledge, but presumed that she must be an effete southerner too. Even in this day and age, no one in Yorkshire would ever name a girl "Angelica."

The professor sighed again, and muttered something that might or might not have been a reference to "lamb to the slaughter"—which, in turn, might or might not have been an attempt at a witty play on words based on the fact that Jason Jarndyke's most profitable mills produced sheepskin by the mile, without the necessity of employing actual sheep.

* * * * * * *

In fact, Jason Jarndyke didn't seem quite as bad as the scurrilous newsfeeds painted him—but that shouldn't really have been surprising, even to an *ingénu*, and Adrian scolded himself for having fallen victim to web-spun prejudice in spite of knowing better.

Jarndyke was a big man, to be sure, with rather coarse features, and he spoke with a broad Yorkshire accent—which had become rare, except as deliberate affectation, since exposure to TV had begun smoothing all regional dialects into subtlety. Once he'd been in the man's company for half an hour, though, Adrian no longer believed that Jarndyke's accent was an affectation, any more than his renowned bluntness was mere rudeness with a tacit apology in tow. Jarndyke gave every sign of being honest, sincere and intelligent.

The textile-manufacturer didn't get down to business right away. For a while, they ate and drank and chatted. Adrian knew that he was being subtly pumped and weighed up all the while, but he didn't mind. He had secrets, of a sort, but he didn't think that they were the kind of secrets that would compromise his usefulness to Jarndyke Industries, and he knew that it was in his interests to be accurately measured for his true worth in purely scientific terms, or even terms of vulgar gold, so he answered all the subtle queries honestly.

Jarndyke was in informal mode, so he wasn't calling Adrian "Mr. Stamford," in the same way that Adrian was addressing him as "Mr. Jarndyke, but he wasn't calling him "Adrian" either. He had settled for the patronizing device of calling him "Son," which Adrian was trying not to mind too much—and succeeding, because he rather liked the old sod, all things considered.

When Jarndyke eventually decided to get to the point, he headed straight for it. "Okay, Son," he said, "you're a bright lad, so you know exactly why I'm interested in you. I've helped to bring about a revolution in the textile industry by growing fabrics from tissue cultures: first wools, then silks. In terms of texture, my products are first-rate, but thus far, I've remained reliant on the traditional dyeing industry for coloring my fabrics. Even if it hadn't been for the provocation of all the stupid media jokes about my supposed quest for the sodding Golden Fleece, genetically-determined pigmentation would be the natural next step in the process."

He tapped Adrian's CV, which was on the table in front of him, with the knuckle of his right forefinger. "I won't try to bullshit you, Son: according to this, and what my spies tell me, you're the best man in England right now to pick up that particular torch and run with it. For that reason, I'd like to hire you, but first, tell me why a bright young reverse engineer like you—a genius of sorts—chose to specialize in a field like pigmentation instead of joining the great crusade to rid the world of disease and make us all immortal."

"You can *see* the results of coloration genes," Adrian said baldly, as he always did when asked that question. "There's no waiting around while the DNA strings you've designed and the proteins they produce go through elaborate testing schemes administered by bureaucrats. Then again, the delicate sculpting of the relevant proteins, not merely to duplicate but also to enhance the extraordinarily elaborate palette of nature's colors, is a technical process that poses fundamental challenges of method and understanding. The fact that you can see the results immediately when working with pigmentation genes, and connect up cause and effect directly, helps to provide a useful insight into the mysterious workings of amino-acid destiny, which is transferable to other areas where the evidence is far less obvious. Mendel started off the entire science of genetics by studying the heredity of manifest characteristics like color, because it was the most practical starting-point. It's still an important gateway to understanding."

"Gateway to understanding," Jarndyke echoed, pensively. "Very neat. Cut the bullshit, Son, and tell me the truth. You're too bright to know that I wouldn't look behind this thing"—

he tapped the CV again—"because you know as well as I do that what's really important is always what's left out. The job offer stands, so you don't have anything to worry about on that score. I just want to know what you're about before you join the crew of the Airedale *Argo*—and I want to hear it from you, as straight as you can."

Adrian gulped—not because he hadn't expected to have to come clean eventually, and not because there was any reason why he shouldn't do so right away, but simply because he wasn't used to being hustled like that. He was used to doing things at his own pace, and he had learned to be wary of letting his secret out too soon in potentially-hostile environments. Jarndyke obviously knew the gist of it, so the sensible thing to do was, indeed, to give his future employer his own account of the truth, and to try to make him understand.

"I do have my own personal reasons for being interested in the genetics of pigmentation," he admitted.

"Well, don't beat around the bush, Son—we don't do that up north. What are they?"

Adrian didn't beat around the bush. "Sight," he said, launching forth into a familiar argument, "is a three-phase process. People differ in all three respects. Phase one is what the retina can register; all eyes are different. You doubtless remember the old schoolboy question about whether what you see as red is the same as what I see as red, even though we've both learned to *call* it red. Physiology tells us that it's a good question. Different people's retinas really do differ in their sensitivity to particular wavelengths and the neuronal signals they transmit in response."

"So?" Jarndyke prompted.

Adrian didn't want to be hurried; if he was going to give Jarndyke the explanation, he wanted to do it his way. "The second phase," he said, "is the other end of the neuronal chain: what the cells of the brain pick up from the signal and how they process it. Everybody's brain is slightly different; identical signals, if there were any, don't always produce the identical results in making raw information available to consciousness."

"Which is phase three," Jarndyke put in, to demonstrate that he was keeping up. "Different minds, different interpretations again. Some people are color blind. Some people have no taste—I'm one of them, according to my wife. This I know. So what? Not in terms of philosophical paradoxes, but in terms of material difference."

"People differ in their perception of color and sensitivity to its nuances," Adrian said, refusing to be hurried, but now deliberately slanting the argument in a direction that might seem relevant to the industrialist, "but the number of people whose physiology makes them objectively incapable of discriminations—as in color blindness—is relatively small. Most insensitivity occurs at the level of consciousness. The individual's brain can discriminate, and does—but the mind takes no notice. Lots of people are unaware of color clashes when they dress, or when they look at other people's costumes—but the fact that they're consciously unaware doesn't mean that they're immune to the subtle effects of color that they're registering physiologically. It really does make a psychological difference what colors you put on your bedroom walls, whether you're consciously aware of it or not. You really can be driven mad by creepy wallpaper. And you might not know, when you look at someone else's outfit, what message it's sending to your brain—but that doesn't mean that it isn't making a difference to your perception of them, and hence to your attitudes and your treatment of them. Power-dressing works, especially if it's cleverly color-coordinated. Color matters, Mr. Jarndyke, in textiles as in everything else. Esthetics matter. Some people might not know exactly how or why they matter, and they might sneer at the people who can bring those things to the level of consciousness, but what we see and what we wear makes far more difference than insensitive people are able to see."

Jarndyke seemed to be busy thinking about that, and thinking hard. Not wanting to let silence fall, Adrian added: "Your business sense and the inventive acumen of your reverse engineers have made you the most successful textile manufacturer in the world, Mr. Jardyke. As you just said, in terms of efficiency of production and texture, your wools, silks and hybrids are near-perfect. In terms of the sense of touch, they're practically unbeatable, but in terms of the sense of sight—especially color—they have a long way to go."

"We're supposed to be talking about you, Son, not me," Jarndyke pointed out. "Personal reasons?"

"That's right," Adrian replied, gathering his courage. "Some people have perfect pitch—they can hear the music more clearly and more subtly than their fellows, because they can discriminate the notes more precisely. I have perfect color sensation—or, at least, far better color sensation than the vast majority of people. My retinas are first-rate in that respect, my brain too, but most importantly, I'm fully conscious of what they're registering. I don't say that there aren't people in the world even more sensitive than I am, but I'm plenty good enough to do anything you need me to do."

Jarndyke frowned at that. "I've told you, Son," he said, "that you don't need the sales pitch. I know you can make me money, with or without being able to see twice as many colors as the man in the street. I gather that you've had difficulty in the past convincing people that you really can see things they can't?"

Adrian nodded. "Some people," he admitted, "think I'm... well, bullshitting. Seeing is believing, they reckon, and if they can't see something, they can't believe in it."

Jarndyke nodded slowly. "But you've met other people who can make the same discriminations?" he said.

"After a fashion," Adrian admitted. "I've run into others who are better than average, but I've never actually met anyone with my degree of sensitivity—not in the flesh. I know they exist, though, because I can see it in their works. Claude Monet. Dante Gabriel Rossetti. Caravaggio."

"Painters."

"That's right. They're probably not the only people who can reflect their perception in their work—some fashion designers can surely do it too—but painters are the most obvious."

"Why didn't you become a painter?"

The bluntness of the question surprised Adrian slightly, but he met it with his customary wry smile. "Because I can't paint," he said. "I can see, but I don't have the hand-eye coordination that would allow me to reproduce what I see. I can visualize shapes very well, even in three dimensions, but I can't reproduce them with my incompetent fingers and a pencil or a brush. I don't even have the kind of design-control that would allow me to be an adept abstract expressionist, like Jackson Pollock. Sometimes, I think that I'm only half the person I might have been, with only half a talent, but I'm not entirely certain that the painters were that much luckier. After all, the number of people who can measure their true achievement—consciously, at any rate—is very small. Can I talk about textiles again now? I know I don't need the sales pitch, but I really would like you to understand where I might fit in with your enterprise."

Jarndyke frowned, and his mouth twisted into what might have been an expression of annoyance, but he nodded his shaggy head. "Go on," he said.

"In the beginning," Adrian said, "what I can do for you is help to produce a basic color range for your various fabrics. I'm a geneticist; I don't expect to be involved in the tailoring end of your operation. I really am interested in the psychology of color as well as its genetics, though, and the way that the two intersect and interact. I'd like to do pure research in that area, for my own esthetic satisfaction—but I'd like it, too, if the results of that research had some practical application for you, and I think they might.

"In the fullness of time, I hope that I might be able to help your designers understand what they need, in terms of coloring your fabrics for particular styles of tailoring. I won't be able to give you natural patterns for a while, yet—even stripes and polka-dots might take a decade or so—when I can, I think I'll be able to work out the best color combinations. I hope that I can not only give you the best reds, the best blues, the best browns and the best blacks, but good combinations and designs—and good advice as to how to use them for maximum subliminal effect.

"I hope that you'll see the effect on your balance-sheet of my initial labors by the end of next year, but that might be only the beginning. With the opportunities you can give me...well, I really don't know as yet what might be possible, but I really would like the chance to find out. There's a lifetime's work in it, and more, but I'm keen to make what progress I can. I can't paint—but I'm a scientist, and I can hope to do what the painters never could: understand. I could do that sort of research in Academe, I suppose, but I really do think I'd have more incentives and more opportunities—and I'm not just talking about salary and equipment—working in your industry, Mr. Jarndyke. That's why I was so pleased to hear from you, and why I'm so grateful to your spies. That's not bullshit—it's the truth."

Jarndyke's eyes looked him up and down, and Adrian felt that every physical symptom of his youth and innocence was being interrogated, skeptically. He knew that he didn't really look the part. He didn't *look* like an Argonaut of science, let alone the possessor of a superpower. He knew full well that, in terms of Yorkshire parlance, he probably looked like "a bit of a pansy"—but every word he'd said really was true, and he hoped that he'd said enough to make Jason Jarndyke doubt the evidence of his own unpolished eyes, and the blunt common sense that guided them.

"So," Jason Jarndyke said, eventually, "you're telling me that, given time you can make me the *authentic* Golden Fleece." He didn't smile ironically, as Professor Clark would undoubtedly have done. "Not just golden, but magical."

"You could put it like that," Adrian conceded. "At least, I can try."

"Then I really don't have any alternative but to hire you, do I?" the businessman said, casually. "And not merely to hire you, but to let you go your own mysterious way. Okay—I'll play. There are three conditions, though."

"No problem," Adrian assured him, but added, for form's

sake: "What are they?"

"One: you move to headquarters, in Airedale. I need you working in *my* lab, behind *my* security-wall, under *my* beady eye. No telecommuting, no gallivanting, no loose talk. We live in an era of intense industrial espionage, and I'm in a highly competitive business. Two: you'd better deliver on your promises, Son, because I don't like to be disappointed, and I really hate it if I find out that someone's been bullshitting me, because it hurts my pride. Once you sign on to work with me, one way or another, you won't ever work for anyone else."

Adrian had already nodded twice, having expected nothing less, and was poised to nod again when everything changed. "Three," said, Jason Jardyke, in exactly the same tone, "you keep your fucking hands off my wife."

Shocked to the core, Adrian blinked hard several times, and forgot to nod.

Then Jarndyke grinned, broadly, and said: "I knew I could throw you off your stride, you cocky little sod. Just winding you up, Son—except, of course, that if you were to violate that partic-ular condition, I'd have to kill you. There are firing offences, and there are shooting offenses." He was still beaming, as if to make it obvious that it was a joke—a Yorkshire joke, orientated to a peculiar sense of humor, but a joke nevertheless—but there was something false in the smile, as if there were some secret behind it that Jason Jarndyke was nursing carefully.

Adrian didn't think that mattered. He felt that he had coped with that aspect of his inadequacies very well, this far, and didn't expect any significant problems in future, even with regard to the kind of Medea that Dante Gabriel Rossetti might have invested with all kinds of subtle charms, imperceptible to the common eye.

"I'm sure I can comply with all your requirements," Adrian said, all too conscious of how frail his voice sounded, all of a sudden. But then, he'd never claimed to have perfect pitch—merely command over a visual spectrum more complete than Isaac Newton had ever been able to see.

"Good," said Jarndyke, extending his meaty hand to be shaken. "We have a deal. Enough of piddling billions—let's make me a *real* fortune."

* * * * * * *

Relocation from London to Jarndyke's estate, in the Aire valley between Bingley and Shipley, was easy enough and almost painless. Adrian didn't really have anyone to say goodbye to except Professor Clark, and the stuff he couldn't fit into the removal van was just stuff, of no intimate significance. He was aware of how sad that might make him seem to an objective but color-insensitive eye, but he didn't care. It wasn't his fault that he was an orphan, after all, and even it was his fault that he had no friends and no girl-friend, he didn't think that it was really a *fault*, as such. Yes, he'd been married to his studies with an obsessive intensity, for seven long years since turning eighteen and leaving school, but that had been required by his life-plan, which couldn't be similar to other people's life-plans, because he wasn't like other people—because he could really *see*, and they couldn't.

Anyway, he thought, *if you're going to be obsessed, you have to take it seriously, don't you? No half-measures.*

Getting settled in to the new labs and the new flat were a little more difficult, because Adrian wasn't all that fond of changes of scene. It wasn't that the flat had nasty wallpaper, or that the new people crowding the labs were unfriendly. Indeed, the wallpaper was a nicely icy shade of egg-shell blue with unobtrusive silver arabesques, and his new colleagues, including the hot-shots from various parts of south-east Asia, seemed to take a conscientious pride in trying to live up to the local delusion that Yorkshire folk were famed for their hospitality. The problem was in him, and the purely psychological discomfort that descended upon him like a particular shade of indigo when his work and domestic routines needed retuning—but because he was conscious of the problem, and knew that it was a problem, he knew that he'd be able to cope, given time.

In consequence, he set about using his time methodically and effectively. He introduced himself to all his colleagues, and tried to figure out how they all fitted into the great genetic project of producing sheet fabrics without such inconveniences as breeding lambs, feeding them, shearing them and then doing all the mysterious things to the bundled fleeces that had once been necessary to turn them into merino sweaters, coats and skirts. He visited the factories too, which were all lined up along the banks of the Aire, because water was their most crucial limiting factor, given the abundance of atmospheric carbon dioxide and the ease of producing artificial light with any spectral composition the doctor ordered.

He allocated five hours a day to the intensive study of all the data hidden behind Jarndyke's security wall, and was politely amazed by its extent, its complexity, and its sheer beauty. Adrian could visualize three-dimensional organic molecules, and even though their colors were invisible in chemical diagrams and computer simulations, he was still sensitive to the esthetics of their topology. He knew—not thought, but *knew*—that DNA was the most beautiful molecule in existence, the standard by which all others had to be judged, just as he knew that there were seven shades of improvement on chlorophyll's green in its super-efficient artificial rivals, especially the ones that the unwittingly half-blind thought of simply as "black."

He could only allocate five hours a day to that essential work because he had to dedicate a further five to setting up his own projects—which was not just a matter of setting up his molecule-modeling programs and establishing a pipeline by which cyberspatial planning could be turned into solid product, but also involved such messy supplements as interviewing and selecting assistants capable of working under his direction, and building them into a team.

Adrian hated messy work; it was too time-consuming— and there were, after all, only twelve hours in a working day, because he had to sleep for eight, having long since given up on trying to train himself to get by on four, and he needed a further four for eating, relaxation and esthetic sensation. Some politicians, he knew, got by on five hours sleep and no relaxation or esthetic sensation at all, but they were just imbeciles who did nothing but messy work—and badly to boot—while he was a true scientist, and a true seer. He had to look after his brain. That meant treating it right in all respects, not just making sure that it got an adequate dose of all the right oils and minerals.

Jason Jarndyke welcomed him when he first arrived, but didn't keep looking over his shoulder thereafter—not obtrusively, at any rate. For the best part of a fortnight, Adrian hardly caught a fleeting glimpse of his employer in the distance, but he knew that it was only a matter of time before he received his first Official Visit. Inevitably, the moment came—but Jarndyke was obviously sufficiently familiar with the new routine that Adrian had set up to slide into one of its interstices, so as not to throw him off his stride.

"How's it going, Son?" the big man asked.

"I'm getting a grip, Mr. Jarndyke," Adrian assured him. "I think I might be ready to set up some experimental runs in a mock-up shed within a month. If they go well, I'll probably be able to bring you a proposal for industrial incorporation in... maybe another five weeks, but say six to be on the safe side. Co-adaptation to your tissue-culture genomes shouldn't be a problem—your genomic designers have done a fine job, fundamentally as well as phenotype-wise."

"Don't be in too much of a hurry, Son," Jarndyke devised him. "This is a marathon, not a sprint. I understand that these things take their own time. Rome wasn't built in a day—and the poor buggers couldn't make it last even with the time they actually took. We're better than that, and we're not slapdash. We want product, but we don't want hitches. Settle down. My spies tell me you're working way too hard."

"I don't think so," Adrian said.

"And you're one of those silly sods who won't ever be told—I know that. I've got half a hundred of your type in the labs already; you probably know who I mean by now. You really do need to get out more, socialize a little. This place might not be London, but it's not a bloody cemetery."

"I've been to see the Hockneys at Salt's Mill," Adrian said, defensively, although he wasn't entirely sure why he needed to be defensive.

"Bully for you," said Jarndyke, with a sigh, like a man who was used to being deliberately misunderstood. "Okay, your own time's your own time. I don't have any right to have an opinion about it, and I'd be an idiot if I started trying to turn my oddball geniuses into ordinary human beings. Come to dinner on Sunday though. Proper dinner—two o'clock. Spend the afternoon at the Old Manse. And don't even think of trying to say no."

Adrian hadn't been thinking of making any such attempt. Sunday afternoon was usually study time, but he wasn't inflexible. Taking obsession seriously was one thing, but being imprisoned by it was something else. Complying with the boss's requests wasn't really socializing, in any case: it was part of the job.

"Thanks very much," he said.

"You don't have to dress up," Jarndyke assured him. "We're very informal. You don't have to bring a bottle, either—I've got the best cellar in England. Yorkshire, anyway. Just turn up, enjoy the grub—and for God's sake try to relax."

Adrian nodded.

Jarndyke had actually turned away, having reached the bottom line, business-wise, but he suddenly turned back. "Have you ever seen the Rothko Chapel in Houston, Texas?" he asked. He had a real talent for the unexpected, when he applied himself.

Adrian blinked several times. "As a matter of fact, yes," he said. "I went to reverse engineering conference in Houston a couple of years ago, and made a special trip."

"I thought you might have done," Jarndyke said, obviously having taken note of the conference in Adrian's CV. "What did you think?"

"Magnificent," Adrian said. "Brilliant work. I'm not sure

I appreciated the religious context, being an atheist, but the artwork...I couldn't help thinking of it as an anticipation of the esthetics of artificial photosynthetics—I find APs beautiful too, if skillfully applied."

Jarndyke nodded his head, as if he'd expected to hear exactly that answer, bizarre as it was, in exactly those terms. "Angie dragged me to see them," he said, thoughtfully. "To me, they looked like so many black rectangles. I just couldn't see what all the fuss was about. Emperor's new clothes, I thought. Nothing there, but these arty types pretend, just to make suckers of the rest of us. I was wrong, eh?"

"Yes, sir," said Adrian, not beating about the bush. "They're not just black. There are other colors in there, if you have the eyes and mind to see them. They really are superb—but it's not your fault if you can't perceive it. It's your eyes, or your brain...."

"Or my stupid consciousness," Jarndyke concluded. "Don't have to sugar-coat it, Son. I know my limitations. Might have a treat for you Sunday. Might not—how can I tell?—but something of interest, anyhow. I'd value your honest opinion—I really would."

Adrian took the inference that Jarndyke had bought a Rothko—or, at least, that he'd put together an art collection of some sort, as all billionaires seemed to feel obliged to do, whether they had any eye for art or not. Apparently, Angelica Jarndyke had an eye for art, or thought she did, and had probably guided her husband's purchases, as many billionaires' wives seemed to feel obliged to do.

"I look forward to it, sir," Adrian said, not entirely dishonestly.

"You can call me Jayjay, now," the industrialist said. "Once you've been invited to Sunday dinner, you're one of the family."

* * * * * * *

Adrian didn't tell anyone that he had been invited to "dinner" at the "Old Manse" on Sunday afternoon, but Jardyke's security walls were specifically designed to keep secrets from getting out, while permitting their free circulation within. That circulation was supposed to be on a need-to-know basis, but research scientists were notoriously liberal in their interpretation of what they needed to know.

"Don't worry about the expedition to Bleak House, Ade," said a Singaporean, who probably hadn't been called Chester Hu by his parents but had followed the common custom of adopting a Western forename for convenience, and who had not been invited to call Adrian "Ade." "It's just a *rite de passage*, to welcome you to the extended family. Watch out for Medea, though."

It was a joke, of course, of the same silly ilk as the Dickensian reference, but because it was the second time that Adrian had heard it, and was a little worried about getting through the *rite de passage* successfully, he paused to wonder whether there might something behind it, and wondered whether Professor Clark's joke had really been improvised out of mythological thin air rather than distant rumor.

"Why?" he asked.

"Oh, don't be scared. She won't try to seduce you, pretty as you are. She's a dutiful trophy wife, faithful to her bargain, and she obviously likes masculine men as well as rich ones—but she's a little crazy, is all. People would probably have nicknamed her Medea anyway, given all the newsfeed jokes about Jason and the quest for the Golden Fleece, and given that Jayjay plays along with it with his Airedale *Argo* nonsense, but...well, I'm not sure that she doesn't think that she actually *is* a witch. Not gene-twisting witchcraft, of course—genuine mumbo-jumbo."

"She has no reason to put a spell on me," Adrian said colorlessly.

"Except that you're the hero who's actually promised to deliver the authentic Golden Fleece," Dr. Hu reminded him. "No—just joking. She's just a little weird, as I say. Don't let her put you off. It's Jayjay you have to impress—and you haven't put a foot wrong so far, Golden Boy."

"Weird how?" Adrian wanted to know, for safety's sake.

"She'll look at you in a funny way—and then, if she doesn't like what she sees, won't look at you again. She doesn't like trivia, or dressing things up—won't have knick-knacks on the mantelpieces, apparently, or paintings on the walls. It's Bleak House up there, as I said. All plain wood paneling—brown by the acre, not a splash of color; more like a monastery than a house. You'll find it even duller than I did, I dare say. Must be other eccentricities, but those are the ones you'll notice. Don't worry about it. I'd say, turn a blind eye, but that's not really your thing, is it?" He smiled.

Adrian ignored the gibe. "What about Mr. Jarndyke's art collection?" he asked.

"He doesn't have an art collection," Hu informed him. "Maybe he wanted one—she probably did—but if so, they shelved the project. Artistic disagreements, at a guess—real ones, not euphemistic ones. Angie paints, so rumor has it—actually has a barn of sorts for her own private space, that no one but her ever goes into, where she does whatever witchy stuff she does, but there are none of her paintings on the walls of the Hall if she does fancy herself as a painter. Not downstairs, at any rate. Maybe they're too pornographic to be allowed out of the bedroom."

Adrian was puzzled, seeing a mystery in the evolving pattern. Chester Hu didn't seem to think that there was anything to what he'd said but a report of arbitrary eccentricity, but Adrian wasn't at all sure, now that he could put what Jason Jarndyke had said to him into a different informational context. Angelica Jarndyke had "dragged" her husband to see the Rothko chapel, but wouldn't tolerate paintings on the walls of their home...not in the spaces that visitors saw, at any rate. She was "rumored" to be a painter herself, but the likes of Chester Hu had never seen any of her work. No one was allowed in her "barn," but Jason Jarndyke had "a treat" for him after Sunday dinner—or maybe not. Something that might interest him, at any rate.

Perhaps, Adrian thought, Professor Clark's Medea joke

hadn't simply been a matter of mythological free association after all. And perhaps Jason Jarndyke's third condition hadn't simply been a random shot aimed to shake his exaggerated complacency and make him blink.

Adrian was almost tempted to ring Professor Clark to ask him for a little more insight into the legend of the Golden Fleece, because he remembered something in that connection, very vaguely, about dragon's teeth. He didn't. He didn't even bother to interrogate a search engine. This was the twenty-first century, after all, and the only magic abroad in the world was that of genetic reverse engineering. A genius of that sort need have no fear of "real" witchcraft.

* * * * * * *

Jason Jarndyke's "Old Manse" was neither old, nor a manse. Not literally, at any rate. It had been completed less than ten years before, having been seven years in the construction, to a design that Jarndyke had imposed on his reluctant architects by sheer will-power and bribery. Unkind people had called it a Folly, but unkind people always said that, and even if it had been a Folly, that didn't mean to say that it was unesthetic. Adrian knew that they could be grandeur in a Folly, and magnificence, even when there was an abundance of mere folly.

In fact, he rather liked the look of the house on top of the moor, although architecture wasn't really "his thing," as Chester Hu would have put it, and fake Portland Stone from northern France definitely wasn't his color. He preferred the honest blacks of the old stone walls on the moors and the old stone buildings in Shipley and Bingley, and thought it a pity that they were gradually being swept away by decrepitude and demolition, and replaced with paler imitations. The Old Manse was an honest fake, not trying to be anything else. Adrian liked it, as seen from distance, and he still liked it at close range, as seen from the driveway, up which he walked because he'd never owned a car and didn't want to face the embarrassment of asking some flunkey where he could put his bicycle. From the outside, the house wasn't bleak in his eyes.

Even though architecture wasn't really his thing, one of Adrian's carefully-planned esthetic excursions, while he was at a GRE conference in Derby, had been to see the site on the Derwent where the nineteenth-century industrialist Richard Arkwright had begun the first revolution of the textile industry, introducing automated machinery into his water-mills, and then replacing water-power with steam engines. The factories had been partially restored as a museum, and the house—the original version of which had been burned down—had served time as a hotel before being fully converted into a museum, but the ghost of Arkwright's intention had still been visible.

As the richest man in the north of England, and the effective kingpin of the *nouveau riche* of the First Industrial Revolution, Arkwright had wanted a palace from which an emperor might look down on his domain, and the source of his own magnificence—a modern palace, of course, not a mere copy of some Roman ruin or some scaled-down Versailles, but a palace nevertheless. Jason Jarndyke's Old Manse wasn't nearly as pretentious as Arkwright's Victorian colossus, but that was just a symptom of marching time: its stone walls and steeply-pitched slate roofs embodied, in essence, the same dream of domination and imperial justice. Not vulgar wealth, or even brute power— Jarndyke wasn't as unsubtle as that—but a testament of *merit*, of due deserts duly enjoyed.

Adrian could appreciate that, and approve of it; he wasn't one of those scientific geniuses who despise men who "make money out of the inventions of others," because he knew how unusual the talent was that such triumphs required—and he knew that Jason Jarndyke, although by no means free of egomania, had his vanity under disciplined control.

Inside, there were, as Chester Hu had said, "acres of brown." Adrian didn't mind that, either, although it did seem austere, and he could understand why some people might find it bleak. Personally, he liked wood, especially old wood, with swirling grain and knots. Whoever had cut and organized the paneling hadn't had perfect sight, but he hadn't been a mug or a skimper.

Anyway, Adrian thought, *better austere and natural than contrived and awful.* He remembered what Chester had said, *en passant*, about Mr. and Mrs. Jarndyke probably having agreed to disagree about matters of decoration, and deciding on minimalism as the best compromise. Adrian got the same impression. They had probably wanted different things, and had decided on neither. He could approve of that.

It was obvious, too, why Dr. Hu had described Angelica Jarndyke as a "trophy wife." In terms of appearances, she was a cliché: fifteen or twenty years younger than her husband, and radiantly beautiful, even now that she was past forty—so beautiful, in fact, as to be out of anyone's league but a millionaire's, at least—and carefully polished to boot, to the extent of seeming an item of artifice, more showpiece than person. Her dress sense was perfect, even though she was displaying "casual," and Adrian perceived at first glance that she was an expert in applying make-up; he had never seen artifice so flawless—but he had had a sheltered upbringing, in that regard, and he knew it.

Angelica Jarndyke was the first trophy wife he had ever actually met, and he knew that all the ones he'd seen in photographs had been airbrushed, so he was slightly surprised to find that she wouldn't have needed airbrushing. If he didn't find her attractive, it was only because he had trained himself, for reasons of self-defense, not to find any woman attractive, in herself. One of the advantages of enhanced color sensation, he'd found, was that a supersensitivity to color allowed him to look beyond the crude kinds of visual cues that stimulated inconvenient hormonal surges. The kind of beauty that formulated his truth was not the coarse beauty of common-or-garden lust.

At least, he liked to think so.

When he was formally introduced to Angelica Jarndyke, Adrian, not knowing what to do, contented himself with a stiff and awkward bow. She looked him up and down, with just a little too much attention. Adrian had expected—hoped, even—that she would simply give him the once over and think: *Just one more mad scientist for Jayjay's collection*, but that didn't seem to be what she was thinking at all. Unfortunately, Adrian couldn't read what the thinking actually was in her lack of indifference, so it just made him feel slightly paranoid. Obviously, Jason Jarndyke had told her something about the latest recruit to his team of geniuses that had been intended to provoke her interest, and it had not been entirely without effect. In all probability, Adrian thought, she wasn't at all sure that she wanted her interest provoked, and resented the fact that it had been.

Even so, and somewhat to his relief, once she had given him a long hard look, Mrs. Jarndyke went on to do exactly what Chester Hu had predicted, and did not look directly at him again throughout the entire meal. That gave him pause to relax, and to avoid looking at her. He concentrated his attention on Jason Jarndyke, the man he was supposed to impress, the helmsman of his destiny.

The cuisine was basic, but top quality. Adrian had never tasted a Yorkshire pudding that hadn't come out of a freezer-bag, and he had to admit that there was a reward in authenticity in that case, as in so many others. The beef was tissue-cultured, of course—there was no point in taking "authenticity" to absurd lengths—but it was top quality, and Adrian would have been willing to bet that it came from cells descended from a local breed, not Aberdeen Angus. He was no wine expert, but he couldn't find any fault with Jarndyke's much-vaunted cellar.

There were no other guests at the table. Adrian knew that the Jarndykes had two children, but there was no evidence of their presence in the house, and Adrian assumed that they must both be away at a fancy prep school, being groomed for Eton or Oundle. Because Angelica Jarndyke made little effort to fulfill her duties as a hostess conversion-wise, and Adrian was too shy to do anything but react to what was said to him, Jason Jarndyke had to guide the chatter and do most of the talking himself, but he was obviously used to that.

The industrialist talked and talked and talked, but he avoided being boring with practiced ease. He didn't come across as too much of a boor, nor as overly arrogant, in spite of his cultivated bluntness and natural ebullience. He discussed current events and future possibilities—in a general sense rather than a specific one—with equal ease, and reminisced blithely without any crass braggadocio. The further the meal went, the more Adrian came to like his new employer, and the more comfortable he began to feel in his presence—until the coffee was saved, and Jarndyke changed the subject without warning, as he was prone to do.

"Angie thinks you're bullshitting me," he said, suddenly. "Not about being a genius geneticist—she's prepared to believe that you can deliver me a Golden Fleece, of sorts—but about the other stuff. I told her what you said about the Rothko chapel, but she thinks you're bluffing, just like I thought she was. She doesn't want to show you any of her paintings, because she thinks you'll bullshit her too, the way half a dozen other so-called art experts have. She doesn't want that. Claims to hate flattery, although I keeping telling her that when people say she's beautiful, it's not flattery because it's the simple truth. So you might not get your treat, unless you can persuade her that it's worth a go."

Adrian made an effort to try to look Angelica Jarndyke in the eyes, but she wouldn't meet his gaze. She had blue eyes, but they were a darker shade than his. She had blonde hair, but it was a lighter shade than his. She and he couldn't have passed for mother and son, even if she'd been old enough—which she wasn't, quite.

Adrian considered going through the whole rigmarole that he'd spun for Jarndyke at the Savoy, but he knew that the old man would have repeated all of that to her, accurately enough to get the gist across. He thought it best to go the philosophical route, with a bit of allegory thrown in.

"The thing about the Emperor's new clothes," he said, "is that the crowd really might have been unable to see them, even if they were real. Not because the members of the crowd were stupid, or uncultured, but because they simply didn't have the right neurophysiological equipment. Imagine the predicament of some poor fellow who, when the kid shouted out: 'The Emperor's got no clothes,' wanted to shout out: 'Yes he has, and they're beautiful! The tailors are right, and they're men of genius. That's the finest suit that any emperor ever had to wear.' What could he possibly say to convince the crowd, knowing that the majority was bound to be against him? How could he ever convince them that he really could see the suit, in all its glory, and wasn't simply crazy or—as Mr. Jarndyke would say—bullshitting? He'd be like the sighted man in H. G. Wells's 'Country of the Blind,' impotent to persuade his hosts that he was anything but a deluded fool, impending rockslide or no impending rockslide. And yet...perhaps the crowd should have been prepared to hear him out. They wouldn't have needed to give him the benefit of the doubt—the *admission* of doubt would have been something, in itself."

Angelica Jarndyke did condescend to look at him then, but not with any sympathy. "I've always thought that the child in the story was a disgrace to youth," she said. "What he should have shouted was: 'Who cares whether the old fool has any clothes on or not? He's the emperor—roll out the guillotine, strike up the *Marseillaise* and full speed ahead for democracy.'"

Her husband laughed. Adrian didn't, although he wasn't at all sure that it wasn't a diplomatic error not to go along with the joke and let the whole issue of who could see what be swept under the carpet and forgotten. He hadn't dared study Angelica Jarndyke as minutely as she'd studied him when they'd first been confronted with one another, and he didn't dare to now, because he knew that staring at someone as beautiful as her was always a *faux pas*, but he tried now to take a better measure of her, covertly.

Then he pointed at one of the panels on the wall behind her head. "That one's wrong, isn't it?" he said. "The designer did a pretty good job with the rest, but that was a slip. Maybe he couldn't find one to fit the scheme and improvised—or maybe he did it deliberately, knowing that ninety-nine people in a hundred would only see a sea of brown, and that most of the one per cent wouldn't know exactly what was wrong, or why, but would just be subtly unsettled by it."

Angelica Jarndyke turned her head. She didn't have to ask him which panel he meant. "I've always thought that it was a deliberate mistake," she said, biting her lip slightly, at the risk of disturbing the gloss. "Cocking a snook, so to speak."

"I can sympathize with that," Adrian said.

She thought about it for a minute, and then nodded her head. "All right," she said. "Let's do it." Then she looked at her husband, who had obviously set up the challenge, perhaps as if to say: *You'd better be right*...or perhaps not.

Adrian could see that the two of them didn't hate one another, even if they had had to agree to disagree more often than they would have liked. They probably wanted to love one another, he thought, but didn't quite trust one another, or themselves, enough to believe that they weren't being bullshitted by the other's affectations of affection.

"That was good," Jarndyke said, nodding toward the panel, when his wife had left the room. "Clever, too. I like you, Son—I really do."

"Thanks," said Adrian, not knowing what else to say. Spotting the anomalous panel had been child's play, though. He knew that the acid test was coming up, and that even though Jarndyke liked him, and had been prepared to hire him on the basis of what his spies had told him, he wasn't yet prepared to believe that Adrian had a superpower. On the other hand, Adrian could now see quite clearly—and cursed himself for not having seen it before—that Jarndyke's peculiar strategy of interrogation at the Savoy had been guided by a hidden motive.

Angelica came back carrying an easel in her right hand and a cloth-swathed canvas tucked under her left arm. Moving with meticulous order, she set up the easel, and placed the canvas on it, still concealed. Then she removed the cloth.

Adrian had been expecting something akin to a Rothko, or maybe a Jackson Pollock: an exercise in abstract impressionism, playing deftly with the subtleties of color, perhaps even the utmost subtleties of color. He had not been expecting what he actually saw. He had been warned, but he had not been expecting witchcraft. He felt his jaw drop, and was uncomfortably aware that he was speechless. These, he knew, were untested waters.

He had seen a lot of paintings in his time, including a lot by people whose color discrimination was unusually subtle, but he had never seen a painting by anyone who used color discrimination in the way that Angelica Jarndyke did, to hide images from ordinary eyes that extraordinary eyes would be able to see, if not exactly clearly and distinctly, then at least in such a way as to make out what they were.

Angelica Jarndyke was no great draughtsman—her figures were a trifle cartoonish—but she knew what it was that she was trying to represent, and she had skill enough to carry off the representation. She was no genius, by any stretch of the imagination—no Monet, no Rossetti, no Jackson Pollock—but what she had tried to do was real, and ambitious, and, in Adrian's experience, unique.

"Now that, to me," said Jason Jarndyke, "is just a big splodge of red with a little dash of orange here and there. Maybe it's a sunset seen in ultra-close-up, or the middle of a rose petal—and a Lancashire rose at that—but I don't get it. I just don't get it. Do you?" The question was addressed to Adrian.

"Yes," Adrian said, faintly. "I get it."

"And what do you think of it?" Jarndyke persisted. "Honestly, what do you think of it?"

"It's very strange," Adrian said, unable to think, for the moment, of a better adjective. "Technically, perhaps not brilliant, but in terms of coloration, in its way, it's magnificent. Magnificent, but...."

"But what?" It was still the husband doing the probing, but Angelica Jarndyke was looking at Adrian again, very intently indeed, search for the slightest sign of bullshit.

"...Unsettling," Adrian admitted.

Jarndyke made a noise with his tongue, like a bullshit-detector going off. "Unsettling! It's a big splodge of red, damn it!"

"It's Dante's *Inferno*," Adrian said, weakly. "It's a depiction of Hellfire—complete with the souls of the damned, in torment. Maybe I can't fully appreciate the religious context, as an atheist, but you don't need to believe in God to have a notion of Hell and retribution. The damned, I can believe in."

Wile he was speaking, Angelica Jarndyke's expression changed. In a trice, she lost all of her artificiality, all of her polish. Amazement broke through, and with it...Adrian couldn't tell. Not delight, not gratitude...something more akin to outrage. Her gaze abruptly shifted to her husband, who met her stare with a bizarre expression of his own.

Adrian realized, a trifle belatedly, that Angelica Jarndyke thought he'd been tipped off. She thought that her husband had somehow found out what the painting represented, even though she'd probably never told him, and that he had formed some schoolboyish conspiracy with Adrian to give her a slap the eye. And ironically, Jason Jarndyke thought exactly the same thing. He thought that his wife had somehow formed a conspiracy with Adrian, so that he could come up with an interpretation of the picture that she would endorse, so that the two of them could give *him* a slap in the eye.

Mercifully, they knew one another well enough, and understood one another's gaze well enough, to know, after five seconds of mutual staring, that they were both mistaken. Then they both turned to look at Adrian.

Adrian had thought, briefly, that if he passed the test that Jarndyke and his wife had faced him with, his employer would be delighted. He *had* passed, he knew: he had proved himself, and his uncanny sight. But his self-satisfaction was undermined by the consciousness that his boast to Jarndyke a few weeks before, though perfectly sincere, had been overstated. He wasn't the only person Jason Jarndyke knew who had near-perfect color vision. He wasn't even the best.

Not only could Angelica Jarndyke see better than he could, she could paint better than he could, albeit in an amateurish sort of way—and not, for the first time in his life, Adrian regretted bitterly that he didn't have the hand-eye coordination to wield a brush with as much efficacy as his sight demanded. Suddenly, being a reverse engineer of genus didn't seem like such a perfect complement to his full-spectrum sight as it had seemed twenty minutes before. His ingenious argument about the emperor's new clothes and the plight of the one man in the crowd who could see the beautiful suit had ceased to be a neat philosophical argument intended for intellectual persuasion, and had take on its full weight as a sketch of an actual, and potentially horrific, existential predicament: his own, and Angelica Jarndyke's.

Angelica Jarndyke was a painter, perhaps not of genius but at the very least of unusual talent, but no one had ever been able to see the results of her particular talent, except very vaguely—until now...and that had shaped her decisions as to what to paint, in a fashion that seemed, to say the least, ominous.

In all his esthetic excursions, Adrian had never encountered her like. He had seen the work of a hundred painters who had real genius, and he had always thought himself better equipped to appreciate their genius than most people—better than anyone else, truth be told—but he had never seen anything painted by someone who had elected to exploit full-spectrum sensitivity in quite that way, and enough skill to complement it...and a subject-matter that somehow seemed altogether appropriate.

Adrian knew, now, that if he did manage to produce some kind of *authentic* Golden Fleece for Jason Jarndyke, that at least one person would be able to see it, consciously, in all its glory—but somehow, that idea didn't immediately fill him with delight. In fact, it frightened him.

Even so, he forced himself to say: "I'd really like to see your other work some time, Mrs. Jarndyke," because he knew that he couldn't *not* say it, whether it eventually turned out to be a bad idea or not.

Jason Jarndyke was ready for that challenge, too, and showed every sign of wanting to watch. Angelica Jarndyke wasn't, and showed every sign of wanting her husband to be a million miles away if ever she condescended to let Adrian into her barn.

The true measure of Jason Jarndyke, Adrian thought, was that he really didn't seem to be jealous. He really did seem genuinely pleased, once he'd got over the initial shock, to know that his wife really hadn't been bullshitting him throughout their married life—and genuinely pleased, too, that she had now found someone who could see what she was doing, someone who could understand, and prove to her that she wasn't alone, and wasn't mad.

Adrian's eyes drifted back to the painting, though. It was amateurish. It was cartoonish. But it was good. In its own way, it was brilliant.

It was also a vision of Hellfire, full of wrath, complete with the souls of the damned, in agonizing torment.

All in all, Adrian, thought, what he'd just learned would have been far less intimidating if the image had been flowers or puppies: something that one could put on the lid of a biscuit tin; the sort of thing that trophy wives, within the scope of his admittedly limited imagination, might be expected to paint.

He knew, for sure, that he was not only out of his social depth now, but out of his psychological depth—which troubled him far more.

* * * * * * *

It wasn't late when Adrian got back home. That was one advantage, he supposed, to eating "dinner" at lunch-time, Yorkshire-fashion. The evening was still young. He could do some work. He could relax for a while.

Or, as things turned out, he couldn't. His head was spinning inside. He couldn't settle to work or relax. He had too much on his mind, too much to work through.

He kept going back to the analogies that he had cited while trying to persuade Angelica Jarndyke to put him to the test. He had, of course, been putting himself in the shoes of the man who could see the beautiful suit, or the Wellsian sighted man in the country of the blind. Like Wells's sighted man, he had always been aware that he was sighted, not mad—not because he came from a country of the sighted, but because he had always been a scientist, at heart and in method. He had been able to subject his unusual sight to experiment and analysis, had been able to prove it to himself, and to explain it to himself. He had never doubted himself, and he had always understood himself.

Now, though, the glimpse he had caught of Angelica Jarndyke—and the sight he had had of her fabulous painting—made him see that it could have be otherwise. All the decisions he had made, with regard to handling his own predicament, seemed logical, even in retrospect. He had known when making them that there had been alternatives, but he had simply made the decisions and concentrated on managing their consequences. He had never wasted time trying to calculate the possible consequences of the decisions he had not taken. Now, he felt compelled to think about that a little more deeply, and to extend his analysis. He didn't suppose that he could work out how Angelica Jarndyke had seen her situation, and how she had tried to cope with it, but at least he could ask himself what might have happened to *him* if he had tried to go in a different direction.

Suppose that he *had* doubted himself. Suppose that the fact that other people couldn't see what he saw had made him doubt that he saw it, rather than providing the stimulus to prove it. Suppose that he had been able to reproduce what he saw, with the aid of artificial pigments, at least to the extent that available artificial pigments would allow—but that people still couldn't see what he saw, or even that there're was anything there to see? Might he have actually stopped seeing it? Might he have adapted and amended his consciousness to what other people could see, psychosomatically rendering himself partially blind?

Yes, he decided, he might. And perhaps some people did. Perhaps it wasn't simply an accident of fate or physiology that so many people who were affected by color weren't conscious of the effects or discriminations they were making. Perhaps it was a psychosomatic compulsion, driven by the need that so many people had to fit in, to be normal...a need by which Adrian had never been unduly afflicted, having always thought it better to be a scientist, a man of logic rather than emotion, and having long ago given up on the possibility of ever *fitting in*.

On the other hand, might he have been able to cling to the conviction that he really could see, and really could reproduce what he saw, even though other people couldn't see the reality or the reproduction—but without the scientific understanding that would inform him as to how it came about?

Yes, he decided, he might. And perhaps people had, long before Angelica Jarndyke. Maybe only a few, maybe more than a few. And might they not, given the conviction without the scientific understanding, have construed what they possessed and could do in consequence as a kind of magic, a kind of witch-craft? Might they not have come to believe that their difference from other people really a kind of superpower: something in defiance of normality, a boon and a curse?

Watch out for Medea, Adrian thought. *Okay. I watched out. I met her. But what now? What now?*

What he meant by that, of course, was what might Angelica Jarndyke want of him, now that she had found him? And what might Jason Jarndyke want of him now, not as a reverse engineer charged with the job of coloring his fabrics, but as a "member of the family" who shared his wife's peculiar vision? But even those two questions, difficult as they were, were only half the problem.

The other half was the question of what he might want himself, given the sudden change in his circumstances, and whether it would undermine all the sterling work he had put into shaping his attitude, planning his career and delineating his goals.

What if Angelica Jarndyke's paintings really did work magic on him, and show him something new, something disturbing?

What if his extraordinary sight, which had already given him a privileged glimpse of hell, were to show him something even more unsettling, which he would be better of not seeing?

The possibilities seemed too confusing for there to be any hope of formulating a strategy in advance.

Of one thing, however, he was certain. He would not be ale to resist the temptation to look. Whatever Angelica Jardyke had to show him, if she consented to show him anything at all, *he would have to look*....and see.

* * * * * * *

The immediate answer to the question of "what now?" seemed to be *nothing*. A good night's sleep restored Adrian's ability to work, and routine did the rest. He didn't forget what had happened at Bleak House, but he was able to compartmentalize it. He did put "Jason" and "Medea" into a search engine, and was glad to find that their mythological relationship didn't seem to lend any other analogies to his situation. He also fed in *Bleak House*, and was grateful to find a similar lack of analogy in Jarndyce versus Jarndyce, with *c*s instead of *k*s—which meant, he concluded, that he need have no fear of ironic fate, and would be free to work things out for himself, on strictly scientific principles. All in good time. For the time being, he shelved the issue. He had work to do.

Jason Jarndyke seemed to respect that. It was Thursday before he dropped by, casually, to tell Adrian what a pleasure it had been to see him on Sunday, even though things had gone "a bit wrong."

"Wrong?" Adrian queried.

"Well, yes. To tell you the truth, I didn't really believe that you would see anything in Angie's picture, and I wasn't immediately convinced that what you thought you saw was what she thought she had put into it. But I *had* expected that if you did see something, which she thought was there, that she'd be pleased. I thought she'd be over the moon at being able to prove to me—or at least put up a good argument to the effect—that she really hadn't been bullshitting me all these years. I thought she'd be grateful."

"But she's not?" Adrian inferred.

"Well, yes and no. Underneath, I think she is—but on top, she's confused. She hadn't expected it, you see—she thought at first that I'd somehow found out what she thought and tipped you off. She knows now, I think, that you really could see it— and I think she's convinced that you'd be able to see what's in her other pictures too, both the ones I've seen and the ones she won't let me see. But I think that scares her, a little. She'd got used to it, you see—people not being able to see, only praising her work, if and when they did, purely for bullshitting reasons. Now, the thought that someone *can* see...*will* see...has taken her aback a bit, given her pause for thought. I'm sure she'll come round, though."

"I don't want to cause any difficulty."

"Difficulty? No, Son, there's no difficulty. In my book, you're a godsend. You have no idea how much she needs you...needs an audience, who can see what she's doing. It'll complete her."

"I don't know about that," said Adrian, warily.

"Neither does she, at present—but she'll come round. It's what she needs—what she's always needed. You must understand that."

Must I? Adrian thought. What he said was: "I'll be glad to help, if I can."

"Don't get any ideas, mind," said Jason Jarndyke, putting on his humorous expression again. "You're a nice looking lad and she's beautiful, but she's damn near old enough to be your mother. You might think she's only with me for my money, but even if you were right...oh, don't blush like that. I'm not entirely color blind, and I know what some red splodges mean. What I'm trying to say is that she's only ever going to be interested in your eyes, and you need to understand that, and not get confused, the way youngsters sometimes do. Because I want this to work, Son—I really do. I adore Angie, and I want her to have what

I've never been able to give her: your eyes. That's worth more to me than the Golden Fleece itself. In fact, if we're being metaphorical, that *is* my authentic Golden Fleece. If you can give me genes to produce colors that can live up to your promises, that might well complete my material fortune...but if you can give Angie faith in her work, and faith in herself, and set her free from the disappointment and anguish that's been dogging her for years....well, Son, you'll have worked a real miracle."

Adrian thought that he could feel his heart sinking. He had thought, a week before, that he could justify all the hopes that Jason Jarndyke had invested in him—but the game had changed now. Now, the Yorkshireman was expecting miracles. Adrian was a scientist; he didn't do miracles. He couldn't even bring himself to say that he would do his best. He would, but he knew that it wouldn't be enough.

"You're still blushing, you silly sod," Jarndyke observed. "But you see what I'm getting at, don't you? She hasn't got used to the idea yet, but she will. Bound to. I can't ask you to dinner again Sunday—I'll have to wait for her to ask me to invite you. She will. Sooner or later, she'll want to show you more of her work...and eventually, even if it takes months, she'll want to take you into the barn to see her latest work. Just your eyes, mind, and your consciousness behind them. No daft ideas—but she'll want you to see...and *I* want you to see. Need to be clear about that." He hesitated, apparently wondering whether he might have gone too far—but self-doubt wasn't in his emotional repertoire. "Not saying that you *can* work a miracle, mind," the industrialist added, cautiously, "and I won't hold it against you if you can't—but the mere possibility justifies the price of your hire...metaphorically speaking, of course. You up to date now?"

Adrian blinked several times, then nodded.

"We're on the same page?" Jarndyke added, wanting to be sure.

Adrian nodded again.

"Good—now get on with making me trillions. Concentrate on your own colors, until you get the call. Okay."

"Okay," said Adrian, feeing that the nodding was becoming too repetitive, and not wanting to be mistaken for an automaton.

"Champion," said Jarndyke, and passed on.

Word that the conversation in question had taken place went round the labs and offices like wildfire, although no one knew *exactly* what had been said or why. Rumor inevitably took wing.

"Made quite an impression on Mrs. Jarndyke, I hear," Chester Hu said to him, when an opportunity arose. "I told you to be careful, didn't I? Don't be fooled by Jayjay's easygoing manner. If he gets jealous, he won't settle for firing you. He's a Yorkshireman. Next worst thing to a Singaporean, when it comes to matters of the heart."

The Koreans, Taiwanese, and even the Scots, made similar comparisons, causing Adrian to realize that every nation on Earth thought that it had a privileged relationship with jealousy and pride. He brushed it all off—which didn't fan the rumors, but didn't extinguish them either. He now felt that it wasn't just Jayjay's beady eyes that were on him, but those of the entire organization.

Mercifully, he had his routines, and a heroic capacity to absorb himself in his work. That was what he did, accelerating the progress of his gene-designing, gene-manufacturing and gene-implanting experiments, looking forward to the day when he could actually begin field-testing. For the moment, he was working almost entirely in cyberspace and headspace, where the hitches rarely showed up, but he did contrive to get half a dozen new pigment genes—all patent-protected—into organic form, and to incorporate them into cultures of both wool and silk. Within a further ten days, he saw the first flecks of color born in his Petri-dishes, and knew that the foundations had been laid for a great ideative and industrial enterprise.

He allowed himself to feel a small thrill of triumph, but not to celebrate. The time for celebration was still a long way off.

For the moment, it looked as if his greens and blues were ahead of his golds, but he wasn't upset by that. The golds would come through, in time; so would the blacks...and the reds too.

Only splodges in dishes to begin with, but in time...maybe he could even produce Hellfire, if there turned out to a market for it. His progress was frustratingly slow, because his ambitions were so large, but he knew that Jason Jarndyke was right. Rome hadn't been built in a day, and the Romans hadn't made as great a job of it as they might have done, although the Goths and Vandals certainly hadn't helped with its preservation. He had to be patient.

He was. He worked with relentless efficiency, by no means tirelessly but always effectively. He ate well. He cycled up and down the moors, enjoying the sun light and the subtle shades of coloration that the mosses and the heather presented, as the season slowly wore on. Everything went like clockwork, uninterrupted by superfluous cuckoos. He had plenty to think about without philosophizing, and he made the most of his opportunities. His head was full of molecules.

Eventually, though, the summons came. Jarndyke dropped round to his computer-station as if for a routine check-in, but added, before turning away: "Can you come to dinner Sunday? Angie has a few things she'd like to show you. Value your opinion." He didn't bother to remind him not even to think about saying no.

"Two o'clock?" Adrian queried.

"Two o'clock," Jayjay confirmed. "Walk or bring your bike— all the same to us."

Adrian decided to walk.

* * * * * *

Dinner went reasonably smoothly. Angelica Jarndyke didn't avoid looking at her guest, and played a much fuller role in the conversation, although she seemed to be avoiding the subject of art.

Jayjay was obviously aware of that, and it eventually offended his rule about not beating around the bush—although, when he eventually steered the conversation in that direction, even he took the scenic route.

"I noticed on your CV that you once went to a GRE conference in Oslo," he remarked to Adrian. "Did you take in Gustav Vigeland's sculpture park? The *Vita?*"

"Of course," Adrian said. "Not really my cup of tea, though. A bit austere. Colorless. Impressive, but...just not my sort of thing."

"I liked it," Jarndyke said, blithely. "What about the other brother? Did you visit *his Vita?*"

That was the point, Adrian knew. Jason Jarndyke was fishing. Gustav Vigeland's little brother Emanuel hadn't been given a park in which to show off. He had been an official recorder, painting portraits of local dignitaries to hang in civic buildings, condemned to a humdrum existence of conspicuous underachievement, living in an ordinary house on an ordinary estate—until he'd ripped out all the floors in his ordinary house and made the entire interior into a single coherent space, on whose black-dyed walls he'd painted his own all-encompassing vision of human life, in all its aspects, which was designed to be looked at in dim light, so that visitors had to be in there for a good half hour before their eyes adjusted sufficiently to see it as it was meant to be seen.

A blind man could have spotted the hidden agenda. Jason Jarndyke had his own theory about what was going on in Angelica's "barn." Doubtless she had "dragged" him to see Emanuel's house, which was only open to the public for a couple of hours a week, perhaps because the local authorities suspected his *Vita* of being pornographic.

"Yes," Adrian said. "I saw it."

"And what did you think?" was the inevitable next question.

"Original. Ingenious. Very effective. A masterpiece, in its way."

"Not brilliant? Not a work of genius?"

"Maybe not entirely my cup of tea," Adrian hedged. "More so than Gustav's *Vita*, certainly, but still...in sum, less than the eye could have desired to see."

"Angie liked it," Jarndyke said, laying down the hook along with the lure.

She bit, but almost dutifully, because it was expected of her—or so Adrian thought. "Mr. Stamford's right," she said. "It's a masterpiece, in its way. Original, ingenious and effective...but it used semi-darkness as a cloak, to shield its weaknesses. I can sympathize with that, I suppose, but...well, I did like it, but not as much as the Rothko chapel. Rothko could use near-black in a way that Vigeland junior couldn't. Rothko understood its subtleties better."

It wasn't really a lead-in, but Jarndyke used it anyway.

"Angie has some pictures set up in the library that she's like to show you," he said to Adrian. "To demonstrate that she *does* understand near-black...as well as red and blue...and maybe even gold."

"If only I were a reverse engineer instead of a mere dauber," his wife retorted, a trifle sharply "what sweet music we might make...not to mention money. I fear that my paintings are never going to find much of a market."

"That doesn't matter," Jarndyke said. "What matters is that *you* know what they're worth."

"I'm sure that Mrs. Jarndyke has always known that," Adrian put in, trying to be gallant. "I'll be very interested to see them. I've been looking forward to it immensely."

"It's only a small sample though," Jarndyke put in. "Old stuff, I believe. All her recent work is in the barn. I haven't seen any of it—she gave up asking for my opinion years ago. Can't blame her."

All that Angelica said in reply to that was: "It's not a barn, Jayjay. It's just an outbuilding. No livestock, no tractor, no bales of hay. Just amateurish dabbling—not worth seeing, really. I wish you wouldn't go on about it so."

"Sorry, Angie," Jarndyke said, contritely.

"And it's not a rip-off of Emanuel Vigeland either," she said. "It's not a collective vision of human life, pornographic or otherwise, to be seen in quiet light as if in a church."

"Can't blame a fellow for guessing," Jarndyke said. "Are we going to the library, or what?"

"No," said Angelica, suddenly stern. "*We* aren't. Mr. Stamford and I are going to the library. *You* are going to stay here, Jason. This doesn't concern you."

That didn't seem entirely fair to his employer, and Adrian felt slightly intimidated about the thought of being alone with Angelica, but he was too scared to say anything.

Jarndyke only shrugged, and said: "You can call him Adrian."

That seemed a bit thick to Adrian, too, especially as Jason Jarndyke had never addressed him as anything but "Son," but he raised no objection, and meekly allowed Angelica Jarndyke to escort him out of the room and along the wood-paneled corridor that presumably led to the library.

It was the kind of library that looked as if it had been put together with books bought by the yard, more to show off their old bindings than to provide reading material. Some were in Latin, others were standard sets of classic authors—but Adrian didn't waste much time examining the bookshelves. He was infinitely more interested in the paintings.

There were seven, each set up on its own easel, the array carefully spaced, as if the intervals had been measured with a ruler.

Like the vision of Hellfire he had already seen, they would probably have looked like "splodges" to the everyday eye, Adrian thought. Like the vision of Hellfire, though, they weren't essays in abstract impressionism. They were representative pictures—very subtle pictures, using extremely subtle gradations of color, but representative nevertheless. Some of them needed careful study, but there wasn't one of them that left Adrian confused as to its subject.

He started with the yellow—or, to be strictly accurate, the gold. It was, as might have been guessed, a picture of the myth-ical Golden Fleece, with a triumphant Jason displaying it to an invisible crowd. Medea wasn't present—unless she was invis-ible, although that would probably have been taking subtlety too far. The Jason in the picture wasn't exactly a portrait, but it was obvious to Adrian that he was based on a real individual. A pity, he thought, that the image in question was invisible to the Jason in question—except, perhaps, subliminally.

The painting reassured him somewhat, after the anxieties he'd built up in consequence of the Dantean image of the inferno. It was a *pleasant* picture, which seemed to have been painted with a degree of affection. Angelica must have known that her husband wouldn't be able to see the image suggestive of himself, but she hadn't been tempted to be satirical in the depiction, let alone cruel. There was no mockery in it.

The blue was a mermaid, or perhaps a siren. It wasn't a Hans Christian Andersen mermaid: the meek self-sacrificing innocent who had consented walk on daggers for a lifetime in exchange for the privilege of being able to keep a fisherman company; it was a temptress, willing and able to lead men to their doom with a seductive song. The limitations of Angelica's draughtsmanship showed up more obviously in the top half of the central figure than the bottom. The fishy part was quite well-done, elegantly curled and beautifully colored in the scales, which were silver behind all the myriad blue reflections of water-modified sky. The human half, by contrast, was vague, the rippling blonde hair seeming in need of the attentions of a good hairdresser, and the features rather flat

Was this a sort-of-portrait too? Adrian wondered. Was the siren a means by which Angelica was trying to represent herself, metaphorically as well as literally? If so, what did her apparent failure—which might, of course be deliberate—signify? Loneliness, no doubt...a sense of difference, obviously...but what else?

Adrian had always felt more comfortable with pure exercises in color and form, like Rothko's or Pollock's. Monet's gardens, too, he felt that he understood very well, and Georgia O'Keefe's flowers. But Dante Gabriel Rossetti...he had appreciated the pre-Raphaelite attention to detail, but not the siren quality of his women's faces, the extreme subtleties of his attitude to the models with which he had had such tortured and convoluted personal relationships....

All in all, Adrian found the blue siren less unsettling than the red inferno, but there was still a hint of damnation about it that seemed menacing as well as uncanny.

The green was forest foliage, with hidden faces peeping through it: nymphs and fauns, Adrian assumed, or maybe mere fairy folk. Again, the faces were too vague to be identifiable, by species let alone as individuals. Some tended to the ugly, some to the beautiful, but none to the meek and sanitized. On the other hand, they were not exactly malevolent either—merely slightly unhuman, weirdly hybridized.

The composition of the picture, and the manner in which the foliage and the faces were intermingled, was very ambitious—perhaps a trifle too ambitious, although it showed off the artist's technique to better effect than the simpler and more straightforward images. Complication helped to offset the slight individual faults of curvature. It was easier to see in this picture that Angelica had had some professional training, and had benefited from it, in spite of being handicapped by insufficient natural ability in her brushwork. Adrian had looked up her biography with the aid of a search engine, and knew that she had done two years at the Courtauld before dropping out—or, more accurately as well as more kindly, moving on. It must have become obvious to her over those two years that she would never be able to create a work of art as wonderful as the one she constituted in herself, even with the aid of full-spectrum color vision.

She had not given up, though. She had carried on painting, in private, concentrating increasingly on work that only she could see.

The pale brown was sand: Egyptian sand, to judge by the ruins and statuary projecting through it at intervals. Some of the half-buried statues had faces, but they weren't human faces; they were the faces of sphinxes. Inevitably, Shelley's immortal line—"Look on my works, ye mighty, and despair!"—sprang to mind, but that wasn't really the tenor of the picture. It wasn't celebrating or regretting the decay that had all but erased the residue of a once-great civilization, but using its extreme subtlety of color to imply a near-identity between the stones and the sand, the shaped and the shapeless. It was an austere picture, but there was nothing sinister about it, and Adrian couldn't get any implication of the supernatural from its peeping sphinxes, which seemed like mere human artifacts, fading into dust in the wake of their makers.

The dark brown, on the other hand, was a calculated exercise in the sinister and the supernatural, which seemed to be aiming to create a sense of unease by concealing its effects just out of the range of ordinary human sight. This one might not have seemed like a mere splodge even to Jason Jarndyke, although he would probably have been hard-pressed to identify anything in it other than trees-trunks and branches. It was another forest, but not leafy forest—there were only a few hints of dark green in the mix. This was a dense forest seen from within, all gnarled tree-trunks and decaying humus. This forest was inhabited, as the other had been, but not by conventional mythological creatures. There were strange squirrels and squatting toads, whose air of menace was not contained in anything as obvious as fangs and claws, but in a peculiar implication of *disease*.

It was an ugly painting, and Adrian wondered whether Angelica had simply found it easier to paint the ugly than the beautiful, given her technical limitations, and had simply decided, in this instance, to play to her strengths. He was reluctant to conclude, now, that there might be any deep psychological significance in it, let alone any attempted magic. He was conscious of the fact that it was supposed to seem scary, but for that very reason, he found it slightly amusing, like a schlock-horror movie striving too hard for effect

The blacks were where the actual witches figured, though. In one, they were traditional witches in black conical hats, gathered around a cauldron. It was like a scene from Macbeth, and might well have been exactly that. It was redolent with tradition—tradition that did not seem to have been excessively tarnished by the travesties of Hallowe'en. The other was quite different; in that one there was a black tower, and black cats, and a black-clad witch standing tall and imperious, mistress of all she surveyed. The witches gathered around the cauldron in the other painting were hagwives, but the witch standing in front of the tower and behind the cat was more Morgan le Fay, a custodian of the kind of cold, implacable beauty that Medusa might have had before her hair became snaky and her gaze literally lethal. Her stare was not murderous, in any straightforward sense, but it was omnipotent.

Again, Adrian wondered if this had been intended as a kind of self-portrait, the dream of some dark *doppelgänger*—but it was not a calculated attempt to produce something frightening, as the second forest scene clearly was. It was an exercise in he deployment of the subtle shades that the common eye lumped together as "black," its them almost incidental. For Adrian, it had all the subtleties of artificial photosynthesis and it was easy for him to imagine it soaking up the sun's energy, in order to generate...what? Perhaps pure magic; raw power of a different sort. He liked it—but on balance, he thought that he liked the picture of the Golden Fleece, from which it was separated by the full length of the library, a little better.

Adrian studied each of the paintings for some considerable time, mentally placing them in a hypothetical chronological order. All in all, he felt relieved. They were experiments, attempts to do different and varied things within the limitation of different but equally slender margins of coloration. Experiments he understood; he was a scientist. Psychologically, he felt that his feet had touched bottom. He was no longer out of his depth.

Eventually, he turned to Angelica Jarndyke and said: "Thank you. I appreciate your letting me look at them."

"Is that it?" she demanded.

Adrian gathered his courage. "Am I still on trial?" He asked. "Do you want me to tell you what I see, just to prove that I can?"

She thought about it for a moment, but then said: "No. I

believe that you can see them. That's not the point. What do you think of them?"

"I think they're superb, in their way. Obviously, I've never see anything like them. I had no idea that anything like them could be done. They're magnificent...if a little esoteric."

"But you don't like then?" she said, flatly.

He hesitated before saying. "They're too varied for a collective judgment. I like some better that others. Less striking than the Hellfire, but that's understandable given that the Hellfire had a thematic advantage as well as the shock of first impact. I *do* like the idea behind them, Mrs. Jarndyke—how could I not, given that they are, in a sense, especially designed for my eyes. If you want me to tell you that they're great art, though, I can't. They're good, but they're not works of genius. They're not comparable with Monet or Rothko, or even the Vigeland brothers. I'm sorry."

"Don't be," she said. "I'd come to the same conclusion myself. Perhaps I've only been hiding them in subtle shades of color so that Jason wouldn't see them, wouldn't see my mediocrity.

"Your husband could never think that you're mediocre, Mrs. Jarkdyke, and neither do I."

"But I can't claim credit for nature's work, can I?" she said, keeping her tone deliberately light. "I wanted to *do* something. You understand that, don't you Mr. Stamford? You're a genius, after all. You can do more than see."

"That remains to be proven," Adrian murmured—but he raised his voice to say: "But you *have* done something, Mrs. Jarndyce. Something nobody else has every done before. Something unique. I'm just a scientist—you can't trust my judgment, but you *can* trust my sight. This is amazing work."

"In its way," she added.

"In its way," he agreed. "That's not an insult, Mrs. Jarndyke. Nobody else in the world could have done this. Nobody else in the world could have shown me this, and I'm truly grateful. And we're not alone, Mrs. Jarndyke. There must be others. We're not as good as bees, because we don't have the same selective pressures operating on us, but we're in the age of genetic engineering now, and we're beginning to understand the physiological bases of esthetics. In time, if they want to, our descendants will be able to see far better than we can—you and me included, Mrs. Jarndyke."

"*Bees?*" she repeated, incredulously.

"I assume so," he said. "There's a wider range of pigmentation in nature—a wider range of pigment-producing genes—than the average human eye can discriminate. Natural selection produced them; ergo there must be organisms that can see them—the organisms to which the colors are, so to speak, addressed. Pollinators that the flowers are competing to attract: bees, among others. Hummingbirds too, probably."

Angelica nodded, in a particular fashion, to confirm that she could follow the argument, and would think about it.

"Perhaps, one day," Adrian went on, "when everyone is able to see as we see, your paintings will be hanging in every gallery on Earth, as the pioneering works of a whole new dimension of artistic endeavor. Maybe others will be better, in time, but you'll always have been the first. No one can take that away from you."

"No one we know of," she said. "But somewhere, lying neglected in some dusty attic or the storerooms of some lunatic asylum...."

"I'm sorry, Mrs. Jarndyke," Adrian said, not interrupting because she had deliberately trailed off. "Your husband believed that you'd be happy to find someone who could see your work—and pleased with him for having found that someone. He wanted you to be pleased. I think I can understand why you're not, but I'm not sure that he can."

"You want me to pretend? For your sake?"

"It's not for me to ask you to do anything—but if I did want you to pretend, it would be for his sake, not mine. He's not at fault, Mr. Jarndyke. He might not give a damn about Rothko or Emanuel Vigeland, but he really would like to be able to appreciate your painting. It worries him that he can't—but it isn't his fault."

Adrian almost continued, but decided that he might already have said too much. Jason Jarndyke was his employer, and he had to make every possible effort not to cause any difficulty. He took a step toward the door, hoping that they could simply go back to the dining room, where he could tell Jason Jarndyke once again what a magnificent artist his wife was, and how grateful he was to have seen her work.

Medea wouldn't let him. She didn't do anything as crude as blocking his way, but she stopped him in his tracks with a glance. Beautiful women could do that Adrian knew, but he couldn't help a slight superstitious shudder.

"Why?" she said. "You think you understand—so why?"

"I thought the trial was over," Adrian countered.

"I believe that you see it. You've yet to convince me that you understand it."

Adrian thought about it, and then said: "I can't, Mrs. Jarndyke. I know that there's been a misunderstanding here—that your reaction to discovering that I can see your paintings wasn't at all what your husband expected, and still isn't. I know that, in a sense, I've let him down. He wanted to make you a gift of my eyes, of my special sight, because he thinks that you've been yearning for an audience for all the fifteen years that you've been married, and maybe longer. I think I do understand why you're disappointed...but I couldn't even attempt to convince you of it without stirring up trouble, and that's the last thing I want to do. Please let me go, Mrs. Jarndyke. You have no use for me; it was very kind of you to let me see your paintings, and I'm truly grateful, but I'd like to return to my own work now."

He had been trying to smooth things over, to worm his way out of his predicament, but he could see in Angelica Jarndyke's marvelously beautiful face that he'd only made things worse. He cursed himself for having been a fool, for not having known what to say and not having the sense simply to keep quiet.

"What would *you* have done?" she asked, in a deadly whisper.

That, Adrian realized, was what she really wanted to know.

She was only a Yorkshirewoman by marriage, he knew, but he didn't think she'd have much patience for beating around the bush, so he stopped trying.

"I've asked myself that, once or twice, since I saw your *Inferno*," he admitted. "What would I have done if, as well as being able to see the full color spectrum, and teach myself to identify and analyze a significant fraction of its psychological effects, I'd also been able to paint? For a little while, it seemed like a conundrum, but then I realized that I already had the answer. I'd have done what I *am* doing, with my own particular talent. Instead of studying genetics, in order to generate as many of the spectrum's gradations of color in different organic pigments, I'd have done what you initially did, and gone to art school to learn technique. And when I'd learned the tricks of the trade, I'd have looked for an opportunity to apply them—but I'd have looked for a way to apply them in such a way that people could see what I was doing, perhaps not entirely consciously, but nevertheless visibly.

"I'd have done what other painters with our particular talent have done in the past, using all the colors of the palette in individual paintings. I'd have painted images that even people like Mr. Jarndyce could see without effort: portraits, flowers, foliage...maybe even sirens, fauns and witches. I'd have used my additional powers of discrimination to build in extra levels of suggestion, tantalizingly beyond the easy reach of commonplace consciousness, but I wouldn't have tried to hide what I was representing; I wouldn't have created an entire occult art that, so far as I knew, *nobody* else would ever be able to see...something for myself alone. Maybe that makes me less than a true artist. Maybe it makes me into a commercial hack, just looking for a way to market my talent. But that's what I do—and that's what I would have done, if I'd been able to paint but had no aptitude for science. I suppose I'd have gone into advertising."

Adrian was afraid that Angelica Jarndyke might take offense at the implicit criticism, and that she might be fully entitled to do so—but if her sentiments inclined her in that direction, she controlled them. She didn't go so far as to nod her head to concede the justice of his case, but she didn't oppose it.

"Would you like to see the barn?" she asked, mildly. It was a hypothetical question, Adrian assumed, not an offer.

"Thank you," he said, "but no."

He knew that it was a mistake as soon as he had said it. He realized immediately that he should have said "Yes please!" as eagerly as possible. That way, she could have asserted herself by refusing. As things stood now, he'd issued a tacit challenge, which she might just fell compelled to meet.

"Liar," she said.

"Honesty doesn't come into it," he lied, clumsily. "I don't think it would be a good idea for me to look at your recent work, given that this isn't working out the way that Mr. Jarndyke hoped it would. There's nothing I can do for him here. I don't say that it wouldn't be interesting to see your work, for myself...but I will confess that I'm a little afraid of the effect it might have."

"Coward, then," she amended.

"Very much so," Adrian admitted. "May I please go back to Mr. Jarndyke now?"

It was her turn to lie. "Nobody's stopping you," she said, and raised her arm as if to show him the way, in case he'd forgotten where the door was.

They both went back to the dining room, and Adrian spent a dutiful twenty minute telling Jason Jarndyke what a magnificent painter his wife was, and what it privilege it had been to see her works.

Angelica Jarndyke made no attempt to challenge him, having reverted to her policy of not looking at anyone, and only making the most blatantly tokenistic efforts to take part in the conversation. Her husband didn't seem offended by that, or even disappointed. His optimism was still intact. He still imagined that she was "coming round," and that she would one day be grateful to him for discovering Adrian, and making her a gift of his miraculous sight.

He had no idea what was really going on, Adrian thought.

How could he, given that he was more than averagely unsighted, even though he was convinced that he could see with perfectly clarity, and was honest enough to call a splodge a splodge?

* * * * * * *

There was no question, this time, of simply waiting for Jayjay to drop by his desk or his lab with another invitation to the Old Manse. The game had gone beyond that. Adrian was expecting a direct approach, and it was almost a relief when he didn't have to remain in suspense for weeks on end.

Three days later, when the doorbell of his flat rang during his scheduled relaxation time, at eight o'clock in the evening, he knew who it would be, but feigned astonishment anyway. He invited Angelica Jarndyke in, and offered her a cup of coffee, which she accepted once he had confirmed that he had no alcohol to hand.

She didn't beat around the bush. "I've been thinking about what you said," she told him.

"I'm sorry about that," he said. "I should have kept my mouth shut."

"No," she said. "I challenged you to prove that you understood, because I still didn't believe that you did. I asked for it."

He didn't try to deny it. He watched her toy with her coffee cup for a few moments, shifting uneasily in her armchair.

"It was a shock," she said. "Much less so for you, it seems. Have you met others?"

"No," he said. "No one as adept as me, at any rate—or you. But because I had a scientific explanation, I was always aware of the theoretical possibility. I was surprised, but I couldn't be shocked. Perhaps I should have been more pleased than I was, because your existence proved me right...but the situation wasn't conducive to that."

"Do you always talk like that?" she asked, with a hint of asperity. "Analytical...pernickety...pedantic."

"Yes," Adrian told her. "I try not to, but the scientific turn of mind keeps coming through. People call it pedantic, but it's not." Only a pedant, he knew, would pull people up on the propriety of their use of the term "pedantic," but he didn't voice the joke. It was hardly the time.

"I'm the one that's at fault," she told him, with a sigh. "If I'd had a more scientific turn of mind...I'd have understood too. If I'd thought like you, I'd probably have gone into advertising as well. What a marriage I'd have had then eh? Jason and I would be partners instead of...not that it would be any guarantee of happiness. Are *you* happy, Adrian?"

"No," he relied, bluntly.

She looked at him carefully: not *hard*, the way she had looked at him up at the Manse, but curiously, inquisitively. He was not the only one, he realized, who had been led by their encounter to re-examine all the decisions he had made, and wonder what might have happened if the flip of the coin had gone the other way.

"Jason says you're not gay," she told him, brutally, "just socially retarded. He had to find out—even in this day and age, closeted gays can be vulnerable to blackmail."

"I don't mind," Adrian said. "My sexuality isn't an issue."

"Which is exactly what's puzzling. Has it anything to do with your supersight?"

Adrian thought long and hard about dropping out of the conversation altogether, but he felt that he had an obligation to help Jason Jarndyke's wife, if he could—to help her to understand, that is.

"Indirectly," he said. "Although it was nothing visible, it still marked me out as different—slightly alien. You must have experienced that too. It's not an insuperable obstacle in itself, even when coupled with the social awkwardness that often comes with a scientific mind, but I had my looks to contend with too."

"You're quite pretty, in a way," she said.

"Exactly," he said. "I've always looked five years younger than I am—not such a handicap now that I'm in my late twenties, and I'll probably be grateful when I'm forty, but as an adolescent... what teenage girl wants to become involved with someone who looks five years younger than she is? It didn't take long to figure out that I wasn't cut out for that side of life, so I decided to concentrate on the other. A little obsession can be a good thing, in science. So can a measure of oblivion to potential distractions."

She didn't sympathize, but she did nod her head to show that she could follow the argument. "It's different for girls," she observed, stating the obvious. "Same problem, in a way—totally different consequences."

Adrian nodded his head, to show that he understood. What man didn't want to become involved with a woman who looked five, ten or twenty years younger than he was?

"Ungrateful bitch, aren't I?" she said. "Four women out of five would kill for my looks, and I just resent the way they define me. I could probably have done with your mentality—but I didn't have that sort of ability, any more than I could cut it as a painter. I have everything I need to be happy—loving husband, nice kids, more money than Croesus—but I'm not. The fault isn't in my stars but in me. I hid it away, where Jason couldn't see it—where no one could see it. But you can, can't you? And you can't even lie about it, like a normal person. You had to tell me."

"I could never understand how liars kept their stories straight," Adrian muttered. "It always seemed simpler just to tell the truth. Normally, it doesn't cause any difficulties."

"Bullshit," she retorted. "In order for it not to cause any difficulties, you have to lead an utterly abnormal life—which yours seems to be, by the way, although Jason has a whole zoo of freaks like you, so you probably feel right at home."

"I'm sorry," Adrian said, flinching under the assault.

"Well, there's one lie you've mastered," she retorted, as if by reflex—but then seemed to realize that she was being terribly unfair. "Sorry," she said in her turn. "Not your fault. Not Jason's either. All mine. I think I'd like it better, through, if your eyes were clouded with lust, like almost all the rest. Just knowing you can see clearly creeps me out a bit, but when you look right through me like that...you don't miss it—that *side of life?*"

"I just learned to tell myself that it doesn't matter—that there are other things in life to pursue."

A lesser person might have said "Money?" but Angelica knew better, She might not understand him as well as he thought he understood her, because he was a scientist and she wasn't, but she knew that he hadn't come to work for Jason Jarndyke for the money. She knew, as her husband did, that he was in quest of a metaphorical Golden Fleece for reasons more intimate than that.

Instead, she said: "I learned that, at least. Don't you find, though, that people *expect* you to be happy—not just to want to be happy, but to *be* happy? I always feel that I'm somehow letting them down."

"I'm not a beautiful woman," Adrian pointed out. "I don't have that kind of burden weighing down on me. Scientists are allowed to be eccentric...cynical and miserable, even. Nobody expects them to be happy."

"It's not as simple as that," she told him—meaning the beauty, he assumed, not the misery and the cynicism, let alone the lack of expectation.

He didn't reply—which was probably a tactical error.

"Come on, then," she said, making as if to get to her feet, even though she hadn't finished her coffee.

"Where to?" He asked, although it was a silly question.

"The barn, of course. I want you to see it. I need you to look at it."

Adrian didn't move. "Thank you," he repeated, stubbornly, "but no." He knew that he wasn't going to get away with it, but felt obliged to put up a show.

She arched her magnificent eyebrows. They were phenomenal eyebrows, and they arched with a perfection he'd never seen before. "Come on," she said. "No more lies—and I know you're not really a coward."

"You shouldn't have come here, Mrs. Jarndyke."

"Why? Because Jason might jump to the wrong conclusion? He won't. He's in London. If he finds out—and he probably will, although I won't tell him—he'll jump to the right conclusion. And he'll be glad. He *wants* me to let someone into the barn: someone who can see. He's glad that he found you. He's not in the least afraid that I might be so glad to have found a sight-mate that I'll screw you."

Given that Jason Jarndyke had mentioned that possibility twice, in seeming jest, Adrian wasn't so sure—but it was a trivial matter. Nothing of that sort was going to happen.

"You shouldn't have come, because you shouldn't want me to see your work," he explained. "Let anyone else into the barn by all means—but not me. Keep your secret."

She pulled a face, without injuring her beauty in the least. "Not the reaction I was expecting," she confessed. "Aren't you curious?"

"Of course I am," Adrian said. "I'm a scientist. But I've seen the direction of your work, from the painting of Jason onwards, all the way to Hell."

Her face lit up then, with a peculiar delight. "You figured it out!" she said. "Well done! And you actually think the trick might work? On *you!*"

She had jumped a little too far with that conclusion, but Adrian couldn't see any point in correcting her.

"I figured out, even though I didn't see the start of the sequence, that you must have had high hopes of your children at one point," Adrian said. "There was a time, I imagine—up to and including the painting of Jason and the Fleece, when you thought that you might one day have an audience—someone with whom to share...but genetics let you down."

She threw up her hands in a gesture of disgust. "They're as bad as Jason," she said. "I tried to teach them, to show them... but they didn't grow into it. They couldn't. Not their fault, poor lambs."

Adrian didn't want to suggest to her that perhaps it had been mistake to marry Jason Jarndyke. She had still been trying to *fit in* at that point, and even if it had occurred to her, it would have been unthinkable to anyone else that having bagged her multi-millionaire, she might turn him down for art's sake, or even for love. She hadn't been a gold-digger, though; she hadn't been thinking in terms of an eventual divorce and a settlement that would make her independently wealthy. She certainly wasn't thinking about that now.

Adrian knew that he ought to be saying something else, in an attempt, however desperate, to lead the conversation on to less dangerous ground, but he didn't know what to say, even to slow her down.

"Now," she said, "you *have* to see it. Even if I have to kidnap you, tie you up and drag you—which I don't have to do, as you know. All I have to do is whisper in Jason's ear. *He* wants you to do it—and you can't refuse him. He owns you. Wouldn't you rather do it now—just the two of us, in private? I really can't believe, you know, that you're actually *scared*. I'd love to think that you ought to be, but you can *see*, damn it! You can *see!*"

Adrian realized that Jason Jarndyke had been right. His wife did lack faith in herself, and she really did need the testimony of his eyes even to begin to believe. Perhaps she knew that she wasn't mad—she did not seem ever given in to that suspicion—but she didn't know that her witchcraft would actually work. Now, she had a chance to find out, or at least to get the opinion of an understanding eye. She really did need his opinion, no matter how resentful she might be of her own need.

And Jason Jarndyke, who hadn't the slightest idea of what his adored wife was up to, would gladly serve as her accomplice. All she had to do was whisper in his ear, and he would grant her wish. He could deliver, because, in every meaningful sense of the word, he *did* own Adrian. Adrian had sold himself into that tacit slavery.

In any case, Adrian thought, wasn't Angelica right? He *could* see, and he *could* understand. There really wasn't any reason for him to be afraid. He didn't believe in magic. He was a scientist.

Somehow, though, Professor Clark's words were still echoing

faintly in his ears—not just "Watch out for Medea" but "lamb to the slaughter."

It didn't matter. He had no alternative but to bow to the inevitable. And Angelica was right about that, too—better now, with her, in private, than on a Sunday afternoon, under Jason Jarndyke's beady eye.

"You win," he said, getting to his feet. "I'm being silly. I ought to be grateful for the opportunity—and I am."

By the time they had reached the top of the hill, he had almost talked himself into it.

* * * * * *

Like the Rothkos in the chapel, Adrian hadn't been able to see Angelica Jarndyke's depiction of Hellfire in its religious context—but that didn't matter at all, because she had wrenched it out of its religious context, or restored it to a context of more primal fears. As he'd pointed out when confronted with the painting, you didn't have to be a Christian to understand the ideas of sin and guilt, and the imagery of eternal punishment; pagans could appreciate that just as well—and atheists too. It was an unsettling picture, even for people who didn't believe in God. That was the whole point of it.

The difference between himself and Angelica, Adrian knew, was that he'd never hesitated for a moment over the explanation of his superpower. He'd always taken it for granted that it was something natural, something explicable in terms of sense-organs neurons and the properties of mind, something that bees could do. He'd never thought of it as a kind of damnation, a kind of curse. A freak he might be, but that was merely a matter of statistical oddity and genetic coincidence. He had always known that it wasn't magic, and every action he had taken in consequence of his perceived freakiness had confirmed and elaborated that conviction. He had explained himself, and he had set out to exploit himself.

He had never thought in any other terms than trying to market his knowledge, not in the vulgar sense of making money from it—what was the point of money if it couldn't buy him love?—but in the sense of making *use* of himself, of giving people what they wanted: of feeding the appetites that their brains had but their consciousness didn't know how to feed. Color matters, he had said to Jason Jarndyke. Appearances control attitudes, manipulate affections, and—ultimately—influence behavior. Clothes maketh the woman and man alike, and if people couldn't dress themselves to maximum effect then they had to look to others to help them out. What Adrian hadn't said, because he didn't think it necessary, was that color sense was *good*; that esthetic sensibility was *good*—because they enabled people to make the best of themselves. They were empowering. In pursuing the quest for Jason Jarndyke's Golden Fleece, and his own, Adrian fully believed that he was on the side of the angels.

But he understood now, never having thought about it before taking ship aboard the Airedale *Argo*, that someone else with his clear sight might have gone the other way. Someone else might not have been able to accommodate the idea of uncanny sight to sensory apparatus, neurons and the capabilities of consciousness. That hypothetical other might have jumped to the conclusion that it was magic, that she really was a witch—and every further investigation she had made, in that context, might have served to make that conviction stronger and more elaborate. If that hypothetical other had then gone to art school—whether or not it involved turning down a modeling career in order to pursue her hopes—she would have realized soon enough, that she was capable not merely of adding a suggestive edge to orthodox imagery, but of hiding imagery away from ordinary sight, of rendering it *occult*, in every sense of the word.

That hypothetical other might have started out the exploration of occult art with a view to finding others of her own elite—others who could see what she saw in her paintings, and would understand and sympathize. Had she been more fortunate, she might have done so, and found a coven. Having failed—

perhaps, at least in part, because she had been sidetracked by marriage—she might have begun looking to the future instead, thinking that if she couldn't discover a ready-made audience close at hand, she could create one. For a while, at least, she might have painted with her children in mind, hoping that they would grow into the ability to see what she was showing them, and that their secret might be all the more precious for being a family affair.

And if that hadn't worked either, she might have started thinking along different lines. She knew that there was a potential subliminal effect to what she was doing—that even people who couldn't see what she was painting could be unsettled and intimidated by the imagery, partly because they couldn't see it and partly because of what it represented: sinister imagery; menacing imagery; the imagery of witchcraft itself. And that knowledge combined with conviction and frustration, might well have led her away from the side of the angels, in the opposite direction.

What Adrian suspected—and, in consequence, feared—was that Angelica Jarndyke, a self-confessed unhappy woman, in spite of her material wealth,had begun to paint curses. Having discovered that her art had the power to unsettle, she had decided to concentrate on that aspect of it, to take it as far as she could. If she believed that her power was magical, she might also believe that she really did have the power to injure people by means of her paintings. And even though she was wrong about the magic, wrong about the witchcraft—in Adrian's scientific opinion—that didn't mean that she couldn't...because color mattered; esthetic sensibility mattered. Appearances could affect attitudes, affections and behavior. The knowledge that Adrian was trying to use to empower people to make the best of themselves—or, at least, to empower Jason Jarndyke to sell them the means to make the best of themselves—could, in theory, be deployed to the opposite effect.

Angelica Jarndyke appeared to be believe that the fact that Adrian could see the images in her paintings would insulate him from their effects, as she clearly believed herself to be insulated. Adrian wasn't so sure—either about his own immunity or hers. She certainly wasn't mad, or bad—but if she had been living among her painted curses for years on end, they might not have been without effect. How could they be? She might still be dangerous to know.

At the end of the day, though, Adrian really was fervently curious to see what was in the barn. How would he not be?

Because it was the end of the day, it was dark when Angelica Jarndyke led him around the back of the Old Manse—walking on the grass so as not to crunch the gravel and attract the attention of the staff. She had no torch, but several of the windows in the house were illuminated, and the light leaking out was adequate to guide them. She took a key out of her pocket and unlocked the barn door very carefully, and then indicated that Adrian should go in.

She hadn't switched on the lights, but he was expecting a *coup de théâtre* of some sort, so he didn't object. He played the game, and stepped into the darkness, which became complete when she closed the door behind her.

She pushed him forward—not brutally, but firmly, the nature of her touch making it clear that she was positioning him. She didn't need light to know how the interior of the outbuilding was laid out. Adrian allowed himself to be maneuvered. When she stopped pushing, he heard her move away, presumably heading for the light witch.

When the lights came on, they were by no means excessively bright—indeed, they were very subtle, but he still had to blink furiously, struggling to adapt his eyes. It didn't take long for him he saw, vaguely at first, and then more precisely, and then as precisely as only he and she could see, what Angelica Jarndyke had been working on for the last seven years or so.

* * * * * * *

The murals were not confined to the walls; they covered the

ceiling and the floor as well. There was a surface area within the barn that represented a place outside the vision, a safe place to stand. Adrian realized that he was standing inside a glass cube, within the walls of the barn.

The barn had a pitched roof on top, with exposed roof beams but the artist's artifice had abolished the angles; the space within the roof now seemed curved, and the entire configuration of the barn's inner walls seemed almost spherical. The viewer within the transparent cube did not seem to be standing on the bottom of something solid, even though he *knew* that he was on a glass plane looking through it at a further floor. Adrian could see the whole spectrum of colors, but when it came to the transparency of optically-perfect glass, he could still be fooled, still subject to illusion. The visual illusion was sufficiently powerful, at least at first glance, to cancel out the tactile awareness of the feet that they were standing on something solid. So far as consciousness as concerned, he seemed to be floating—and Angelica, who was standing between him and the entrance door, seemed to be floating too.

That illusion, rather than anything painted on the walls, made Adrian glad that Angelica was there—that there was something else he could see as well as the painted imagery. She, of course, had never had that advantage before—but she had built the illusion from scratch, highly conscious of its growth and development, and had spent most of her time outside the glass cube, working on the walls. She was not disconcerted; she was at home. She was not even looking at her own work: she was watching him.

Slowly, painstakingly, Adrian looked around.

At first he was disappointed. It was not what he had expected, and he felt that all his anticipations and anxieties had been for nothing, all his hypotheses mere fantasies. There was no Hellfire to be seen there, no witches, no demons, no sinister mythological creatures. Nor, for that matter, were there any vast "splodges" in which figures were lurking, outlined in subtle variations that most human eyes and minds could not discern, although there were several patches of seemingly-limitless darkness, of true unameliorated blackness, including a large rectangular section directly opposite the entrance door, suggestive of a tunnel or an abyss: a portal to oblivion.

Perhaps, Adrian thought, the paintings he had seen so far had only been one phase of her work; Angelica seemed to have moved on. She had used all the colors of the palette in decorating the walls of her "barn," and had produced images that even Jason Jarndyke could have made out, and recognized. He would have been able to see all the faces looking up at him, and the starry sky above him, and the horizons surrounding the enormous crowd, and the true blackness in front of him.

Jason Jarndyke would even have been able to recognize the expressions on the faces of the people in the painting—their superficial expressions, at any rate—and he would have been able to experience vertigo in looking up at the sky and sideways at the distant horizons. He would even have understood, without any prompting at all, why his wife had told him that her masterpiece was not a Vita, a compendium of human life in all its aspects. He would have been able to understand, simply on the basis of what he could see, that it was quite the opposite: that this was a representation of human death, in all its aspects.

But he would not have been able to see all the detail of the depiction of death: not consciously. He would not have been able to see the leering skulls within and superimposed on every agonized face. He would not have been able to see into the graves of the cemeteries filling the horizon. Perhaps he would not have been able to see, as clearly as Adrian could, that the blackness behind the stars really *was* absolute, that the space depicted really was infinite in its appalling emptiness, and that the stars themselves, even though they were distant suns, were merely futile flickering flames, helpless to stave off the empty dark, save for the illusions they created on the surfaces of absurdly small surfaces of orbiting planets, in the deluded eyes of the minuscule creatures warming there—but he would have been able to get the gist of the message.

In theory, Adrian supposed, the faces looking up at him were countable. There must actually have been a specific number, which could be calculated and recorded—but in terms of perception, in psychological terms, there was no way to number them. They were as many as all the human that had ever lived and ever would, as different as all those human faces could be, and as similar. There were children among them, but none of them was truly alive; all of them were dying—not just the ones that bore the visible stigmata of torture and disease, but those that were seemingly healthy. He could actually see evidence of the truth that humans begin to die even before they are born, that they are sculpted by death and that death works within them.

Angelica had apparently come to the conclusion, after due experimentation, that supernatural imagery, stripped of its ancient contexts of belief, had lost its power to horrify. Even if she believed in her own witchcraft, she did not believe in its power to terrify directly. She seemed to have come to the conclusion that she needed to go directly to the source of human angst, and all her subliminal imagery was calculated to appeal to that fundamental existential dread. Perhaps that was the substance of her curse—the curse she had aimed at anyone who might see her work without being able to see it all, and without being able to understand it, out of resentment at her isolation.

There was nothing insane about it—quite the reverse. It was supersane, aimed to corrode, undermine, and perhaps eventually to break down the most cherished illusions of the human mind.

Eventually, Adrian spoke: "Not quite what I expected," he admitted.

Then she threw another invisible switch, and he realized that she had been playing with him. This time, the light was dazzling, at least momentarily—and when his madly blinking eyes had adjusted to it, he saw the remainder of the work.

The trickery of the inner cube was far more subtle than he had imagined; its transparency was manipulable. Now, thanks to the glass, the hellfire sprang forth to consume the dead, to wrench them from their rest, but not their pain. The red was superimposed on everything—and not just red, but all the subtle wrath of flame. And the black rectangle that had seemed to be a door to oblivion was now filled, with a self-portrait, of the face alone, detached from any body, and magnified to seven or eight time life-size, like a cinematic close-up.

It was a very accurate self-portrait. In fact, Adrian realized with barely a second's relay that it had actually started out as a photographic reproduction, before Angelica had begun applying her expertise in make-up to its features. Perhaps she had, in purely literal terms, used an air-brush, but she had not been aiming to erase flaws in her skin exposed by the camera. She had been aiming for a different effect, She had been aiming for Morgan le Fay, Medea, or Medusa. Using nuances that the common eye could not see, she had made every effort to give her face the power to command, the power to curse.

Adrian felt his heartbeat accelerate, his thoughts reel. Momentarily, he felt the magic, and knew that there was a sense in which he was not merely as vulnerable to it as any other man, but more so.

Then the scientist kicked in. He could *see*. He *knew* what was there, and what effect it was supposed to have on him. He could see it clinically as well as esthetically. He could analyze as well as appreciate. He wasn't required to react in purely emotional terms, or even with any emotion at all. He steadied his thoughts, and would have steadied his heartbeat too had he had the time to concentrate on relaxation. In fact, he let his heart race. It wasn't engaged in any other way.

"Holy shit," he said, eventually. "That's really something, Mrs. Jarndyke. You really have come on."

"Were you right to be frightened of what you might see?" she demanded.

"I don't know," he answered, truthfully. "I don't know yet what effects I'm going to carry away. Probably not. Probably, being able to see it *all*, to fathom it all, will be more than adequate protection, for a scientist. Don't ever let your children in here, though—and make sure that the lock is strong enough to defy their curiosity.

"They're like Jason," she said. "Fully insulated. Not as rare as our condition, but not commonplace, so far as I can tell. I do keep the door locked, mind—for now, it's hidden away. I've no intention of putting it on exhibition any time soon. For now, it's just for my amusement...and yours." The correction was telling, as was the use of such phrases as "any time soon."

"It's unsettling," Adrian said, "but it's only metaphorical magic. Even the people who'll only be affected subliminally will only get a frisson."

"Don't be disingenuous, Mr. Stamford," she said. "You know that's not the point."

Adrian knew what she meant. The point was not to scare people who might look at the work of art, or mock them with subtle *memento mori*. She had not painted this with any present or future audience in mind. She had painted it for herself, as an attempt to see herself and understand herself. It was an attempted analysis of her own unhappiness—but on that level, it was just pantomime. It had no real depth or accuracy. She was too sane for that. Perhaps, too, she was too good an artist not to let contrivance overwhelm truth. He couldn't say any of that to her, however. It wasn't for him to play the psychoanalyst. At best, he could only sympathize. That was what she wanted. That was what Jason Jarndyke wanted.

"It's brilliant, Mrs. Jarndyke," he told her. "It's unique, and it's exceedingly well done. It's beyond apprentice work—it's a masterpiece. Not your last, I dare say. Just a beginning."

"You're a scientist," she said, seemingly ignoring the flattery. "You're in the business of cutting through illusions—of making people see the truth, however unpalatable. That's what I'm trying to do...or, at least, to create the possibility of doing. I'm trying to see, and to reproduce what I see...."

She was fishing for some response to what she'd done to herself, or tried to do to herself, but she didn't want to be told that she was beautiful, or even that she was a witch. That would just have been flattery.

"I'm sorry that you're unhappy, Mrs. Jarndyke," Adrian said, colorlessly, "but I can't tell you how to be happy. I'm the last person in the world who can do that. But for what it's worth, when I look at you, *that*'s not what I see. And the fact that it's not what your husband sees isn't because he's blind to the subtleties of the color that you and I can see—it's because he's looking from a different standpoint."

"Do you think I'm crazy?" she asked, bluntly.

"No," he said, "you're not. I'm not. We're not. We just have a sensitivity that's normally the prerogative of bees and humming-birds—something that enables us to make clothes worthy of emperors, which mere street-urchins can't comprehend...but which we might be able to turn to our advantage anyway."

"I have the option of painting over it," she said. "I could do something pretty instead. Is that what you think I should do?"

Adrian knew that she wanted him to tell her that it was far too brilliant to be destroyed—that it was a precious work of art, and justified itself on those grounds alone.

"Maybe you were wrong about science, just now" he said, reflectively—because, after all, he was entitled to take his time coming to terms with what she'd shown him, and because Rome hadn't been built in a day. "If it strips away illusions and casts down idols, perhaps that's a means, not an end. The aim, ulti-mately is to enhance life, not corrode it. Religious people have never been able to see that, because they have an artificial view of what life is, and ought to be, but it isn't the case that once you lose faith, you have nothing. The truth is that, once you lose faith, there's a chance of having anything...and maybe, in the fullness of time, everything. It's not the case, Mrs. Jarndyke, that everything leads to death and to hell. It doesn't have to be. To help people to see, it might be better to make them *want* to see. Feeding their fear of seeing, by creating anxiety at the edge of perception—punishing them for not being able to see—might be counter-productive."

"So you *do* think I ought to paint over it and start again?"

"That's not for me to say," he replied, proving his cowardice. "But I really am grateful to you for letting me see this. It's very impressive—perhaps a work of genius."

"But it's not the Golden Fleece?"

"No," he agreed. "Not to me."

* * * * * * *

Adrian had hardly started working at his terminal the next morning when Jason Jarndyke appeared beside his desk.

"You got into the barn last night," he stated.

"Yes," Adrian replied, cautiously.

"My spies tell me that Angie seemed disappointed when she came in. Should I conclude that you didn't like what you saw there?"

"It's impressive," Adrian told him. "But no, I didn't like it. I'm truly sorry—but I could hardly lie about it, could I?"

"You didn't like any of her stuff, in fact, did you? Including the ones you saw at the house?"

"I liked the one of you."

"There's one of me?" Jarndyke visibly brightened.

"Yes—you've seen that one, I think. You're hidden in a yellow splodge, but I could see you."

The Industrialist shook his head. "I've been doing her an injustice all these years," he said, ruefully, "I really thought there was nothing there. Made me feel quite uncomfortable at times. I'll try to make it up to her, if I can."

He could have gone away then, but he didn't. There was something more.

"I've been in the barn, you know," the industrialist confessed. "I couldn't resist the temptation. Ange would kill me if she knew, but I had to. I had to try. I saw it all: the faces, the red light, the self-portrait. I didn't understand it, because I don't understand that sort of thing, but it seemed very clever. You saw more, though, didn't you. There are things hidden in it that I can't see—that I'm not meant to see—aren't there?"

"Yes, there are," Adrian confirmed.

"If I knew what they were...would I be worried? Should I be worried?"

"I don't think so, Mr. Jarndyke," Adrian. "To tell the truth, I was a little worried myself, beforehand...scared even...but that was silly. As you say, it's very clever. Very clever indeed. You're wife is a real artist. She still has a lot of future ahead of her."

"You won't tell her I've seen it, will you?" the industrialist said, anxiously.

"Your secret's safe with me," Adrian assured him. "All your secrets are safe with me."

"I took a risk hiring you, you know, Son. Not with respect to the product—it was obvious that you were the man for the job—but with respect to the other thing. I didn't know whether you were going to see anything at all, and I still don't know what it is you saw...but I knew that it would make a difference, either way. It was a risk."

Adrian nodded, to show that he understood.

"I'm happy," the big man told him, out of the blue. "I've always been happy. I'm a happy man. Maybe it's because I can't see things that other people can, and maybe I'm just made that way. I'd like Angie to be happy too, if that's possible. Do you think that's possible, Adrian?"

"I don't know," Adrian told him. "I'm the last person in the world who can offer an opinion on that matter."

"You think that," Jason Jarndyke said, "but I wonder if it's really true. To me, you see, it seems that you just need to get out more, to get a girl-friend, to have some fun. I think you could and should be happy—unless there's something I'm just not seeing, just not understanding."

"It's not in your interests for me to be happy, Mr. Jarndyke," Adrian reminded him. "It's in your interests for me to be single-minded, obsessive, utterly committed to the quest for the Golden Fleece. If you want to surround yourself with happy people, you could hire idiots. If you want to make trillions...."

Jarndyke cut him off. "Are you calling me an idiot?"

"Certainly not, Mr. Jarndyke," Adrian said blushing deeply. "I think you're a genius, in your way. You have everything—and it wasn't blind luck. You've *earned* everything, including happiness. Not many people can say that."

"Bullshit," said Jarndyke, although he didn't mean it, and it wasn't true.

Again, he could have left on that note and let Adrian get back to work, but again, he didn't.

"I want you to tell me what you saw in the barn," Jarndyke said. "I want you to explain to me what it was that you saw but I couldn't."

"I can't," Adrian told him.

"Because Angie forbade you to?"

"No, because I literally can't. Sometimes, you have to be there. Sometimes, it just isn't possible to explain what I can see to people who can't see it for themselves."

Lying, Adrian thought, wasn't as difficult as it sometimes seemed—and sometimes, it wasn't all that difficult to keep the story straight, even when the reasons were tangled.

"She still won't let me in, you know. You're privileged—and she doesn't hold it against you that you didn't like it. Told me this morning that you were a real treasure, and that I should be sure to cherish you. Said she wished that she could do what you can do. Can't all be scientific geniuses, though, can we? How are things coming along?" The last question was just for form's sake, to transfer the dialogue back to safe ground, to the *terra firma* of business.

"The deep reds are coming along nicely now. The test genes are ready for implantation for preliminary trials. The true blues are very slow—but organic chemistry's always had difficulty with true blues. I hope to have first of the lemon yellows ready for implantation next week...but I still haven't mastered the configuration of the perfect gold. I'll know it when I've imagined it, because it will be the most beautiful DNA sequence in the world. It's just a matter of racking my brains, reaching out a little further...eventually, I'll find it"

"It's a marathon, not a sprint," the big man said, automatically. "Making progress—that's the main thing."

"It's the only thing," Adrian replied. "It's all we have, this side of the grave. All else is illusion."

SOME LIKE IT HOT

"Gaia likes it cold."

> James Lovelock,
> *The Ages of Gaia*

Gerda Rosenhane fell in love with Kelemen Kiss—who did not like his forename and insisted on being called Kay—at the age of six, and somehow avoided ever falling out, in spite of all the customary childish quarrels and jealousies, adolescent metamorphoses and adult shifts in perspective. She was able to fall in love with him in the first place, and to sustain their relationship for many years thereafter, because they spent their childhood living on the same street in Strasbourg, within walking distance of the European Parliament.

The resilience of their relationship was greatly aided by the fact that Gerda and Kay had the same birthday, March 12th; they always celebrated it together as children, thus founding a tradition that extended far into adulthood.

Under other circumstances, the cultural differences between Gerda, who was Swedish, and Kay, who was Hungarian, might have been immense, but they not only lived on the same street but attended the same school: the so-called New International School, whose pupils came from the assorted nations of the EU, but where all the classes were taught in English. Everything in their world tended to be prefaced with the label "New", even though the practice was getting rather old. As beneficiaries or victims of New Internationalism, however, they were certainly united in their cultural affiliations in a way that even their immediate families did not entirely understand.

Another circumstance that helped Gerda and Kay find common cause in their early days was that they only had one parent each, and that the parents in question, busy about the ever-problematic business of running Europe, were almost entirely absent from their quotidian lives. Gerda's father, an EU bureaucrat, had died on a fact-finding trip to the vanishing Arctic ice-cap before her second birthday, a victim of the treacherously-melting ice; Kay's mother—a much-married woman—had resumed her briefly-interrupted career as a celebrity model as soon as she had recovered her figure after the relevant divorce, which was finalized not long after her pregnancy came to term.

At six, Gerda believed, with an innocently boundless conviction of which only six-year-olds are normally capable, that Kay was her other half—or, because she had a precocious love of language, her "inevitable counterpart". They did, in fact, look uncannily alike, apart from the fact that Gerda was very pale of complexion, blonde and blue-eyed, while Kay was dark, black-haired and brown-eyed. "Like opposing pawns on a chessboard," Gerda's mother once observed, rather unkindly—quickly adding, for the sake of kindness, even though it wrecked the analogy: "But one day, when you're grown up, you'll be a queen."

Even at the age of six, Gerda had been able to reply. "I can't, Mummy. We live in a democracy."

When Gerda and Kay started at the NIS, the fact that all its classes were taught in English was only mildly controversial, but by the time they reached their final year it had become a running sore of angry contention. This was not because anything had happened in the meantime to the ever-dubious reputation of the United Kingdom, which was still the Crazy Man of Europe, but because it was universally recognized that the NIS practice of offering classes in English had nothing to do with far-from-Merry England and everything to do with an "American cultural hegemony" that was supposed to have died in the first half of the twenty-first century, and whose inertial persistence within the World Wide Web generated a good deal of World Wide Resentment. Pragmatism insisted, however, that if any language were ever to get the children of Europe's elite talking like a true community, English was the only possible candidate, so English survived while "American cultural hegemony" became effectively synonymous, on European lips, with "the poisonous ideas that got us into this unholy mess".

The unholy mess in question was, of course, the CC. Hardly anyone called it the Carbon Crisis any more, as if merely spelling out its name might somehow make the catastrophe worse. Indeed, such were the mysterious ways in which euphemism operated, that it was often re-expanded, with calculated absurdity, as "the Cubic Centimeter"—except in England, where the cultural significance of the letters CC was as farcically out of step with the rest of Europe as everything else. There, the unholy mess was routinely referred to, in a similar spirit of perverse flippancy, as the Cricket Club, even though—as the smart kids at the NIS were fond of pointing out, in order to demonstrate that the Second Great Depression hadn't entirely robbed the world of its sense of humor—the only things England had that remotely resembled crickets were itsy-bitsy grasshoppers, which no one ever hunted with clubs, or even packs of hounds.

Long before she came to the end of her schooldays, Gerda had grown used to thinking of her relationship with Kay as an unholy mess, but it wasn't the same kind of unholy mess as the CC, even though the CC had already become tangled up in it. The CC was all about unwelcome overheating, but Gerda's love for Kay had never had a chance to overheat, because Kay had never given it a chance to do so. When Gerda first confessed to Kay that he was her other half, her inevitable counterpart, he agreed, but his casual manner made it obvious that he didn't really understand. It soon became painfully clear to Gerda that he understood the analogy in a very different way. He thought that they were like non-identical twins: that his idea of "inevitability" was that they were and would always remain pseudo-siblings, as close as close could be but in an inviolably non-erotic sense. As time passed, although his sexual indifference never became a hostile jet of ice-cold water chilling the force of her emotion, it definitely functioned as a frustrating gust of carbon dioxide, warm enough in its fashion but fatal to wholehearted flamboyance.

Because she continued stubbornly to yearn for him, in a pathetically desperate fashion, Gerda grudgingly accepted and adapted to Kay's insistence on thinking of her as a sister. By slow degrees, as she passed through puberty and matured into an adult, she even managed to half-convince herself that perhaps it was for the best; romance was, after all, an obsolete twentieth-century delusion born of a world careless of the deadly Cubic Centimeter, blithely unconscious of the holocaust to come. She, as an apostle of New Internationalism, owed her first and greatest dedication to whatever part she might be able to play in the Great Crusade for the Salvation of Civilization.

There were, of course, many parts available in that great drama, which was an end that lent itself to many means, but Gerda and Kay were MEP kids in an era when European politics was proudly recovering the old dynastic dimensions that it had briefly forsaken in the twentieth century. There was a tacit expectation in the NIS that the best of its students would become the MEPs and EU bureaucrats of the future, and that all other vocations were second-rate. Kay was never in any doubt that he would follow in his father's footsteps, but Gerda was not at all sure that she wanted to follow in her mother's. This was not because of any difference in the quality of the role models that Miklos Kiss and Selma Rosenhane provided, but did have something to do with the fact that they were routinely opposed in key debates, Miklos being an orthodox Gaian utterly dedicated to the war against global warming, while Selma represented a constituency that had seen significant local benefits from the shift in climate and were not at all averse to keeping them, in spite of the nasty problems that were being caused elsewhere.

While Gerda and Kay were children, their parents flew home

on a regular basis to visit their constituencies—Selma Rosenhane to Kiruna, Miklos Kiss to Szeged—but the need to maintain the continuity of their NIS schooling and conserve their NIS-based social lives meant that the only times Gerda ever saw Sweden and Kay saw Hungary were during the long summer vacations. There was a sense in which they both felt even closer to the beating heart of EU politics than their parents did, but that sense of closeness affected them differently. The fact that it was his father who currently had a seat in the chamber never seemed to Kay to be anything more than a mere technicality, and Kay lived in the expectation not only of one day stepping into his father's shoes but also of finding them a perfect fit. Gerda, on the other hand, was not so sure that her mother's shoes were the correct size, or the most apt design; in particular, she was not sure that her mother was sufficiently passionate in the cause she represented.

Kay and Gerda remained united, however, in the conviction that they had been born with a mission to change the world, and that their schooling constituted an intense training-program that would allow them to carry their mission through. The Strasbourg chamber was still afflicted by the Curse of the Thousand-and-One Interpreters, but in the corridors of the NIS there was no need for such barriers to understanding. Even the six-year-olds there knew that they were the future in embryo, whose responsibility it would be to steer the New Old World through the climatic ravages of the CC. Such subsidiary tasks as defending the EU against the economic ravages of the New New World of Asian Slow Developers—whose brief days as Asian Rapid Developers had recently run into the bumpers at the end of the Great Historical Track—were also on the agenda, but the focal point of all their hopes, fears and endeavors was the Cubic Centimeter.

* * * * * * *

Kay was a trifle envious of Gerda's summer holidays in the

Far North, not because they took her away from him for weeks on end—which always left her own heart more than a trifle desolate—but because they gave Gerda an opportunity to see snow. The snow in question was not, admittedly in her immediate vicinity, but on the as-yet-undefrosted mountain-tops that formed Kiruna's western horizon. Snow was snow, though, and everyone knew that it was soon to become extinct, except in Antarctica, where the colossal mass of the great ice-sheet was not yet in a tearing hurry to be gone. Snow was symbolic of Gaia's ongoing decline; it was her favorite dress, and all true Gaians loved it. Gerda had never known the ravages that snow and ice could inflict on populations for whom winter was Hell, but she nevertheless contrived, during her summers in Kiruna, to absorb something of the traditional local terror. She never like snow herself, and became impatient with Kay's reverence.

"Green is supposed to be Gaia's color," she told Kay, ostentatiously when they came together again after the summer that divided the Elementary and Secondary sectors of their NIS education. "There's plenty of green in Kiruna nowadays. The New Agricultural Revolution is just as spectacular in Sweden as it is in Greenland and Siberia. Nobody there wants the old winters back."

"Szeged may not be the hell on Earth that Southern Italy and Spain have become," Kay retorted, dutifully reciting the Gaian party line, "but it's still bearing the cost of your New Agricultural Revolution. I know that your population's expanding as people from the drowned coasts are relocated, but it's tiny by comparison with the numbers whose livelihoods have been wrecked. We live in a democracy, remember. Anyway, I hate spending summers in Szeged. My great-great-great-grandfather should never have moved from the mountains to the city. It's still tolerable up there, even in July—so they say."

Everyone in the International School was an expert in European geography by the age of eleven, and most of the pupils were fairly well up in European history, in spite of its appalling intricacies, so Gerda was able to reply: "But the mountains that

your ancestors came from are in Rumania now. If your ancestors had stayed where they were, your father wouldn't be a
Hungarian MEP. He'd be a tourist guide showing crazy English
people round one of Count Dracula's alleged castles."

"The real Dragulya was a Magyar, and therefore quintes-
sentially Hungarian," Kay pointed out, attempting to claim the
intellectual high ground, as he always did before going on to
state the obvious. "Anyway, he'd be a Rumanian MEP instead.
He was a born politician. Everybody says so."

Even at eleven, Gerda knew that Kay's arguments carried
real weight. The Greenlanders, Laplanders, Siberians and
Kamchatkans were tiny in number by comparison with the
southern Europeans who had been displaced by rising sea levels
or seen their agricultural bases shrivel beneath the effects of
devastating heat-waves and violent storms. Even the Siberian
Oligarchs paid lip-service to Gaian ideals, like ancient would-
be saints crying "Lord, give me chastity—but please, *not
yet*!" Even so, it never occurred to her to modify her gathering
political convictions simply because Kay, whom she loved so
desperately, did not share them.

Much later in life, Gerda came to suspect that the peculiar
dynamics of their personal relationship might have intensified
their political opposition. She suspected, too, that the true—
subconscious—reason for Kay's failure to understand that her
beliefs were correct, while his were seriously misled, was his
refusal to admit that he really was her other half, her inevitable
counterpart. Even while they were still at school, she could not
help believing that there was a sense in which Kay could not
really believe what he claimed to believe, but must be a victim
of delusion, of some strange arcane spell cast upon him by an
inability to connect with or comprehend the wisdom of his heart.

Although Kay claimed, as all committed Gaians did, that his
ambition to reduce the levels of greenhouse gases in the atmosphere was purely based in reason and utilitarian calculation,
Gerda came to suspect, even before she completed her education, that it was really based in unthinking idolatry, and that in

worshiping Gaia, he and the rest of the vast democratic majority that he aspired to represent were merely cherishing the chains of an ancient bondage.

Gerda, on the other hand, became firmly convinced that the world needed a new Mother, if it needed a Mother at all—and her conviction of that was as firm as her love for Kay. Her love for her own mother was just as firm, but it was increasingly infected with a conviction that Selma Rosehane was a member of the opposition for all the wrong reasons. Had Selma been born in Szeged, like Miklos Kiss, she would have been a committed Gaian, because that would have been the obvious way to gather votes and the most useful source of profitable alliances. Hungary was hardly in the front line of the CC, having no coastline and still being ten degrees north of the Creeping Tropic, but the only pro-change nation with which it had a border was Ukraine, which was only pro-change because it was in Russia's pocket, and Moscow was now the hapless puppet of the Siberian Oligarchs.

Selma Rosenhane was no Laplander, ethnically speaking, but Lapland was her vote-cropping turf; her political allegiances and alliances were forged in the hinterlands of the Arctic Circle, on the shores of the New Blue Ocean, whose present shore-dwellers—especially the immigrant "converts" to whom it seemed a land of limitless opportunity—did not take kindly to the fact that the rest of the world had taken to calling it "the Methane A-Bomb" since the ice-cap had disappeared and the waters had started soaking up the sunlight. Selma was, however, too canny a politician not to play the Gaian game; she not only paid lip-service to the idea that the CC was a global disaster, but accepted it. Even in her own opinion, she was merely one of the worst of the vast multitude of bad Gaians who deplored the way the world was going but did not want to make the personal sacrifices required to return it to its old stability.

Gerda, by contrast, became an honest and devout anti-Gaian, who wanted to find a new stability rather than returning to the old one: a warmer, more passionate Earth Mother, who did not care to dress in snow and ice, who did not love a world that was cold and bleak. She admitted that the ecosphere might not be able to find a new stability unaided, but that was because the ecosphere was under Gaia's dominion. If the ecosphere could not achieve a new stability unaided, Gerda thought, then it was up to humankind—a humankind intellectually and materially liberated from Gaia's dominion—to discover and impose one. That would certainly require a more profound change in human behavior than a patchy migration from the Creeping Tropics to the New Temperate Zones—but who, in their right minds, could possibly believe that Gaia's humankind was so perfect as not to require real and profound change?

* * * * * * * *

Kay did not seem to understand, at first, that Gerda was not simply following in her mother's footsteps in taking up an anti-Gaian stance. When they both stood for election as Student President in their final year at the IS, thus coming into open conflict for the first time, Kay tried to take advantage of their mutual birthday party to persuade her not to do it—and, indeed, that that the platform on which she intended to stand made her a traitor to her own people as well as the entire human race. It was, by coincidence, the first birthday party they had entirely to themselves, in one of Strasbourg's most carefully air-conditioned restaurants—an indulgence for which Selma Rosenhane and Miklos Kiss had grudgingly agreed to pay the bill.

"Just because you've seen snow in the distance, my dear sister," he said, sternly "doesn't mean that you're a real northerner. You're Strasbourg through and through. Your mother might have been sent here to give the barbarians a voice, but your mission in life ought to be to carry the good word in the other direction. It's up to the children of the Arctic MEPs to explain to the up-and-coming generation why the fact that atmospheric warming might make Novaya Zemlya into the new Caribbean and turn Siberia into the world's grain basket is not adequate compensation for the devastation of the Mediterranean, even if one only takes economic costs into account. We all have to be better Gaians now than we've contrived to be before—better *practicing* Gaians I mean—else the world is doomed. All opposition, wherever it's based, lends dangerous support to the reckless and the gluttonous, encouraging them to continue their bad habits. Anyway, I'm bound to win—you'll be humiliated."

"The point, beloved," Gerda riposted, affectionately, "is not to worship Gaia more devoutly, but to cast her idol down. She has held the world in icy thrall too long. Now that spring is here, the task at hand for humankind is not to preserve what vestiges of winter we can for as long as possible but to make proper preparations for glorious summer. And whether you win or not, and however large your majority might be, you're backing the wrong horse. We're the third or fourth generation that has battled with its conscience over carbon restraint, and people will soon be exhausted by the toils of the losing battle. Gaian politics is on the point of collapse; it's only a matter of time before the balance tips and the opposition catches fire. All the true cause will need to bring about a revolution in ideas is a clever torch-bearer."

"You?" he said, with an unintentional hint of a sneer that was a stab in the heart, not so much because it was a sneer as because it was so utterly casual.

"Maybe not," she admitted. "But somebody with ideas similar to mine. The slogans that will win the future are ours:

FREE THE CARBON
WAKE UP TO WARMTH
BIOMASS IS OPPORTUNITY
HEAT IS GOOD
GO WITH THE FLOW, NOT AGAINST IT
EVOLUTION, NOT DEVOLUTION
PROGRESS, NOT REGRESS

Shall I go on?"

"Do you really think the voters will go for that sort of crap?" he asked her bluntly, effortlessly coming all the way down from the intellectual high ground he had initially tried to occupy. "Here in Strasbourg I mean, not in the ex-frozen wastes of northern Sweden."

"Maybe not," she replied, "but a true statesman's job is to change public opinion, not to reflect it. You might win this battle, by courtesy of historical inertia, but you can't win the war. You can't stop progress, and the CC really is progress, no matter how frightening it seems."

"Frightening? It's more than frightening, sister. It's costing live—billions of lives."

"Everybody has one life, my love, and nobody loses it more than once. It's Gaia's world that can't sustain the present population, and Gaia's people who've produced it regardless. Maybe a better, warmer world can sustain a larger human population, and maybe it can't—but there's every chance that it will sustain a wiser population, because it will need a wiser population to create and sustain it."

"You can't dismiss the misery of billions of people with that kind of smart rhetoric."

"And you shouldn't try to sustain that misery with stupid rhetoric."

It was at that point that the argument came close to spoiling the meal, and the birthday—which was something that neither of them wanted.

"Anyway, this student presidency thing is kids' stuff," Kay told Gerda, relenting his tone a little. "It's a game. We won't be going into battle until we actually graduate from uni—which is why you still have time to switch sides and join the White Knights. In real life, if not in proverbial wisdom, it's the side that wins the battles that wins the war, and the Gaian majority is solid. It won't disappear in our lifetimes unless the methane bomb goes off and the CC turns into the Venus Effect. School politics is only play-acting, but we'll be embroiled in the real thing soon enough. Do you really want to be stuck in the struggling opposition? You don't have to step into Selma's shoes, flying the flag of prevarication for avaricious Eskimos and the Siberian Oligarchs—there are plenty of other things you might do. Your father was a bureaucrat, working on the day-to-day amelioration of the crisis, and there'll always be more than enough to do in that direction. If you don't want that, you could always work for me. We've always had a useful camaraderie, and every great front man needs great back-up."

"There's a world of difference," Gerda replied, sadly, "between being friends and being a team." Because she was exactly the same height as he was, she was able to look him straight in the eye without any implicit disadvantage, and she knew full well that blue eyes were better equipped for staring, but she took the fact that he eventually looked away as solid evidence of the virtue of her cause.

Kay won the NIS presidential election hands down, just as he had predicted, but Gerda wasn't unduly downhearted. The game had a long way to go before the final whistle. Kay might have put the first point on the board, but Gerda felt, passionately that history and evolution really were on her side. As with all the other gods and goddesses that humankind had ever worshipped, the ideals that Gaia stood for were more honored in the breach than the observance. In Christendom, the meek had conspicuously failed to inherit the Earth, and even the loudest of Gaia's preachers continued to breathe out more than their fair share of carbon dioxide, without ever managing to dampen civilization's industrial flamboyance.

* * * * * * *

Gerda and Kay never discussed the possibility of going on to the same university after leaving the NIS. Kay took it for granted that the tacit parting of their ways introduced into their lives by their increasing commitment to opposing political ideologies would extend to an actual parting of the ways, and Gerda accepted the assumption—but she was able to leave it to

Kay to insist that they meet up at least once a year to celebrate their birthday.

"I'll never give up hope of bringing you into the fold," he told her. "I'll keep on trying to win you over."

"So will I," she promised.

Even Kay, of course, could not step directly into his father's shoes after university, mainly because his father was still wearing them and fully intended to go on doing so for another ten or twenty years. That was a normal situation for ex-IS students to be in, and the conventional career-path of the school's elite had to accommodate that period of delay. Most went to Brussels, which had clung on to the greater part of its bureaucratic functions when the legislative chamber had revised the whole system, in order to serve as cogs in the administrative machine while they waited for power-charged slots to open up, and that was what Kay did. Gerda, on the other hand, decided to stay on at her own university—Bern—as a postgraduate researcher.

When she communicated this decision to Kay on their twenty-second birthday, when they met up in Budapest, where he had taken his own degree, he was not at all surprised. He even seemed to take a certain satisfaction in her decision, as if he imagined that he could take some credit for it. Mistakenly—mistaking her motives had become second nature to him by now—he jumped to the conclusion that she was planning to abandon politics permanently, having realized the folly of setting up a campaign-tent outside the Gaian encampment.

"It's a wise move," he told her, smiling to demonstrate his goodwill. "Academic life is a safe haven, especially for...what was the title of your course, again?"

Gerda knew that Kay had studied International Relations, as a good MEP kid should; he, on the other hand, only contrived to remember that she had not. "Practical Botany," she reminded him.

"Right," he said, putting on a show of vagueness. "I knew it sounded as if it had something to do with flowers, even though it was really about crop engineering. Good decision—plant engineering is hotter than ever. It's not just a matter of tweaking staple crops to help them adapt to changing climatic conditions, is it? The necessity of compensation for insect decline has forced the engineers to be more adventurous. And it's still the cutting edge of carbon sink technology, even if it hasn't delivered yet."

"Plant engineering is crucial to the world's future," Gerda agreed, as she had at least twice before, when Kay had condescended to make similar remarks on their previous birthday meetings. His affected vagueness was intended to assist him in maintain the appearance of knowing where the intellectual high ground was, even though his ignorance of the intimate details of genetic engineering prevented him from operating there. It never worked, and Gerda always took a certain delight in watching him flounder as he tried to pretend that he knew and understood more than he did.

"I've heard good things about contemporary work on hemp and...er...those primitive trees that were among the first colonists of the land," Kay said, blushing when he was momentarily unable to conjure up the second term.

"Cycads," said Gerda, helpfully. "Gymnosperms that look like crosses between tree-ferns and palms. Very interesting to engineers because of their lack of attention to strict speciation."

"Right," said Kay. "Will you be doing anything with hemp or cycads?"

"As a matter of fact," Gerda said, "I will."

"Which?" was all that Kay was able to say by way of follow-up.

"A bit of both," she said. "I'm not a front-line engineer, modifying small sets of genes to produce new strains of existing species. I'm more of a genomic designer—a strategist rather than a tactician. Making incremental improvements in the old staples is all very well, and there's certainly a spur of urgency driving such work right now, but the process is too much like the early development of systemic computer code—or natural selection, for that matter. It's just one quick fix after another, improvised patches gradually building up into nightmarishlyconfused strata. Somebody has to think on a bigger scale, and in a longer term."

Kay obviously had little or no idea what she meant, but he wasn't about to ask for enlightenment in any craven fashion. "At least you'll be working for the cause," he said. "The Heavy Metal brigade still favors engineering solutions to the problem of getting carbon dioxide out of the atmosphere and turning the methane-bomb problem into an energy-producing opportunity, and they have industry's inherited quadrillions behind them, but I'm all in favor of the natural approach. Gaia made trees to secure her own carbon balance, so that's probably the wisest way to get back to twentieth century carbon dioxide levels, if we can only make the crucial breakthrough. That's what the current work on hemp is all about, isn't it?"

Gerda flashed him a broad smile, as she always did—without always being conscious of it—before she set out to lead him up the garden path. "Hemp's old news," she told him. "It's a perfect carbon-sink crop, I suppose—it grows like wildfire, and every part of the crop is useful."

Kay knew enough to amplify that. "The fibers have always been used to make rope," he said, "but modern engineers have expanded their textile versatility marvelously. The woody shiv produces building-materials—properly processed, the material is as strong as concrete. We've got several initiatives in hand to increase its use, although your mother's friends keep making smart remarks about rebuilding the Kremlin, the Taj Mahal, the Vatican and the White House out of matchsticks. Is that the sort of thing you're working on?"

"No. Insofar as hemp figures in my genomic schemes, it's the leaves that are the interesting part. We all know what sort of potential the leaves of *Cannabis sativa* have as brain-food."

Kay furrowed his black eyebrows at that. "I thought the engineers were trying to take the psychotropics out of the leaves," he said. "Even the industrial varieties that have been tweaked to make the leaves usable animal-fodder only preserve a mild tranquilizing effect."

"That's the present situation," Gerda agreed. "All of the research to date has focused on adapting the foliage as a foodstuff or a biofuel source—but that's a bit wasteful, in my view. If we've got abundant potential already there for the production of cannabinols, why not exploit it? That's where the wise money is going now. Give the world a better building material, and people will shake you by the hand; give them a better way to get high and they'll love you forever."

"I don't know about that," Kay said, dubiously—and accurately.

"If Gaia made trees to strike the right compositional balance in the atmosphere," Gerda told him, carefully keeping a straight face, "she must have made psychotropics to strike the right compositional balance in the noösphere. She's an all-round chill-out fan, after all."

* * * * * * *

After that exchange, Kay didn't bother to ask about the cycads, any more than he probed any deeper to find out whether Gerda really had been converted to the Gaian cause—but the cycads were, in Gerda's opinion, far more important than hemp to the cause of remaking the word. Hemp was a Gaian agent through and through: an old-school carbon sink that loved a relatively cool environment. If the newly-fertile lands of northern Europe were to be planted with vast forests of generically-engineered hemp, the rains that fell on them would continue to be dutifully temperate, and the northward progress of the Creeping Tropic would be inhibited, even if it were not eventually reversed.

If Gaia were to be permanently toppled from her icy throne and replaced by a Mother with fire in her loins, in Gerda's opinion, hemp could only be awarded a peripheral role in the deicidal army, perhaps as a sly double agent. A host of new cycads, on the other hand, might well provide shock-troops capable of turning the battle into a rout.

For the moment, research on cycads, like research on many

other species, was being driven by anxieties about the global decline of insect populations. People who thought botany had "something to do with flowers" considered flowering plants to be one of Gaia's artistic masterstrokes, and were horrified by the thought that much of that beauty might be lost because many of the nasty insects that had long undertaken the duty of pollinating them were in danger of extinction. Flowering plants had, of course, been so outstandingly successful in the eternal war of natural selection precisely because insect pollination allowed them to range further and faster than plants relying on less agile and versatile pollination-mechanisms. Where the insect-pollinated angiosperms had led, the sturdier varieties had been able to follow, including the fruit-producers that used evolutionary johnny-come-latelies like birds and mammals as seed-transmitters.

Now that the insects, birds and mammals were all on the decline as rapid climate change took its punishing toll, the pressure on agriculturalists and genetic engineers to save the angiosperms had become intense, but the difficultly of the task was such that biotechnologists had been forced to examine the possibility of a bolder substitution, responding to a potential angiosperm die-back by introducing new and carefully-enhanced models of the various kinds of plants that the angiosperms had replaced, especially the most ancient: tree-ferns and cycads. The primitive nature of their genomes gave them a certain precious flexibility, which more recent species had forsaken. Cycads, in particular, seemed remarkably amenable to exotic genetic augmentation, unusually hospitable to gene-complexes transplanted from very different species, including fungi and animals. They had never made much appeal to tactical engineers because they had few economically-useful properties to be enhanced, but from the viewpoint of genomic strategist they were raw clay, which might be molded into anything at all by flesh-sculptors of genius.

Gerda knew that it was the versatility of specialized angiosperms, more than any other single factor, that had facilitated

Gaia's manifestation as the Snow Queen, cooling the Earth down from the much higher temperatures that had been normal when gymnosperms ruled the climate. Gerda was interested in cycads not because they might have the potential to take up slack as Gaia's favorite carbon sinks ran into difficulties, but because they might have the potential to initiate a much more profound metamorphosis in the ecosphere. For the neo-cycads, Gerda thought, the imaginable might be only the beginning. The ultimate objective of human intelligence, as she saw it, was to roll back the horizons of the presently-imaginable into the realms of the previously-undreamed-of—and for that, flesh-sculptors of genius would require the proper clay.

Gerda was perfectly well aware, of course, that humankind had been a casual by-product of Gaia's fondness for a cool throne. It was not so much that *Homo sapiens* was a mammal, designed to live in a cool environment—its ancestor-species had, after all, evolved in the tropics—but that its great leap forward, in evolutionary terms, had resulted from the sequence of Ice Ages in which Gaia had displayed her most recent ward-robe. It had been the domestication of fire—the foundation of all technology—that had allowed human beings to colonize almost the entire land surface of the globe, including such inhospitably cold regions as northern Sweden. Gerda was not prepared, however, to draw the conclusion from this intrinsic indebtedness that humankind was bound to remain Gaia's slave forever, trying loyally with all its collective might to restore the world to the climate *she* liked best.

In Gerda's view, such ecological conservatism could only lead to evolutionary petrifaction and an end to progress. If humankind were to continue to advance, it needed to evolve; and to evolve, it needed new challenges, new pressures and new opportunities.

Gaia had cooled the world down by putting carbon that had once been incorporated into living organisms into a whole series of inert deposits: coal and oil sealed up in geological strata, methane held in crystalline clathrates in permafrosts and on the sea bed. The cost of the ecosphere's cooling had, in consequence, been a massive loss of biomass: biomass that had once been embodied in species that thrived in the heat, based in jungles and swamps that must have made angiosperm-dominated rain-forests look like mere kitchen-gardens by comparison. There had been no deserts in those days, when it really had never rained but it poured.

Unlike Kelemen Kiss and his pusillanimous majority, Gerda Rosenhane did not want to design new carbon sinks in order to calm the atmosphere down and make the Earth cool again. She wanted to design new carbon *carriers*, in order to liberate all the dead carbon from Gaia's miserly hoards, to give it life again and to restore the ecosphere to all its prodigal glory. She believed that humankind, armed with a sophisticated biotechnology, could not merely come through that transition but thrive on it, emerging stronger than before—and she also believed that if the species' statesmen would only condescend to become constructive strategists instead of mere reactive tacticians, they ought to be able to take control of the metamorphosis and guide it.

Cycads were to be her secret weapon; they had lost their first battle against the angiosperms, but the war was not yet over. With the right scientific allies, there was every chance that they might be re-equipped to take full advantage of the trouble that the angiosperms had run into as their traditional pollinators died in droves. If they were to do so, however—if the world were to be fitted out with a new and enduring heat-loving ecosphere—they would need human foot-soldiers to clear their way. Gerda knew full well that the war would first have to be won in the political arena, and that was where she intended to fight when the time was ripe.

In Gaia's cool world however—in spite of the fact that it had now been in dire danger of becoming seriously uncool for the better part of a century—time, like fruits, did not ripen overnight.

* * * * * * *

While Gerda labored patiently and unobtrusively in Bern, Kay's career went from strength to strength. He inherited his father's seat in the Strasbourg Parliament at thirty, became EU ambassador to Beijing at thirty-three, and at thirty-six was one of the key architects of the fifty-first Global Carbon Treaty—the first one, in the estimate of many cynical observers, that actually stood a slim chance of remaining unbroken for more than a decade. By the time he turned forty he was widely known as the Hemp King, not so much because he had made billions of euros investing in hemp biotechnology, planting and processing, as by virtue of the fact that he had become such an enthusiastic propagandist for the existential benefits of neo-cannabinols.

When he met up with Gerda in Brussels for their private fortieth birthday celebration—he had such an elevated public profile that he had now to have an "official" one as well, although she did not—Kay was careful to give Gerda due thanks for this particular aspect of his success.

"You were absolutely right," he told her. "Carbon sinks, polite handshakes; better highs, unconditional love."

"Not unconditional," she corrected him, blandly. "There's no such thing as unconditional love in politics."

"That's true," he admitted, "but the principle holds good. The utilitarian aspects of Gaia-worship will save the world, but the spiritual aspects help it to want to be saved. Good Gaians need to get their heads straight."

"That's a trifle glib too," she pointed out. "Neo-cannabinols reduce appetites, in more ways than one. They enable people to be happy in consuming less and doing less, but that's not really *the spiritual aspect of Gaia-worship*, is it?"

"You really have turned into a scientist, haven't you?" he retorted. "Full marks for pedantry. Mind you, you were never the easiest person in the world to compliment. Perhaps I should content myself with simply saying thanks."

"You're welcome," she said.

"Mind you," he said, "we're still running faster just to stay in the same place. The pace at which things are getting worse probably isn't accelerating any more, but we're going to need something new to help us turn the corner. The methane bomb hasn't stopped ticking, and it has to be defused. If something were to trigger a massive clathrate-release, we'd really be sunk. You biotech wizards haven't got any ingenious new algae in the pipeline, by any chance? Ideally, something that we can sow on the surface of the New Blue Ocean to help stabilize its temperature and soak up an extra measure of carbon dioxide. The Heavy Metal brigade are still pouring their inherited quadrillions into the search for a mechanical solution, of course, trying to find a mining technology that will allow them to strip the methane out and process it for use as household gas, but you know my take on the problem. Mother Gaia gave us seaweed to help keep the world in balance, so that's probably the best way to get the balance back again. Edible fish stocks have recovered somewhat since the CC wiped out the dolphins and all those other greedy predators, but all the reports say that the plankton are almost at the end of their tether, and that we need to rebuild the marine ecosphere from the bottom up, if we can. I've heard some good things about kelp, but I'd appreciate an off-the-record opinion from someone who isn't primarily concerned with protecting their EC funding."

"Algae aren't the answer," Gerda told him, bluntly. "I suppose Kelemen Kiss the Kelp King has a certain ring to it, but I wouldn't put your own hard-earned billions into it if I were you. Not that I'm an expert on algae, mind. Modern classification has excluded them from the plant kingdom, so they're not in Practical Botany's bag any more."

"You could have made billions too, if you'd been prepared to take risks," Kay pointed out, his features briefly exhibiting what might have been a twinge of guilt. "You can't blame me for getting rich on your advice. You should have had the balls to act on it yourself."

"The comment about giving people a better high wasn't advice, Kay," Gerda told him. "It was a flippant remark—just idle rhetoric. Only politicians can't tell the difference."

He might have blushed at that had his complexion been paler, but any hint of emergent pink was lost in the bronze. "So what *is* the answer, sister mine?" he asked. "Biotechnically speaking, that is."

"There was a time," she said, "when algae pioneered the conquest of the land—but they didn't hold the lead in that particular race for long. They adapted well enough to fresh water, but the vast expanse of the primal continent required something cleverer. That's where the plants came in, and never looked back, even though they might have taken a wrong turn or two on evolution's highway. Maybe it's time to start looking back, investigating unexplored avenues of potential—or unexplored plunges of potential."

Kay took a moment or two to catch her meaning. "Oh," he said, when he had. "You mean reversion to the sea—like the poor old dolphins."

Gerda nodded. "Not a bad analogy, my love," she conceded, graciously. "Reptiles and mammals both evolved on land, participants in a selective process driven by the imperatives of land life—but both orders produced species that successfully re-adapted to life in the sea, where many of them preyed very successfully on the fish that had stayed there all along, and others became world-champion plankton-filterers. You're right—given that plants are so much cleverer than algae, why shouldn't they produce species better adapted to sea life than the algae are?"

Kay caught a glimpse of a patch of intellectual high ground and raced to occupy it. "Difficult for plants to work on the sea bed, though," he said. "Chlorophyll only works close to the surface, so that's where the green algae are, and the food-chains that depend on them; the sea-bed food-chain thrives on the dead bits that sink down."

"Trees thrive on land," Gerda said, nodding in agreement, "because there's considerable selective advantage in lifting foliage up, above the competition—but in the sea, living organisms can float. Even kelp, which often anchors itself to the bottom even in deep water, in basically a floater rather than a sturdy-boled thruster. Only corals build marine dendrites on a truly heroic scale."

"They used to," said Kay, glumly. "Almost extinct now. You reckon that could change, though, with a little help from biotech? You think plants might be able to take over the niches that corals have left vacant? You think they might take the shallows back, at least? The forests drowned by rising sea-levels don't seem to be coping very well on their own, though, and the vast increase in swampland has been disastrous for serious economic activity."

"That," said Gerda, "is because it's the wrong type of swampland. Angiosperm swamplands have always been precarious things, never capable of much in the way of versatility and aggressive expansion. Gymnosperms had a lot more practice at swamp life, especially in the days before the primal continent broke up and continental drift began to open up the deep trenches and push up the high mountains, so that much larger tracts of land dried out completely. Mother Gaia's drainage system didn't do the gymnosperms any favors, alas."

"Cycads!" Kay exclaimed, getting there at last. "I've heard good things about cycads too. Primitive, but lots of untapped potential, according to the reports I've scanned. You think they might be able to take back the new shallows—and maybe, in time, the continental shelves—in a manner that will permit agricultural exploitation?"

"Thus far," Gerda said, as if she were merely following the meandering course of an improvised reverie, "the rise in sea levels has been an unmitigated nuisance—but it might yet provide opportunities as well as threats. With the bulk of the Antarctic ice-cap still to melt, it might be advisable to look harder at the potential opportunities. The ideal sea-bed plant, you know, isn't one that simply sends up kelp-like fronds to float on the surface...."

"It's one that extends foliage above the surface," Kay continued, allowing his imagination to be gripped. "Trunk below, crown above. Algae can't do that—not without massive genetic modification, at least—but plants might be more readily adaptable...if only we can identify the right kinds of plant. Plants grow best on land where there's a lot of leaf litter and other organic debris in the soil...if marine plants were able to mop up methane from the sea-bed and dissolved carbon dioxide as well as extracting carbon dioxide from the atmosphere, they could be really useful. How easy will it be?"

"Fiendishly difficult," Gerda admitted. "Lots of problems, including the salt in the water, the destructive potential of tides and waves—but even some of those problems might be turned into opportunities, if the genomic strategists are ingenious enough."

"The reports I get," Kay mused, "keep telling me that it will take a long time to get the sea-level back down to where it was in the twentieth century, even if we can stabilize the atmospheric temperature. The next best thing, in the short term, is to find a means of making the inundated land economically viable. If it were possible to develop off-shore orchards...it wouldn't be much, but it would be better than nothing. What are the chances of putting living accommodation in the crowns of your sea-dwelling trees, and connecting up the individual crowns with rope-bridges or something similar? We could really do with some new rope technologies, to help maintain the price of hemp."

"It would certainly be possible for people to live in the kind of swampland I envisage," Gerda said, guardedly, "provided that they were prepared to adapt their lifestyles to the necessities of the situation. With population pressure the way it is, there'd be every incentive."

"How far away are we from initial viable product?" Kay wanted to know. "Are we talking years, decades or centuries?"

"Decades, probably," Gerda said. "Faster, of course, if a few extra trillions of research money were diverted in that direction. It might pay off extravagantly to investors prepared to be a little bit patient."

"Is that advice, or just idle rhetoric?" he wanted to know.

"It's an off-the-record opinion from someone who isn't as unworried about her funding as you might like to believe. It isn't just money the neo-cycads need, though—they could really benefit from the services of a top class propagandist: a man with the balls to get involved on every level."

"For the sake of Mother Gaia," Kay told her, "it's worth taking the trouble."

To which Gerda said nothing at all, lest she give the game away.

Kay took the opportunity to change the subject and bring in something else that was on his agenda. "Forty's still a critical age," he observed. "More so for you than me. Responsibility urges women not to bring children into a world teetering on the brink of total ecological meltdown, but the species can't leave reproduction entirely to the irresponsible. Have you made arrangements to put some eggs in cold storage?" He was allowed to ask her questions of that personal nature, because they'd been close friends for such a long time.

"No," she said, increasing the steeliness of her gaze slightly. "Have you made some provision for your own genetic future?"

This time, there was enough pink to defeat the bronze mask. "There's not so much urgency in my case," he said. "As it happens, though, I am planning to get married this year—June, to be exact."

"Congratulations," Gerda said, including herself in the congratulations for showing no emotion at all. "Who's the lucky lady?"

* * * * * * *

Kay's lucky lady was a nice Magyar girl named Magda, who was a full ten centimeters shorter than Gerda. She did have blonde hair and blue eyes, but they were the consequence of somatic engineering rather than her natural genetic heritage. Gerda honestly couldn't see what Kay saw in her, given that, whatever it was, he had obviously never bothered to look for it in Gerda. She went to the wedding, though, and didn't cry or forget to smile.

Gerda also waited until Kay had plunged a substantial fraction of his own fortune into cycad futures, as well as persuading a substantial fraction of the Gaian Economic Priesthood to follow his lead, before she put herself forward as a candidate for the European Parliament in northern Sweden. Because Selma Rosenhane was still going strong as Kiruna's leading lady, Gerda had to run as a second string on the regional ticket, and only just squeaked home under the labyrinthine rules of the PR system. Once she was in the chamber, however, she soon began to outshine her mother as an orator, if not as a deal-maker behind the scenes.

If Selma was jealous of her daughter's sudden emergence from academic obscurity on to her own stage, she kept the feeling well-hidden. She soon began telling her daughter what a great team they made, and advising her as to what offices they might both aspire to attain, with the benefit of their combined skills and Siberian backing. The Siberian backing did not materialize, though; as soon as the Russians discovered the full extent of Gerda's radicalism, they decided that she was too far off message to be accommodated within their tactical schemes. Selma then began lecturing Gerda on the necessity to be pragmatic, and the terrible danger of taking up a position too far away from the parliamentary consensus.

"The Parliamentary consensus is rotten at the core, Mummy," Gerda told her patient advisor. "It's due for collapse, and when it does come down it'll shrivel like a burst balloon. The future lies in providing a nucleus for the new consensus that will take its place."

"You may think forty's old," Selma informed her, sternly, "But it's not. Starry-eyed ideals are all very well, but politics is the art of the possible."

"Biotechnology," Gerda told her, "is the art of the possible too—but strategic genomics is the art of the imaginable...and the genius of the unimaginable."

"That kind of glibness might play well to the media," Selma said, with a hostile edge to her voice, "but it doesn't wash in the back rooms where the deals are made. If you're wise, you'll let me be your guide now that you're in my world."

Gerda smiled at the time—and then ignored her mother completely. From her point of view, the decision of the Siberian Oligarchs to oppose her and isolate her within the opposition ranks was a relief and a blessing, because she didn't want to be stuck with any of their baggage. She had no alternative but to begin her work as a propagandist within the ranks of the existing opposition, but she knew that she needed to build her own constituency in order to steer it in an entirely new direction.

There were two sets of vested interests that sprawled across the political boundary separating the confirmed anti-Gaians from the increasingly-disgruntled bad Gaians, and those were the groups that would have to be captured in their entirety if the old Gaian majority were to be conclusively punctured. One set, familiarly known as the "littorals" consisted of the already-dispossessed inhabitants of the inundated coastal regions and the about to-be-dispossessed inhabitants of the present coastal regions. The other comprised the persistent complex of old industrial interests that Kay called "the Heavy Metal brigade". Gerda set out to capture them both, beginning with the factions that were already loosely associated with the so-called opposition.

The particular neo-cycads in whose preliminary genomic design she had been involved, she told the two groups, over and over again in every possible venue and context, offered enormous potential, not merely for enhancing the economic potential of the new shallows, but also for developing the economic potential of the old shallows. They would do it not merely by producing new and useful biomass, but also by doing something that had never been done before, which would involve a new collaboration between organic and inorganic technologies, and forge a vital economic link between Big Tech and biotech, living fibers and heavy metal.

On the one hand, Gerda argued, neo-cycads could provide vast tracts of new lebensraum of an admittedly-challenging but extremely promising sort; on the other hand, they would generate bioelectricity on a massive scale to feed and replenish the Heavy Metal brigade's ailing distribution-networks. They would achieve the latter trick by taking an entirely new approach to bioelectricity generation: the conversion of tidal energy. The stout boles by which the cycads would attach their ambitious crowns to the sea-bed would not be mere supportive trunks, but would extend net-like and sail-like structures to capture a substantial fraction of the enormous energy imparted by the moon's gravity to the ocean on a twice-daily basis. The realm of human habitation would become larger than before, and its energy-supply would be secured.

All of this, she assured her potential followers, was both possible and practicable. Previous attempts to develop bioelectrical facilities by genetic transplantation had gone awry because natural bioelectricity was an animal monopoly, whereas commercial bioelectricity required plant-like supportive structures. That kind of ambitious hybridization had never succeeded using angiosperm stocks—but she and her former collaborators had devised a potential means of achieving the desired end in neo-cycads. Organic and inorganic technology had been estranged for far too long, and had grown accustomed to regarding one another as mere casual acquaintances, if not as enemies—but the time had come for them not merely to become friends, but to indulge in passionate intercourse. A new era was dawning.

At first, everyone thought that she was crazy. Indeed, they never actually stopped thinking that she was crazy—but they did not take long to remember how desperate they were to find some way out of the imprisoning Cubic Centimeter, or at least of making it a more comfortable confinement in which to dwell. Crazy or not, she was offering them a new hope: an alternative to yet more lectures on the Gaian vices and the need for everyone to become more virtuous.

Gaian vices and virtues did not figure in Gerda's argument at all, even in the beginning. Even then, she did not seek to conceal—although she refrained from laboring the point—that neo-cycads could not and would not flourish in a cool world. If they offered hope now, it was only because the world had already warmed sufficiently to let them offer it. If they were to fulfill that hope generously, they would need to be gifted with the climatic environment that suited them best. Much more active than the trees that had driven their primitive ancestors into tiny corners of the land tens of millions of years in the past—living fast and dying young, by tree standards—the neo-cycads needed a higher ambient temperature in order to do their work, and bioelectric neo-cycads were especially thermophilic. Unlike Gaia's favorite species, and Gaia herself, neo-cycads liked it hot.

The Gaian reaction was entirely predictable. Humankind, the Gaians argued, was the species that Gaia had favored more than any other, the one that had benefited most from a relative cool Earth whose carbon was mostly locked away in inert deposits. The new ecosphere that Gerda's radical biotech would eventually produce would be intrinsically inimical to human beings and human life; that was far too high a price to pay for effective bioelectricity. The core members of the great Gaian coalition regarded this argument as conclusive—but it failed to deliver the expected killer blow, and the coalition found itself leaking support on a serious scale for the first time in a century.

Gerda's initial support base came from the first of her two potential constituencies—not merely from the Netherlands and Belgium, whose densely-packed populations had suffered greater setbacks than any other European nation from the erosions of the sea, but most extravagantly of all from Britain, the Crazy Man of Europe, whose crazy jingoists saw the potential to become an even bigger sceptred isle than before, expanding gradually but majestically into the wilderness of the North Sea until it finally reached the continental shore again.

The Heavy Metal brigade was a little slower to come aboard, even though she took great care to emphasize out that it was they who could provide the definitive answer to the Gaian challenge. Heavy Metal, Gerda reminded its power-brokers, often and insistently, had always taken the blame for the CC, but it was also Heavy Metal that had made it possible for at least some people—the rich—to live quite comfortably in tropical heat, by means of air conditioning.

The spread of air-conditioning had long been inhibited by problems of energy-generation, but now that those problems were potentially soluble, there was no reason why the Heavy Metal brigade had to continue thinking in terms of air-conditioned buildings or air-conditioned domed estates. The time had come—or soon would come, if the political will could be mustered—to think in terms of air-conditioned cities. If the neo-cycads could be gifted with the hothouse climate they needed and deserved, then Big Tech could start fulfilling its age-old dream of building glittering crystal cities, hermetically sealed by external membranes, whose internal atmospheres could be differentiated at will from the one that the neo-cycads breathed and sustained.

Privately, Gerda did not imagine that enclosed environments would be anything more than a stop-gap solution; her belief was that the *lebensraum* offered by the neo-cycads would inevitably give rise to a new human species that would love the heat as much as they did, whether by means of genetic engineering, natural selection or cyborgization. As a practicing politician, however, she stuck to more pragmatic issues and carefully-limited imaginative horizons. She was, after all, her mother's daughter.

* * * * * * *

Gerda knew, and had always known—or at least felt—that she was bound to win in the end. The only real point at issue was how long it would take for the rotten *ancien régime* of the

Gaian majority to crumble away, and for the new consensus to consolidate a step-by-step program.

Many a politician, from Moses onwards, had sown the seeds of Promised Lands without living to see more than the faintest glimpse of their reality, but Gerda had always hoped that things might move faster for her, even in a world that was still essentially cool. As things eventually turned out, she was luckier than most, even though she shared the fate of many of those same visionaries in being forced to hand the reins of power over to others some time before the seeds she had sown began to germinate.

By the time Gerda's sixty-fifth birthday came around, an unholy alliance of Heavy Metal entrepreneurs, Siberian Oligarchs and resurgent Asian Not-So-Slow Developers had hijacked her prospectus and her party—but it was her slogans that they continued pushing and polishing. She lost the battle for personal control, but she won the war.

When Gerda and Kay met up in London to celebrate their sixty-fifth birthday, seven years had passed since they had last shared such a celebration. The previous one had ended badly, after Kay had accused Gerda of betraying him, by tricking him to invest not merely his own funds but those of hundreds of his allies and acquaintances in research in neo-cycad biotechnology. He really had felt betrayed, and really had believed that she had cruelly taken him for a ride in order to pursue an agenda directly opposite to his, with no other motive but malice aforethought.

When Kay agreed, in response to her urging, that they could get together for their sixty-fifth "to talk over old times", he still had not forgiven her, but he had accepted the inevitability of circumstance. He had not deserted the ailing rump of the old Gaian coalition, but he had accepted that he was now doomed to be a has-been, to the extent that he had ever *been* at all, within the political arena. Gerda guessed that he only felt able to face her again because he now considered that she too was a has-been, having been deposed from her various positions of nominal political authority.

"You might have won the war," he conceded, ungraciously, "and you'll doubtless say that all's fair in war, and that there's no such thing as betrayal in politics, but that's not what rankles. We were friends—practically brother and sister. It's the personal betrayal that I can't stomach. You didn't have to play me for a sucker. You could have won without doing that."

"I didn't play you for a sucker, my love," she told him. "Everything I told you was true."

"But it wasn't the whole truth," he pointed out. "You never said anything to me about neo-cycads needing a higher atmospheric temperature. You let me believe that they'd be living carbon sinks, just like all the other trees we'd been planting for the last hundred years to soak up carbon emissions. You took advantage of my ignorance. You didn't have to do that. You didn't have to involve me at all. You could have left me out of it. That would have been the sisterly thing to do. When we were kids, you told me that we were two halves of the same whole— you should never have betrayed that just to score a point when we happened to end up on opposite sides of the chamber. You didn't have to oppose me, you know, back in that stupid high school debate. You could have seconded me instead. We could have worked together."

"You could have seconded me," she pointed out.

"But you were on the wrong side!" he complained. "You still are, even though you've hooked the majority with your counsel of despair. The people who've usurped your throne aren't saving the world—they're changing it out of all recognition. We could have saved it, Gerda, you and I, if we'd only joined forces in the same cause. I don't believe for a moment that neo-cycads were the only game in town, or even that your kind of booby-trapped neo-cycads were the only possible means of reclaiming the inundated shallows. We could have taken a different route entirely, biotechnologically speaking—and you should have. You didn't just betray me; you betrayed the species and the ecosphere."

"You're a tactician, Kay," Gerda told him. "I'm the strategist, remember. I'm the long-term thinker. I didn't betray you; I saved you—you just haven't realized it yet. And you did make billions out of cycad speculation—far more money than I ever did."

That shot struck home, just about—but there was no hint of a blush on Kay's slightly-tightened features. "Well, yes," he admitted. "If it had only been about the money...but why *didn't* you make billions? Twenty-five years ago, when you gave me the tip about hemp, I thought it was because you were too cautious, too risk-averse...well, I have to admit to being wrong about that. So why aren't you super-rich? Why didn't you back your winner, financially as well as in the chamber?"

"It wasn't about the money, Kay, It never was."

"Just a matter of wining the war, then? I never realized that you were so intensely competitive. Sibling rivalry is a terrible thing—and we *were* practically siblings, weren't we? Only one barely-functional set of parents between the two of us...not that Miklos and Selma ever....did they?"

"I don't think so," Gerda said. "Mind you, there's time yet—they're both retired from the chamber now, so they must be desperate for something to fill in time."

"Perhaps we should have invited them along—maybe fixed them up?" Kay said, obviously not meaning it. The fact that he now felt able to say something that he blatantly didn't mean seemed to Gerda to be progress. He couldn't meet her stare, though, even though an unbiased observer glancing at their table would have taken him for the stronger and younger of the two. They no longer looked uncannily alike, or even remotely similar.

"Perhaps we should have invited your ex-wife," Gerda countered, "or your son, at least."

"I haven't even let on that we're meeting," Kay confessed. "Lothar would consider it to be consorting with the enemy, cherishing the blade that stabbed me in the back."

"And Magda too?" Gerda queried.

"Oh no—she never considered you an enemy or a threat. She always understood our friendship...at least until you started your great crusade. Like you, she always took the trouble to point out that I had made billions out of neo-cycads, even if I hadn't fully understood what the cost of the profits would be. She was delighted to take her share—if she were here, she'd be gladly proposing toasts in your honor."

"For her," Gerda said, casually, "it was only a matter of love, not war. She must have had a markedly different notion of what was fair—even if her blonde hair was only cosmetic."

"It's red now," Kay told her. "Hot colors are back in fashion, thanks to you. Mind you, silver doesn't look too bad on you—although you might want to think of having some skin-work done." Kay's own face and forehead, needless to say, had not a wrinkle in sight.

"I'm young at heart," Gerda assured him. "Just like the New New New New World. We are up to four now, aren't we?"

"Alas yes," he said—and then paused, apparently for reflection. Eventually, he went on: "You know, setting all joking and resentment aside, I believe that you and I really might have made a difference, as individuals. If you had only sided with me instead of reacting against me, it really might have been the salvation of the Gaian cause instead of its damnation. If only I had been able to keep you with me, instead of somehow contriving, unknowingly and unwillingly, to turn you against me...."

Gerda didn't bother to point out that his manner of framing the argument was outrageously egocentric. Instead, she said: "No, Kay, we couldn't have made that sort of difference. We couldn't have made much more of a difference even if you'd sided with me instead of relentlessly following the herd. Gaia was always gong to lose the war, no matter how many successful defensive actions her myrmidons completed. The neo-cycads were always bound to carry the day. The Heavy Metal brigade, the Siberian Oligarchs and the Asian Developers were always bound to end up in bed together, running the show. The only difference I made, and the only difference I was ever capable of making, was to warm things up a little, and hurry them along."

"You must have felt rather lonely doing it," Kay observed, retreating into pensive reflection. "It's still different for a woman, isn't it? Your mother managed to have it all, though, at least until that stupid accident. Maybe you felt that no one could ever quite live up to the memory of your father."

"He was dead before I learned to talk," Gerda said. "I never knew him."

"My mother's still alive, but I've hardly ever exchanged two words with her. To me, she's just a sequence of pictures—but that didn't stop me marrying Magda."

"No," Gerda agreed. "It didn't." And it was then, oddly enough, rather than at any of the more weighty or awkward moments in the conversation, that Gerda suddenly realized that her love for Kay had cooled somewhat while she had thrown her heart and soul into her cause, and that its once-fiery passion had been transformed by time and tide into something mellower and more even-tempered. It was still most definitely there, and still unfulfilled, but it no longer felt like a dagger of glass rudely jammed into her beating heart. By the same token, she no longer hated Gaia the Snow Queen quite as much as she had before. Their conflict had, after all, merely been a difference of opinion.

"It says something for us, I suppose," Kay observed, glumly, as he raised his wine-glass in a vaguely celebratory gesture, "that we can still be friends, in spite of everything. The fact that, no matter who's won and who's lost, and no matter what becomes of the world now it's all turned upside-down, we can still hold on to something of what we had when we were six years old says something good and precious not just about us but about the world. I can still think of you as my twin sister, my inevitable counterpart."

"The world was upside-down before, my love," Gerda told him, softly. "From now on, it'll be able to right itself, slowly but surely. The deadly CC is no longer deadly—or, as they say here in dear old England, all's now well at the beloved Cricket Club."

"The trouble with you, darling," Kay replied, with a contrived sigh that was as insincere as it was insulting, "is that you never could take anything seriously."

ALFONSO THE WISE

Alfonso the Wise was king of Castile in the thirteenth century. He is now entirely forgotten but for one attributed remark. "Had I been present at the Creation," he is reputed to have said, "I would have offered some useful advice as to the better arrangement of the universe." It is, of course, mere coincidence that the man who discovered meta-DNA was also called Alfonso—and the coincidence is partly spoiled by the fact that it was his surname rather than his given name.

Professor Alfonso had always felt that life had made a slight mistake in selecting DNA as the carrier of its genetic code. DNA is, after all, highly unstable under physiological conditions. As long-chain molecules go, it lacks resilience; given half a chance it is apt to denature. He realized, of course, that there were advantages to this condition as well as disadvantages. The readiness of DNA to throw a chemical wobbly is, in essence, the root of all mutation, and hence of evolution by natural selection. Anyhow, the ability of DNA to form a double-helix and to serve as a mount for long strings of base-codons was what had selected it out to be the parent of all life as we know it; the more stable natural molecules whose names were legion had no such faculty, and had always been non-starters. All things considered. Creation had done what it could, and hadn't made such a bad job of it.

It had, after all, produced Professor Alfonso.

Alfonso reasoned, however, that now that humans had invented genetic engineering, Creation no longer needed a source of random mutations. That job could be taken over by careful planners who could produce useful innovations deliberately, without bothering to go through all the messy cut and thrust of natural selection. By the same token, he figured, it ought to be possible to design a molecule of which Creation had never dreamed, which would combine DNA's codon-carrying ability with a bit more backbone.

As soon as organic molecule design program became sufficiently sophisticated, Alfonso and his desktop supercomputer were on the job—and such was the brilliance of their partnership that they came up with a brand new super-tough coding-molecule in a matter of months.

Out of respect for the excellent job that the old model had done during the previous four billion years, Alfonso called his new coding-molecule meta-DNA, although it wasn't a particularly close relative, chemically speaking. Its greatest asset was that its simplest version retained the same ACGT genetic code that was already built into DNA, which meant that it could actually copy all the codes already in existence in order to build on them further. It was rather like designing an update for a word-processing program, so that it could process all existing documents but also incorporated lots of extra features that could be exploited in further edits.

Professor Alfonso hoped that he might be able to sell his new product as a longevity serum. He reasoned that the one intractable and untreatable aspect of the aging process was the accumulation of somatic mutations and copying errors in DNA. Meta-DNA was much more resilient, and it had the useful ability to colonize the cells of a mature organism one by one, replacing the obsolete programming without any loss of routine function. Because meta-DNA was self-replicating, a single injection would suffice to set in train the rebuilding of any existing organism as a souped-up meta-DNA version of its former self.

As things turned out, of course, Professor Alfonso didn't make any money out of his immortality serum, because it was far too good at its job. Meta-DNA didn't stop with single individuals; it transformed all their passenger bacteria too, and thus became highly infectious. It only required the transformation of a single individual to ensure the eventual transformation of every living organism on Earth.

As soon as Professor Alfonso put his brainchild to the test on a single laboratory rat, the die was cast. DNA was on the way out and meta-DNA was on the way in, permanently.

Alfonso was right about meta-DNA ensuring longevity; it succeeded in doing that without any problem at all. Unfortunately, he had not given overmuch attention to the question of what it might do to the physiological apparatus of reproduction— specifically, to the process of meiosis, by means of which fusing gametes produced whole new genomes. Meta-DNA was far too stable to go in for that kind of molecular balletics, so every organism that took it aboard became irredeemably sterile.

In a way, the sterility was convenient, for the long-lived organisms that were inheriting the world would soon have become exceedingly crowded had they continued to reproduce at anything like the old rates. This convenience was, however, limited to those organisms that specialized in sexual reproduction; organisms that went in for vegetative reproduction had no such check on their proliferation.

Fortunately, bacteria reproducing by binary fission were soon cut back by ferocious new meta-DNA bacteriophages, and plants suffered similar plagues, while the meta-DNA-reinforced immune systems of higher animals prevented their suffering similar catastrophes. Even so, the Earth's ecology went pretty wild for a decade or two before a new generation of meta-DNA genetic engineers got to grips with the problems of ecospheric control. After that, change was pretty much a thing of the past. Chaos was gone and order had triumphed. *Homo sapiens* had been replaced by *Homo alfonsiensis*: an ultra-rational species no longer troubled by emotions, dreams or other disturbances of flesh and spirit.

Asked whether his fellow men might, if given a choice, have

selected some alternative destiny, the new Alfonso the Wise said: "Had God been present when I injected that first rat, he would doubtless have regretted that I had not been available for consultation when the Big Bang was but a twinkle in His eye."

And no one could any longer be found to disagree with him.

NEXT TO GODLINESS

As the cab drove away Adam looked down, checking his clothing carefully from the bottom up. The black moccasins, charcoal-grey slacks and chocolate-brown sweater looked supremely casual—which was exactly how they were supposed to look. They seemed slightly loose, but that was a carefully-contrived surface effect; like all smart clothes, they clung fast to his own skin. He took out a pocket mirror in order to make sure that his hairpiece was on its best behavior, spruced up the petals of the scarlet roses he was carrying and finished up by taking one last look at the label on the bottle of wine expertly clutched in the same hand, to reassure himself yet again that it was the '98 and not the '99.

The gate didn't creak and the path to the Millers' front door was entirely free of weeds. The smart WELCOME mat was spotless. The stained glass panels in the front door depicted characters from Greek mythology: Tantalus and Sisyphus to the left and the right, Ixion upraised in the centre. The door chime was as mellow as a concert grand.

"Adam!" said Nick, responding to the signal with wonderful alacrity. "It's great to see you again. Come into the kitchen for a moment and say hello to Eve."

Adam was ushered through the hallway and into the kitchen, where he presented Eve with the roses and Nick with the wine, swiftly fulfilling the true purpose of his abrupt summons to Eve's inner sanctum by admiring the astonishing cleanliness of the cooking area.

Even while cooking a four-course dinner for six, Eve Miller was in total control; there was not a drop of spatter anywhere on the gleaming tiles, dumb as they were, not a crumb or a flake on the polished work-surfaces. The crockery for the later courses was stacked with military precision; the knives, ladles and spatulas assembled in wall-racks were gleaming so brightly they might have been chrome-plated. Eve was wearing a frilly apron that was as dead as a doornail, but the blood-red dress she was wearing underneath was vibrant with artificial life.

Nick, like Adam, was conscientiously clad in drab plumage; a superficial glance might have rated them as nearly alike as two peas in a pod, although Adam saw things very differently. He always had, even before the divorce from Lilith, but his new circumstances had sharpened his regrets considerably. Reducing the dosage of his patches might have helped with that particular problem, but that kind of retreat was unthinkable for a man of Adam's stripe.

The door chime resounded again, impossibly mellow, and Nick rushed off to admit Seth and Ruth Wright, leaving Adam alone with Eve. That hadn't been in Nick's script—the effusive host had to tidy his inconvenient guest away into the sitting-room as soon as the perfection of the busy kitchen had been dutifully observed—but Eve had known Adam far too long ever to be flustered by his presence. She gave him a swift peck on the cheek and whispered: "How are you holding up?"

"Pretty well," Adam replied—but his hands were now free, and he couldn't help a reflexive twitch of the right hand towards the left bicep, where his patch was. Eve pretended not to notice, but he knew that she had. Her fake ruffled sleeves were amply long enough to conceal her own patch. The day was not far off, Adam knew, when the work of patches would be fully integrated into the smartness of clothing, but the time was not quite yet. Lilith was still working on the problem, among others, but she was unlikely to win the race to the crucial breakthrough.

Nick hustled Seth and Ruth into the kitchen, creating a crowd. There was a further handover of flowers and wine, efficiently executed, given the crowding. Adam was relieved to note that Seth had brought silver carnations and Chilean wine. Seth and Ruth were both solicitors; he was a specialist in company law while she was in criminal—another marriage made in Heaven, but one more likely to survive infernal corrosion. Legal minds always tended, in Adam's slightly churlish estimation, to be somewhat lacking in the aesthetic department, although legal stomachs certainly seemed to enjoy fine food.

Adam was proud of his own aesthetic sensibilities, even though he was a scientist through and through. He was always prepared to argue that there was as much aesthetics as logic in bioscience, especially its creative aspects.

At least, Adam thought, neither Seth nor Ruth would be inclined to spend all night explaining to him how badly the divorce settlement had been mismanaged by his solicitor. He greeted them both politely, but with a certain reserve. They were among Nick's newer acquaintances—of which he had made a great many since he had become a successful corporate analyst, assessing the potential of takeover targets for a mysterious cabal of private equity investors—but they had already achieved a remarkable closeness, to Eve as well as Nick.

Nick had assured Adam when issuing the invitation, with all the sincerity he could fake, that the sixth guest would merely be making up the numbers, but Adam knew well enough what his fate and his role now was within all the overlapping social circles in which he moved. Wherever he went, there would always be "someone to make up the numbers", until he was "fixed up" again. It would become a telic objective, with an appropriate psychological reward attached.

The Millers' sitting-room was as spick and span as the kitchen, though not as conspicuously polished. There was not a speck of dust on the carpet, nor a thread of lint on the sofa, nor the remotest ghost of a cobweb in the corners of the ceiling. Adam, determined not to be consigned to the sofa with an empty space yawning beside him, beat Seth to the armchair without seeming to make a race of it.

Nick was busy with the cocktail-shaker when the chime sounded again; politeness demanded that he pass it to Adam, who was the older friend, and Adam stood up to pour, allowing him to turn his back to the door when it eventually opened after the obligatory sidestep kitchenwards. Nick would, in any case, have introduced the newcomer to the couple first, leaving Adam for last.

"And this is my old friend Adam Goldsmith," Nick finished, as Adam handed round the chartreuse-tinted cocktails. "He lectures in biotechnology at the Uni—the old one, not the new one. Adam, this is my new friend Judith Apter. She's a web developer."

There was something about the combination of a female Christian name and the term "web developer" that made Adam think "black widow", but Judith Apter wasn't dressed in black and he had no reason to think that she was a widow. The miracles of cosmetic somatic engineering made it impossible to judge anyone's age simply by looking at them, but there was something about Judith's smile suggestive of authentic innocence. Her purple sleeves came all the way down to her wrists. There wasn't the slightest hint of a bulge, but Adam guessed readily enough that she'd be wearing a patch the size of a five-pound coin, just like his own. Even if she were just making up the numbers, there had to be something at stake between her and Nick, business-wise. She had to be feeling the stress of opportunity and expectation, and must have taken extra precautions in the interests of maintaining focus and incentive.

"What sort of biotech to you do?" Judith asked, politely.

"Mostly artificial," Adam replied. "Some microbial, some textile. What sort of web development do you do?"

"The usual cocktail of commissions—two-thirds ads, one-third edutainment."

"Are you doing some work for Nick?

"Consultancy for one of his takeovers. You?"

"We've never worked together," Adam said. "We used to play together, when we were young—back at the dawn of time." He looked away, slightly discomfited, when the careless metaphor stirred up ideative echoes. At the dawn of time, according to *Genesis*, Adam and Eve had been happy in the garden, until Old Nick had come along in serpentine guise—but Adam had had another wife before then, if you believed the Apocrypha: a non-conformist Lilith who would doubtless have insisted on baring her arms to demonstrate her independence, her "ownership of her emotions", her "responsibility for her own telic intensity". Adam felt an urgent necessity to change the subject.

Fortunately, Judith did it for him. "Are the Wrights old friends too?" she asked.

Seth Wright, having left his wife to entertain Nick, immediately elbowed his way into the conversation. "I only met Nick a few months ago," he volunteered. "We came into the Propriotech takeover from different directions and joined forces to manage the leverage. We've become thick as thieves, though—we live within walking distance, although we'd never dream of actually walking. Adam was somewhere in the Propriotech battle-line too, although I didn't meet him at the time—he made a small killing when the buyout went through."

"*Killing*'s a corporate lawyer's term," Adam said. "He means that one of my patents was among the assets that got stripped."

"*Stripped* isn't a corporate lawyer's term," Seth quipped, "and my lovely wife has far more to say about killing than I do. She sometimes defends killers of the literal kind—paratelic killers, of course. There's no point defending telic murderers— no arguments to be made in mitigation."

"Patches aren't supposed to encourage violence, let alone murder," Judith observed, gauchely—making it obvious that she really was as young as she looked.

What she said was true, of course—PIA patches were only supposed to encourage *socially acceptable* telic behavior, although they couldn't forbid natural telic behavior, or the association of such behavior with inappropriate neural rewards. The sin that Judith had committed was an error of judgment rather than fact. Discussions of that particular topic were already passé, quite worn out.

"Adam's a bioscientist," Seth observed, dismissively. "He can give you all the technical details, if you're really interested."

"Actually," Adam said, "the problem with designing patches to promote telic violence is economic rather than technical. There's no substantial black market in them. Patches promoting paratelic violence, on the other hand, are always in demand."

"I thought that was a tabloid myth," Judith said.

"Just because it's a tabloid myth," Seth put in, beating Adam to the punch, "doesn't mean that it's untrue."

Nick ushered them into the dining-room then, and promptly disappeared into the kitchen, from which he returned bearing bowls of asparagus soup, a basket of French bread and a bottle of Chardonnay in a portable cooler. Adam had to count Nick's hands twice to make sure that he still only had two. Eve emerged in his wake, bearing more soup-bowls, a second bread-basket and Adam's bottle of '98 Bordeaux. There were no place-cards on the oval table, but Nick and Eve cleverly maneuvered all of the guests into their carefully-allotted seats. Adam was set between Eve and Judith, directly but rather distantly opposite Ruth.

The soup, as was only to be expected, was divine. Seth was the first to spill a stray drop on the tablecloth, but the smart cloth swallowed it with alacrity. Adam could not suppress a pang of regret as he looked at the place where it had vanished; in a kinder world, that might have been one of his patents, worth a great deal more than the one that had brought him such a derisory windfall in the Propriotech takeover. It might even have been a shared patent, cementing his Heaven-made marriage and protecting it against disaster—but treacherous Lilith had refused to take advantage of the technology that could have facilitated their partnership.

* * * * * * *

"It's obscene," Lilith had said, when the first PIA applicators came on to the market, eighteen months after the first TGAD applicators. Until then, TGAD patches had been called "pleasure patches" by their users and detractors alike, but as soon as the new antithesis was established the popular parlance shifted. TGAD stood, somewhat euphemistically, for Third Generation Anti-Depressant but PIA wasn't so stubbornly descriptive; it stood for Pride In Achievement. From that day onwards, the rival product-categories were known as Pride and Joy, at least among the users who loved Joy. Those who preferred Pride eventually came to favor a sterner terminology; it was they who had taken up the telic/paratelic dichotomy.

"It's inevitable," Adam had assured his wife. What had begun as a mild philosophical debate had then turned into their fiercest and most enduring argument; at its beginning they had not been long out of the honeymoon period, and the sporadic continuation of the quarrel hurt them both more deeply than they knew.

Adam took the position that people had been using drugs to control their moods for millennia, ever since the primal discovery of the intoxicating effects of fermented grains and the hallucinogenic effects of certain fungi. Organic chemistry had made that kind of artificial intervention far more sophisticated, eventually leading to the invention of the first- and second-generation anti-depressants. It was inevitable, he argued, that genomic augmentation would lead to a further order of sophistication, ensuring not only that people would never have to feel miserable again if they didn't want to, but that they could actually employ artificial happiness as a carrot to encourage them in productive endeavor.

"That's the beauty of it, you see," he told her, when he still thought or hoped, that he could make his point by the sheer force of reason. "The problem with TGADs is that all they do is make people feel good, with no regard to circumstances. They're just the latest opium of the people, blotting out the pain and misery of poverty and failure with blunt neurochemical instruments. They take away incentives, facilitating bliss in ignorance. PIAs are different. PIAs recognize and accommodate the fundamental principle that feeling good—happiness, joy, pleasure, or whatever label you care to use—ought to be *earned*, as a reward for some task completed, some artistry attained. What PIAs do is enhance the neural pathways that connect the pleasure areas in the brain with purposive action, with physical and intellectual accomplishment. They guarantee that people can take an entirely proper delight in the results of their creativity, and an entirely appropriate pleasure in the products of their labor. Whereas TGADs drag their users down, forging a society of modern lotus-eaters, PIAs will lift their users up, reopening the road to Utopia."

"That's a foolishly optimistic expectation, Adam," was Lilith's bitter riposte. "These things have more in common with the old nicotine patches than mere appearance. What they're peddling is poison; while pretending to help us free ourselves from addiction, they're actually feeding and enhancing addiction. We've grown used to thinking of TGAD reliance as the ultimate in addiction, but that's because we couldn't see PIA coming. You can trumpet all the slogans you want, but at the end of the day, all PIAs offer is the opportunity to become happier workaholics. When you talk about enhancing the neural pathways connecting to the pleasure areas in the brain, you mean that it will intensify the rewards associated with the pathways that are already there, not that it will encourage the development of new pathways. In fact, it will discourage the development of new pathways, preventing the further elaboration and sophistication of an individual's spectrum of rewards. PIA isn't a road-map to Utopia, Adam; it's a recipe for a society of obsessive-compulsive freaks who rejoice in their obsessive-compulsiveness."

Adam had done his level best to refresh his arguments when the new terminology became fashionable. "It's always been the case," he told his wayward wife, "that people have indulged in some activities for the sake of the ends to which they serve as means—purposive, or telic, behavior—while indulging in others purely for the sake of the momentary, or paratelic, sensations they produce. The most obvious instance is the difference between eating food for its nutritive value and eating for the sake of taste sensations. What PIAs are doing is redressing a balance that had been tipped in favor of the paratelic—one of whose consequences was a society in which more than half the population was morbidly obese. It wasn't just that we'd become a consumer society, but a society that found pleasure in the act of consumption rather than using its purchases to building anything substantial. PIAs will restore the balance; while TGADs allow us to maximize paratelic pleasure, PIAs will allow us to maximize telic pleasure in accomplishment and achievement: Pride *and* Joy. We'll all have the means to become better people, Lilith."

"But that isn't what will happen, Adam," she had insisted, stubborn in her rebellion. "What will actually happen is that an already-divided society will become even more divided, between people without opportunities, who blot our the misery of their circumstances with TGADs, and people with opportunities, who'll delight in addiction to more-or-less rewarding kinds of work, wallowing ecstatically in the saintliness of deferred gratification. What will happen, in the long run, is that the members of the middle class will become even more insanely smug than they are now, thanks to the focusing powers of PIA. I don't want to be a part of that, Adam. I want to be a *whole person*. I want to be *my own* person, not some drug-addled slave to concentrated ambition."

And so the argument had rumbled on, while Adam experimented with various kinds of PIA patch, until he found the one best suited to his particular vocation, while Lilith had worn the shortest sleeves she could find—in dead and living clothes alike—to show the world that her arms and mind were clean. That kind of cleanliness, in her perverted opinion, really had been next to godliness—but the conventional kind had fallen increasingly under the responsibility of Adam, who had become more and more intent on keeping a tidy house, as well as a tidy appearance and a tidy mind.

In retrospect, he should have realized five years before it actually came about that the break-up was inevitable, but he really had loved his wife, just as she had loved him, in her fashion. That was one thing the patches seemed impotent to affect; all the telically-focused bioscience in the world had not yet succeeded in manufacturing a reliable love-potion—nor in finding a cure for love-sickness, for those of a contrary disposition.

* * * * * * *

After the soup, following tradition, came the fish course. The sole was, of necessity, farmed and genetically modified—which led the conversation in a perfectly natural way to the prospects for the revivification of the oceans. Adam, as the party's bioscientist, was forced to take on the role of expert judge, even though he had never worked with vertebrates and had no expertise in ecological engineering.

"We're winning the battle," he assured Judith, who seemed genuinely interested. "The declining pH and the extinction rate grab all the headlines because even blissed-out paratelics can understand simple numbers, but they don't reflect the complex truth of the situation. The key to the whole problem—global warming included—is new and better algae. Get the algae right and not only will the fish will flourish, but the problematic surplus of carbon dioxide will be mopped up with far greater efficiency than any mere forest will ever be able to achieve."

"And it tastes good too," Eve put in, referring to the marine salad garnish, which had been transported from the Atlantic littoral that very morning.

"My mother used to give us seaweed to eat when I was a kid," Nick recalled. "Laverbread, they used to call it. Extinct now, I dare say."

"Only in the shops," Adam assured him. "The sole's magnificent, Eve—done to perfection.

"Thanks," Eve said. "It's very difficult to judge the frying time, especially when you're doing six at a time in a mammoth pan, but if you can get the butter to exactly the right temperature...."

"Eve's a genius in the kitchen," Nick put in, cheerfully interrupting her.

"Not just in the kitchen," Eve supplied, blushing slightly as she realized that the remark might be taken for a *double entendre*. She hadn't been intent on advertising her skills in the marital bedroom, but her expertise as a mother. Baby Samuel—who was two years old now and not, technically speaking, a baby any longer—hadn't uttered a sound thus far, and probably wouldn't.

There, but for fortune, Adam thought, allowing himself another twinge of regret as he pretended not to notice the delicate pink flush that had stained Eve's pale porcelain cheeks. He knew, though, that there had been more than one kind of fortune involved in Eve's decision to abandon her career in accountancy to concentrate on household management. Nick Miller made more money than all four of his guests put together; Ruth could no more afford to give up her career than Lilith had, even though a solicitor specializing in company law probably commanded a substantially higher salary than a university teacher who was still four or five years away from a professorship. If he'd been slightly more fortunate in filing patents, Adam's might have been a different story, but he was convinced that Lilith's detachment and eventual defection from their joint enterprise had cost him dear in more ways than one.

When Eve and Nick got up to clear the plates for a second time, Adam turned to Judith and asked whether her edutainment work ever involved her with the university.

"Not really," she said. "It's mostly aimed at younger agegroups. I'm not much of a talking head farmer in any case, more an infrastructure planner. What sort of web resources do you use in your teaching?"

"I don't do that much teaching, to be honest," Adam admitted. "Lecturer's just a title. I have postgrad students, but they're really my research assistants. Basically, I'm a lab rat." He added one more mental click to the tally of things that he and Judith didn't have in common, and assumed that she was doing the same.

He was almost grateful when Ruth leaned forward across the table to address them both in a quasi-confidential manner, saying: "I really envy Eve. I know the domestic goddess thing is supposed to be old-fashioned, but it can't ever go out of style, can it? And she's so utterly perfect in the role. Seth does more than his share, bless him, but even between the two of us we just can't find the time to do the housekeeping to this standard, let alone entertaining."

Adam knew that it was a matter of focused attention rather than time, but it would have been impolite to say so. "Eve is an artist," he said. "Even when she was training to be an accountant, she was an artist. Whatever she does, she does with an unmatchable flair. It's Nick I envy."

"And I envy you for being able to say so without fear of reprisal," Seth said, smiling at Ruth to emphasize that he was only joking.

Ruth smiled back as if she believed him. No matter what somatic engineers might accomplish in the future, Adam thought, Ruth would never look half as beautiful as Eve.

In spite of all the food-bearing skills they had developed, it still required all Nick and Eve's collective effort to carry in the silver platter bearing the roasted suckling pig, neatly encircled by a chain of roast potatoes, topped and tailed with conical heaps of diced carrot and broccoli florets. They had to make a second trip to bring the plates, which they had left behind in order to give their guests an adequate interval to admire the meat.

Once the plates had been distributed, Nick began to carve. Adam was the only person at the table who had ever practiced dissection, but he had to concede, to his secret chagrin, that Nick was a better slicer than he would ever be. The chorus of murmurous admiration went on for a long time, renewed when Eve brought out the sauceboat. Adam, in his capacity as oldest friend, helped out by pouring more wine, making sure that he got a particularly opulent glassful of the '98—which he then had to gulp, in order to pretend that he'd been more scrupulous in his division. Nobody seemed to notice, except Eve, who didn't seem to mind.

Adam observed that Eve waited until everyone else had started eating before she picked up her fork; even then, she took up her wine-glass in her other hand instead of her knife, in order to have a few more moments to watch her guests' reactions.

Their reactions would have been effusive in any case, but Adam's was perfectly sincere. The pork was superb, the sauce ambrosial. He saw Eve smile as she put her wine-glass down to take up her knife, and knew that for her, that had been the critical point of the whole evening. The dessert was still to come, and would doubtless be unimaginably sweet, but he and Eve both knew that the heart of any meal is the main course, and that the moment when the main course is put to the test is the first succulent mouthful.

Adam smiled discreetly sideways at Eve, to signal his recognition of her contentment, and gave her a near-imperceptible nod. That brought an extra twitch of broadness to her smile, which she maintained while she cut the meat on her plate, added a moderate complement of sauce-steeped vegetables and slowly brought the fork to her mouth, savoring every instant of expectation. Adam was still staring at her as her head snapped back, and then jerked forward. The mouthful of food was blasted out again, scattering its glutinous fragments in every direction before they cascaded down upon the tablecloth and her immediate neighbors' plates.

Ruth screamed. Seth's jaw dropped. Adam couldn't see Judith's reaction because he had already turned his back on her as he leapt to his feet, but he saw Nick's.

Nick was utterly horrified, and for one fleeting moment the expression on his face was pure wrath: anger that his dinner party had been spoiled, and that his carefully-laid plans had *gone wrong*. By the time the anger was replaced by concern,

Eve had fallen to the floor, jerking uncontrollably.

Adam knelt down beside her, supporting her head and forcing the edge of his napkin into her mouth to make sure that she couldn't bite through her tongue. "Phone an ambulance, Seth!" he said, trying not to shout. "Tell them it's a type-two NA seizure. Ruth, get me a cushion from the sitting-room. Judith, get these chairs out of the way and help me pull her clear of the table-legs. She'll be okay, as long as she doesn't damage herself." The last assurance, meant for Nick—whose concern was mounting exponentially—was not entirely honest. Adam was no doctor, but he was a bioscientist, and he knew perfectly well that the world had not yet seen the worst of type-two seizures, and that no one had any idea as yet of the full scope of the damage they might do.

Everyone did as Adam told them to do; he was, after all, the only bioscientist in the room, fully entitled to set goals and benchmarks in a situation of this sort. When Eve was clear of any hard surfaces, laid on her side with Adam and the cushion both supporting her head, everyone became preternaturally still, as if they could somehow force motionless on the victim of the fit by means of their own contrived inertia.

"Call a cab, Judith," Adam said, when the silence became unbearable. "Nick can ride with Eve in the ambulance; Seth, you and I can follow it with Judith. Ruth will have to stay here, with Samuel." When Ruth opened her mouth to object he added: "Samuel knows you, probably better than me. I need to go with Eve." He didn't explain why he needed to go with Eve, allowing Ruth to infer that it was some kind of medical necessity.

Nick was becoming hysterical, in spite of Adam's brief reassurance that all would be well. The future possibilities opening before his vivid imagination were putting his earlier horror to shame. For a moment or two, Adam thought that he might have a second seizure victim on his hands, but then Ruth grabbed hold of Nick and hugged him, babbling that it would all be okay, that type two seizures were eminently treatable, and never fatal. *Hardly ever* would have been more accurate, but it wasn't an occasion for accuracy.

By the time the ambulance arrived, well within the official response-time target, Eve had passed into a quieter phase of unconsciousness and Adam felt sure in his own mind that she really would be okay. He gave a curt report to the senior paramedic, and then stood aside as Eve was loaded on to a stretcher and borne away. The cab that Judith had called was already waiting; it followed in the ambulance's slipstream all the way to the hospital, with Adam, Seth and Judith wedged in together on the back seat.

Once they reached the hospital, however, there was nothing to do but surrender control to the staff and wait. Adam knew that the waiting would be hard; telics always found waiting hard, especially in the wake of something going wrong. Open-ended waiting was the worst of all. Pleasure In Achievement was all very well, until achievement was frustrated—as Adam had had abundant opportunity to discover during and after the divorce. He left the job of calming Nick to Seth, who seemed both willing and able to take it on, while he sat down, uncomfortably aware that all the color must have drained from his cheeks, and that his distress must be clearly visible.

Judith sat down beside him, awkwardly tense. "Are you all right, Adam?" she asked, in a low voice—as if she feared that the question, or its answer, might somehow upset Nick if he were to overhear it.

"Fine," Adam lied. "It gave us all a fright, I dare say—but she'll be fine now. It won't take the doctor long to give her the all-clear."

"I've seen it on the news plenty of times," Judith said, "but never for real. They're adamant that it isn't the patches that cause it, but that can't really be true, can it? As Seth says, just because something's a tabloid myth doesn't mean it's a lie."

"PIA patches don't cause the seizures," Adam told her. "They just make them possible. It's always been possible, of course, for that kind of neural amplification to happen naturally, but it almost never happened before PIA. Now, it's much easier to die of happiness than it ever was before—or at least to go into literal fits of ecstasy."

"It can't be the pleasure that does it," Judith objected, again displaying her naivety. "Paratelics don't have fits like that."

"No, they don't," Adam admitted, dully. "The new epilepsy is strictly a middle class disease. It's not the pitch of the joy so much as the tautness of the obsession. Thank God Lilith's not here—the conflict of emotions would probably tear her apart."

"What conflict of emotions?" Judith asked, keeping her voice strictly neutral. She obviously knew that Lilith was the name of Adam's ex-wife.

"She's known Eve for as long as I have," Adam said. "Loved her just as much, in her fashion. She'd be heartbroken—but Lilith, being Lilith, wouldn't be able to hold back a surge of triumph. She'd see this as proof that she was right, you see—it isn't, but that's the way she'd see it."

"She's a dissenter," Judith observed. It was a comment, not a question.

"Is she? Is that what we're calling refuseniks these days? She's clean; she doesn't use patches. Never has, never will—and I really do mean *never*."

"That's why you divorced," Judith said, maintaining her tentative tone.

"Irreconcilable differences," Adam replied. "When they say mixed marriages don't work they usually mean telics and paratelics, but that can sometimes be a winning combination. Refuseniks and paratelics can get along too, if the rest of the chemistry's right. I loved Lilith and she loved me, in her fashion, but there's no hope for a marriage between a telic and a...dissenter. Didn't Nick and Eve give you strict instructions to avoid the subject of Lilith when they invited you along to balance the numbers at the party?"

"Of course they did," said Judith, but carried on regardless. "What does she do for a living?"

"Industrial biotech. Textiles."

"And she doesn't feel the pressure to compete? She doesn't

feel she's losing out to her PIA-enhanced peers?" Judith's voice had suddenly become more intense, and Adam guessed that she was not disobeying orders just for the hell of it; it was her own situation that she was thinking about.

"No," Adam said, shortly. "She insists that they're the ones who are losing out. There's none so blind as those who will not see."

"I wouldn't dare to try," Judith told him, confirming his conclusion, "but when you see something like that...."

"There's no need to worry," Adam told her, not meaning it kindly. "There's no reason to expect anything like that to happen to you. You're not Eve."

Judith looked at him sharply, but Adam judged that she hadn't taken offence, or even been aware that she might have done. Judith wasn't wondering what Eve had that she didn't; she was wondering how Adam had ended up with Lilith instead of Eve, if he felt as intensely about Eve as he seemed to do. That was something that Adam had no intention of explaining.

Nick interrupted them then, having been brought back down to earth by Seth. He was still exceedingly fretful, though, even by the standards of a telic forced to wait. "She is going to be all right, isn't she?" he said, to Adam.

"She'll be fine," Adam assured him. "It's just nature's way of telling her to take it a little bit easier. She's bright enough to heed the warning."

"It's not that easy, though, is it?" Nick said.

"Yes it is," Adam told him. "It really is."

* * * * * *

The reason why Adam and Lilith had ended up together, instead of Adam and Eve—if there really had been a reason, rather than a mere freak of circumstance—was that Adam and Lilith had had the potential to change the world, whereas Adam and Eve would only have changed one another.

Adam and Eve might have been—*would* have been, Adam

now felt sure—the happier couple, but Adam and Lilith had planned to be collaborators as well as eternal lovers. They were both bioscientists, and their specialisms had an obvious overlap in the economically significant field of smart clothing. If only they had been able to sustain an adequate level of domestic harmony, they might have worked together as closely, and as productively, as Pierre and Marie Curie—but they hadn't. The patent applications they might have formulated and filed together had never come to term, and they had missed out on their due share of the big boom. They had had their separate successes, but they had been very minor ones compared to what they might have done together.

Adam knew that he ought to phone Lilith, to tell her what had happened to Eve. After all, she'd known Nick and Eve as long as he had, and just as well. But for a whim of circumstance, it might have been her they'd invited to dinner tonight, along with some unattached Byronic hunk who cherished his satanic gloom far too much ever to surrender to the joys of PIA...except that it wasn't a whim of circumstance at all. There was no way Eve Miller would ever tolerate a refusenik at her dinner table, even one she had known since childhood and loved, in her fashion. Lilith knew that too, and the knowledge would only add to the awful confusion of her emotions when she heard the news.

It was better, Adam decided, not to phone her. Not now, at any rate. Instead, he rehearsed the argument in his mind that he would have been forced to put to her, to prove to her that Eve's misfortune wasn't any kind of proof that she was right about the awful iniquity of PIA patches.

"The problem," he would have told her, "isn't the enhancement of pleasure in achievement. The problem is the complexity of the enhanced neural pathways that are set up. It's a matter of focus. Common-or-garden workaholics like me and Nick, or Seth and Ruth, can narrow the scope of our potential achievements, so the neural pathways enhanced by the patches are relatively simple and direct—motorways of the mind. Common-

or-garden mothers can do the same—but Eve is an artist, who brings an unmatchable flair to *everything*. She could never be content to concentrate on motherhood. She might have given up her own career, but she hasn't given up her involvement in Nick's, and she hasn't give up her determination to maintain a social life outside of motherhood and Nick's work alike. She's tried to maintain too many strings to her bow, that's all. The enhanced pathways she's built in her brain, with the aid of PIA, are too complicated and intricately tangled. All she needs to do is slow down, take things a little easier, lower her standards just a little."

Unfortunately, Adam had known Lilith for far too long not to be able to synthesize the arguments she would have constructed in opposition to his. "That's exactly what I've been telling you all along," she would have retorted. "PIAs are creating a culture of obsession. They help people with unhealthy tendencies to become even more unhealthy, even more manically focused on their petty specialisms. To a mentally healthy person—a *well-rounded* person like Eve—they're a curse, which can only lead to neural overload and mental breakdown. How can she slow down, take things easier and *lower her standards a little* while she's addicted to her PIA cocktail of choice?"

"She's not addicted," Adam replied, reflexively. "PIAs aren't addictive."

"Not *physiologically* addictive," his Lilith-anima countered, "but in psychological terms, they're as addictive as addictive can be. Who can't get hung up and strung out on *success*? Who can resist the temptation to *excel*. But we have to resist it, Adam, don't you see? We have to retain mastery of our own motivation."

"But we could have had success," Adam objected, plaintively. "We could have *made a killing*. We could have done our bit to change the world."

* * * * * * *

"Are you all right, Adam?" Judith asked, yet again.

Adam woke up with a start, convinced that he had not really been asleep. He became aware that the fingers of his right hand had been plucking at his left arm—not, he realized, to test the patch beneath the fleshcloth but to tease the garment itself, the living clothing to whose evolution he and Lilith might have made a crucial contribution, if only they had not been torn apart by a difference of opinion.

"Yes," he said. "I'm fine."

"Eve's awake," Judith told him. Nick popped his head out just now to say that you can go in to see her if you want. Seth and I just waved at her from the doorway.

Adam looked around and saw that Seth was in the far corner of the waiting room, muttering into his phone while staring at his wristwatch—the perfect image of Telic Man. He was presumably bringing Ruth up to date, and assuring her that they would soon be back on track, back on the timetable.

Adam stood up, and went in to see Eve. The room she was in was very clean, although it wasn't easy to find telic cleaners, but Adam couldn't believe that it seemed clean to Eve. To her, it must seem gloomy, dingy and dangerous. She was desperate to be out of it and home, but she had the obligatory fluid drip attached to her arm and a whole battery of electrodes clustered on her skull, feeding data to an EEG. The doctor had doubtless set a deadline for the completion of his enquiries, but the waiting would be agony for the patient.

Nick stayed where he was, sitting on the right-hand side of the bed holding Eve's right hand. Adam brought a chair up to the other side.

"You gave us a fright," Adam observed, as Eve's anxious blue eyes met his.

"I ruined the dinner," she said, tearfully. "The whole evening."

"The dinner was fabulous," Adam told her. "You know as well as I do that no further mouthful can ever match up to the first. It was a kindness to interrupt us, really. Imagine the emphasis your performance lent to the memory of that perfect moment. It was a masterstroke—pure *coup-de-théâtre*."

Eve smiled.

"I wish I could bullshit like that," Nick said. "You should never have been a scientist, Adam—with a talent like that you could have worked for the tabloids."

"I wanted to change the world," Adam said, pretending to answer Nick's veiled insult. "I still might."

"You never got dessert," Eve lamented, losing her smile again.

"It's dessert," Adam said. "It'll keep."

"You didn't even get to finish the '98 Bordeaux."

"It's a full-bodied claret," Adam said. "It'll be all the better for a chance to breathe."

"You really should have decanted it instead of just uncorking the bottle," Eve immediately said to Nick. "We really must try to get things right."

"Not according to Adam," Nick retorted, a trifle spitefully. "Slow down, take it easy, lower our standards—that's his advice. Did the doctor say anything?"

"The same, but not as economically. Is Samuel all right? He won't like it if I'm not there when he wakes up."

"Ruth's with him," Nick assured her. "He'll be fine. You'd better go now, Adam—it's getting late, and you must have things to do tomorrow. You ought to take Judith home—this isn't really her concern, and she must be in a bit of a state."

"What must she think of us?" Eve wondered, aloud. "Do you like Judith, Adam?"

"Yes," said Adam, dutifully. "She's very nice—brought a perfect balance to the party."

"I picked her," Nick said, proudly.

"And you're absolutely right about my seeing her home," Adam said. "Be sure and take the doctor's advice, Eve. You don't have to be perfect in *every* respect, and you're already perfect in more ways than any normal human being could ever hope to be."

"You really ought to phone Lilith too," Nick suggested.

"After all, she's known us as long as you have. She'd want to know what happened wouldn't she?"

"I'll phone tomorrow," Adam said, still looking into Eve's eyes, and knowing that she would understand that he intended to phone her, not Lilith. "It was the single greatest mouthful of roast pork I've ever tasted, or ever hope to taste."

"I know," said Eve, softly. "It blew my mind."

* * * * * * *

As Adam and Judith arranged themselves in the back seat of the cab they were both careful to leave a symbolic margin between them. He was glad that they seemed to be in agreement on the issue, although there hadn't been much doubt about it. It would have been embarrassing if one of them had been interested if the other wasn't, but the catastrophic interruption of the party would have put paid to any chance either one of them might have had of forming such an interest. Contrary to what Nick had said, Judith was in far less of a "state" than any of the other diners, but she was still a telic whose purpose had been interrupted and frustrated. She was in no condition to form attachments, no matter how tentative.

"One thing I've never understood," Judith said, by way of making conversation, as the cab set off in the direction of her home, "is why the patches work so well in helping people to work harder and more effectively, but don't seem to have any effect at all on personal relationships. You'd expect them to reward success in marriage just as much as success at work, wouldn't you?"

"No," Adam told her, slipping easily enough into his lecturing mode now that he was sure that he and she were ships that would pass in the night without a flicker of remorse. "The whole point about PIAs is that they assist *telic* behavior. They can only increase the pleasure derived from the completion of goal-orientated tasks."

"You're saying that marriages—romantic relationships in

general—aren't goal-orientated?"

"Yes."

"But TGADs don't affect them either."

"Of course not. TGADs are their own reward—that's the essence of paratelic experience."

"I don't believe that relationships are paratelic," Judith said, flatly. "They're not just things to be enjoyed for the sake of the experience. They *are* goal-orientated. At least, they can be. They *should* be."

"I thought so once," Adam admitted. "I changed my mind."

"Thanks to bitter experience?"

"Thanks to more careful theoretical analysis, and the lessons of objective empirical observation. If romantic relationships were as telic as mythmongers sometimes pretend, there really would be PIAs that function as love potions. There aren't."

"There aren't any that enhance the rewards of telic violence," she observed, "but you wouldn't rule out that possibility on theoretical grounds when we were talking earlier."

"There's no substantial pressure of demand on that particular innovation," Adam reminded her, "in spite of the potential military interest. The demand for love potions, on the other hand, is potentially immense—and so are the potential commercial rewards."

What a terrible thing it would be, he heard Lilith whisper, in the depths of his mind, *if we could choose who to love, and who would love us, and make our choices stick with the aid of drug-induced reinforcement.*

Would it? Adam asked, silently. *Would it, really?*

"I still don't think that you can rule out the possibility," Judith insisted. "We can't know today what we might discover tomorrow. The world is changing more rapidly now than ever before—human society as well as the climate—and we have no idea where it might end up."

"The road to Utopia isn't closed," Adam said. "It's just that there aren't very many of us capable of following the map."

The cab drew to a halt then, and Judith got out.

Adam didn't bother to get out with her. He already knew that she wasn't going to invite him in. He leaned over before she shut the door to say: "I'm sorry the evening was such a disaster."

"It wasn't," she said. "I've never seen a house so perfect, and a meal so perfectly planned and executed. It was quite an inspiration, in its way. I'm sorry for Eve, of course—but I hope I'll have the opportunity again. Perhaps they'll invite us both." She tried hard to sound enthusiastic, but couldn't.

As soon as the door closed, the cab got under way again. Adam's flat was only five minutes away.

As he paid the driver, Adam was struck by a gust of cold wind, whose suddenness overwhelmed the compensatory capacity of his smart sweater. He shivered. The patch on his left arm made itself felt, although the heat it seemed to generate was illusory. As the cab drew away Adam paused to scratch his arm, resolving not to use such a heavy dose the next time he went out.

The problem with being wired to obtain superabundant pleasure from success, he thought, framing the words as carefully as he would have done had Judith still been there to hear him, *is that when, in spite of one's best efforts, one can't seem to succeed, life becomes very difficult indeed.*

As he walked up the stone steps to his front door, he heard someone in one of the other flats laughing excitedly. *Bloody paratelics*, he thought, uncharitably. *It's all so very easy for them.*

Lilith, he felt sure, would not have laughed, any more than Eve would. She had loved him, after all, in her fashion.

MORTIMER GRAY'S HISTORY OF DEATH

1.

I was an utterly unexceptional child of the twenty-ninth century, comprehensively engineered for emortality while I was still a more-or-less inchoate blastula and decanted from an artificial womb in Naburn Hatchery in the county of York in the Defederated States of Europe. I was raised in an aggregate family which consisted of six men and six women. I was, of course, an only child, and I received the customary superabundance of love, affection and admiration. With the aid of excellent role-models, careful biofeedback training and thoroughly competent internal technologies I grew up reasonable, charitable, self-controlled and intensely serious of mind.

It's evident that not everyone grows up like that, but I've never quite been able to understand how people manage to avoid it. If conspicuous individuality—and frank perversity—aren't programmed in the genes or rooted in early upbringing, how on earth to they spring into being with such determined irregularity? But this is my story, not the world's, and I shouldn't digress.

In due course, the time came for me—as it comes to everyone—to leave my family and enter a community of my peers for my first spell at college. I elected to go to Adelaide in Australia, because I liked the name.

Although my memories of that period are understandably

hazy I feel sure that I had begun to see the fascination of history long before the crucial event that determined my path in life. The subject seemed—in stark contrast to the disciplined coherency of mathematics or the sciences—so huge, so amazingly abundant in its data, and so charmingly disorganized. I was always a very orderly and organized person, and I needed a vocation of that kind to loosen me up a little. It was not, however, until I set forth on an ill-fated expedition on the sailing-ship *Genesis* in September 2901, that the exact form of my destiny was determined.

I use the word "destiny" with the utmost care; it is no mere rhetorical flourish. What happened when *Genesis* defied the supposed limits of possibility and turned turtle was no mere incident, and the impression which it made on my fledgling mind was no mere suggestion. Before that ship set sail, a thousand futures were open to me; afterwards, I was beset by an irresistible compulsion. My destiny was determined the day *Genesis* went down; as a result of that tragedy my fate was sealed.

* * * * * * *

We were en route from Brisbane to tour the Creationist Islands of Micronesia, which were then regarded as artistic curiosities rather than daring experiments in continental design. I had expected to find the experience exhilarating, but almost as soon as we had left port I was struck down by sea-sickness.

Sea-sickness, by virtue of being psychosomatic, is one of the very few diseases with which modern internal technology is sometimes impotent to deal, and I was miserably confined to my cabin while I waited for my mind to make the necessary adaptation. I was bitterly ashamed of myself, for I alone out of half a hundred passengers had fallen prey to that strange atavistic malaise. While the others partied on deck, beneath the glorious light of the tropic stars, I lay in my bunk, half-delirious with discomfort and lack of sleep. I thought myself the unluckiest man in the world.

When I was abruptly hurled from my bed I thought that I had fallen—that my tossing and turning had inflicted one more ignominy upon me. When I couldn't recover my former position after spent long minutes fruitlessly groping about amid all kinds of mysterious debris, I assumed that I must be confused. When I couldn't open the door of my cabin even though I had the handle in my hand, I assumed that my failure was the result of clumsiness. When I finally got out into the corridor, and found myself crawling in shallow water with the artificial biolumines-cent strip beneath instead of above me, I thought I must be mad.

When the little girl spoke to me, I thought at first that she was a delusion, and that I was lost in a nightmare. It wasn't until she touched me, and tried to drag me upright with her tiny, frail hands, and addressed me by name—albeit incorrectly—that I was finally able to focus my thoughts.

"You have to get up, Mr. Mortimer," she said. "The boat's upside-down."

She was only eight years old, but she spoke quite calmly and reasonably.

"That's impossible," I told her. "*Genesis* is unsinkable. There's no way it could turn upside-down."

"But it is upside-down," she insisted—and as she did so, I finally realized the significance of the fact that the floor was glowing the way the ceiling should have glowed. "The water's coming in. I think we'll have to swim out."

The light put out by the ceiling-strip was as bright as ever, but the rippling water overlaying it made it seem dim and uncertain. The girl's little face, lit from below, seemed terribly serious within the frame of her dark and curly hair.

"I can't swim," I said, flatly.

She looked at me as if I were insane, or stupid, but it was true. I couldn't swim. I'd never liked the idea and I'd never seen any necessity. All modern ships—even sailing-ships designed to be cute and quaint for the benefit of tourists—were unsink-able.

I scrambled to my feet, and put out both my hands to steady

myself, to hold myself rigid against the upside-down walls. The water was knee-deep. I couldn't tell whether it was increasing or not—which told me, reassuringly, that it couldn't be rising very quickly. The upturned boat was rocking this way and that, and I could hear the rumble of waves breaking on the outside of the hull, but I didn't know how much of that apparent violence was in my mind.

"My name's Emily," the little girl told me. "I'm frightened. All my mothers and fathers were on deck. Everyone was on deck, except for you and me. Do you think they're all dead?"

"They can't be," I said, marveling at the fact that she spoke so soberly, even when she said that she was frightened. I realized, however, that if the ship had suffered the kind of misfortune which could turn it upside-down, the people on deck might indeed be dead. I tried to remember the passengers gossiping in the departure lounge, introducing themselves to one another with such fervor. The little girl had been with a party of nine, none of whose names I could remember. It occurred to me that her whole family might have been wiped out, that she might now be that rarest of all rare beings, an orphan. It was almost unimaginable. What possible catastrophe, I wondered, could have done that?

I asked Emily what had happened. She didn't know. Like me she had been in her bunk, sleeping the sleep of the innocent.

"Are we going to die too?" she asked. "I've been a good girl. I've never told a lie." It couldn't have been literally true, but I knew exactly what she meant. She was eight years old and she had every right to expect to live till she was eight hundred. She didn't deserve to die. It wasn't fair.

I knew full well that fairness didn't really come into it, and I expect she knew it too, even if my fellow historians were wrong about the virtual abolition of all the artifices of childhood, but I knew in my heart that what she said was right, and that insofar as the imperious laws of nature ruled her observation irrelevant, the universe was wrong. It wasn't fair. She had been a good girl. If she died, it would be a monstrous injustice.

Perhaps it was merely a kind of psychological defense mechanism that helped me to displace my own mortal anxieties, but the horror which ran through me was all focused on her. At that moment, her plight—not our plight, but hers—seemed to be the only thing that mattered. It was as if her dignified fear and her placid courage somehow contained the essence of human existence, the purest product of human progress.

Perhaps it was only my cowardly mind's refusal to contemplate anything else, but the only thing I could think of while I tried to figure out what to do was the awfulness of what she was saying. As that awfulness possessed me it was magnified a thousandfold, and it seemed to me that in her lone and tiny voice there was a much greater voice speaking for multitudes: for all the human children that had ever died before achieving maturity; all the good children who had died without ever having the chance to deserve to die.

"I don't think any more water can get in," she said, with a slight tremor in her voice. "But there's only so much air. If we stay here too long, we'll suffocate."

"It's a big ship," I told her. "If we're trapped in an air-bubble, it must be a very large one."

"But it won't last forever," she told me. She was eight years old and hoped to live to be eight hundred, and she was absolutely right. The air wouldn't last forever. Hours, certainly; maybe days—but not forever.

"There are survival pods under the bunks," she said. She had obviously been paying attention to the welcoming speeches which the captain and the chief steward had delivered in the lounge the evening after embarkation. She'd plugged the chips they'd handed out into her trusty handbook, like the good girl she was, and inwardly digested what they had to teach her—unlike those of us who were blithely careless and wretchedly sea-sick.

"We can both fit into one of the pods," she went on, "but we have to get it out of the boat before we inflate it. We have to go up—I mean down—the stairway into the water and away from the boat. You'll have to carry the pod, because it's too big for me."

"I can't swim," I reminded her.

"It doesn't matter," she said, patiently. "All you have to do is hold your breath and kick yourself away from the boat. You'll float up to the surface whether you can swim or not. Then you just yank the cord and the pod will inflate. You have to hang on to it, though. Don't let go."

I stared at her, wondering how she could be so calm, so controlled, so efficient.

"Listen to the water breaking on the hull," I whispered. "Feel the movement of the boat. It would take a hurricane to overturn a boat like this. We wouldn't stand a chance out there."

"It's not so bad," she told me. She didn't have both hands out to brace herself against the walls, although she lifted one occasionally to stave off the worst of the lurches caused by the bobbing of the boat.

But if it wasn't a hurricane that turned us over, I thought, *what the hell was it? Whales have been extinct for eight hundred years.*

"We don't have to go just yet," Emily said, mildly, "But we'll have to go in the end. We have to get out. The pod's bright orange and it has a distress beacon. We should be picked up within twenty-four hours, but there'll be supplies for a week."

I had every confidence that modern internal technology could sustain us for a month, if necessary. Even having to drink a little sea-water, if your recycling gel clots, only qualifies as a minor inconvenience nowadays. Drowning is another matter; so is asphyxiation. She was absolutely right. We had to get out of the upturned boat—not immediately, but some time soon. Help might get to us before then, but we couldn't wait, and we shouldn't. We were, after all, human beings. We were supposed to be able to take charge of our own destinies, to do what we ought to do. Anything less would be a betrayal of our heritage. I knew that, and understood it.

But I couldn't swim.

"It's okay, Mr. Mortimer," she said, putting her reassuring hand in mine. "We can do it. We'll go together. It'll be all right."

* * * * * * *

Emily was right. We could do it, together, and we did—not immediately, I confess, but in the end we did it. It was the most terrifying and most horrible experience of my young life, but it had to be done and we did it.

When I finally dived into that black pit of water, knowing that I had to go down and sideways before I could hope to go up, I was carried forward by the knowledge that Emily expected it of me, and needed me to do it. Without her, I'm sure that I would have died. I simply would not have had the courage to save myself. Because she was there, I dived, with the pod clutched in my arms. Because she was there, I managed to kick away from the hull and yank the cord to inflate it.

It wasn't until I had pulled Emily into the pod, and made sure that she was safe, that I paused to think how remarkable it was that the sea was hot enough to scald us both.

We were three storm-tossed days afloat before the helicopter picked us up. We cursed our ill-luck, not having the least inkling how bad things were elsewhere. We couldn't understand why the weather was getting worse and worse instead of better.

When the pilot finally explained it, we couldn't immediately take it in. Perhaps that's not surprising, given that the geologists were just as astonished as everyone else. After all, the sea-bed had been quietly cracking wherever the tectonic plates were pulling apart for millions of years; it was an ongoing phenomenon, very well understood. Hundreds of black smokers and underwater volcanoes were under constant observation. Nobody had any reason to expect that a plate could simply break so far away from its rim, or that the fissure could be so deep, so long and so rapid in its extension. Everyone thought that the main threat to the earth's surface was posed by wayward comets; all vigilant eyes were directed outwards. No one had expected such awesome force to erupt from within, from the hot mantle that lay, hubbling and bubbling, beneath the earth's fragile crust.

It was, apparently, an enormous bubble of upwelling gas that contrived the near-impossible feat of flipping *Genesis* over. The earthquakes and the tidal waves came later.

It was the worst natural disaster in six hundred years. One million, nine hundred thousand people died in all. Emily wasn't the only child to lose her entire family, and I shudder to think of the number of families which lost their only children. We historians have to maintain a sense of perspective, though. Compared with the number of people who died in the wars of the twentieth and twenty-first centuries, or the numbers of people who died in epidemics in earlier centuries, nineteen hundred thousand is a trivial figure.

Perhaps I would have done what I eventually set out to do anyway. Perhaps the Great Coral Sea Catastrophe would have appalled me even if I'd been on the other side of the world, cocooned in the safety of a tree-house or an apartment in one of the crystal cities—but I don't think so.

It was because I was at the very centre of things, because my life was literally turned upside-down by the disaster—and because eight-year-old Emily Marchant was there to save my life with her common sense and her composure—that I set out to write a definitive history of death, intending to reveal not merely the dull facts of mankind's longest and hardest battle, but also the real meaning and significance of it.

2.

The first volume of Mortimer Gray's *History of Death*, entitled *The Prehistory of Death*, was published on 21 January 2914. It was, unusually for its day, a mute book, with no voice-over, sound-effects or background music. Nor did it have any original art-work, all the illustrations being unenhanced still photographs. It was, in short, the kind of book that only a historian would have published. Its reviewers generally agreed that it was an old-fashioned example of scrupulous scholarship, and none expected that access demand would be considerable. Many commentators questioned the merit of Gray's arguments.

The Prehistory of Death summarized what was known about early hominid lifestyles, and had much to say about the effects of natural selection of the patterns of mortality in modern man's ancestor species. Gray carefully discussed the evolution of parental care as a genetic strategy. Earlier species of man, he observed, had raised parental care to a level of efficiency which permitted the human infant to be born sat a much earlier stage in its development than any other, maximizing its opportunity to be shaped by nurture and learning. From the very beginning, Gray proposed, human species were actively at war with death. The evolutionary success of *Homo sapiens* was based in the collaborative activities of parents in protecting, cherishing and preserving the lives of children: activities that extended beyond immediate family groups as reciprocal altruism made it advantageous for humans to form tribes, and ultimately nations.

In these circumstances, Gray argued, it was entirely natural that the origins of consciousness and culture should be intimately bound up with a keen awareness of the war against death. He asserted that the first great task of the human imagination must have been to carry forward that war. It was entirely understandable, he said, that early paleontologists, having discovered the bones of a Neanderthal man in an apparent grave, with the remains of a primitive garland of flowers, should instantly have felt an intimate kinship with him; there could be no more persuasive evidence of full humanity than the attachment of ceremony to the idea and the fact of death.

Gray waxed lyrical about the importance of ritual as a symbolization of opposition and enmity to death. He had no patience with the proposition that such rituals were of no practical value, a mere window-dressing of culture. On the contrary, he claimed that there was no activity more practical than this expressive recognition of the value of life, this imposition of a moral order on the fact of human mortality. The birth of agriculture Gray regarded as a mere sophistication of food-gathering, of considerable importance as a technical discovery but of little significance in transforming human nature. The practices of burying the dead with ceremony, and of ritual mourning, on the other hand, were, in his view, evidence of the transformation of human nature, of the fundamental creation of meaning that made human life very different from the lives of animals.

Prehistorians who marked out the evolution of man by his developing technology—the Stone Age giving way to the Bronze Age, the Bronze Age to the Iron Age—were, Gray conceded, taking intelligent advantage of those relics that had stood the test of time. He warned, however, of the folly of thinking that because tools had survived the millennia, it must have been tool-making that was solely or primarily responsible for human progress. In his view, the primal cause that made people invent was man's ongoing war against death.

It was not tools that had created man and given birth to civilization, Mortimer Gray proclaimed, but the awareness of mortality.

3.

Although its impact on my nascent personality was considerable, the Coral Sea Catastrophe was essentially an impersonal disaster. The people who died, including those who had been aboard the *Genesis*, were all unknown to me; it was not until some years later that I experienced personal bereavement. It wasn't one of my parents who died—by the time the first of them quit this earth I was nearly a hundred years old and our temporary closeness was a half-remembered thing of the distant past—but one of my spouses.

By the time *The Prehistory of Death* was published I'd contracted my first marriage: a group contract with a relatively small aggregate consisting of three other men and four women.

We lived in Lamu, on the coast of Kenya, a nation to which I had been drawn by my studies of the early evolution of man. We were all young people, and we had formed our group for companionship rather than for parenting—which was a privilege conventionally left, even in those days, to much older people. We didn't go in for overmuch fleshsex, because we were still finding our various ways through the maze of erotic virtuality, but we took the time—as I suppose all young people do— to explore its unique delights. I can't remember exactly why I joined the group; I presume that it was because I accepted, tacitly at least, the conventional wisdom that there is spice in variety, and that one should do one's best to keep a broad front of experience.

It wasn't a particularly happy marriage, but it served its purpose. We went in for a good deal of sporting activity and conventional tourism. We visited the other continents from time to time, but most of our adventures took us back and forth across Africa. Most of my spouses were practical ecologists involved in one way or another with the re-greening of the north and south, or with the reforestation of the equatorial belt. What little credit I earned to add to my Allocation was earned by assisting them; such fees as I received for net-access to my work were inconsiderable. Axel, Jodocus and Minna were all involved in large-scale hydrological engineering, and liked to describe themselves, light-heartedly, as the Lamu Rainmakers. The rest of us became, inevitably, the Rainmakers-in-Law.

* * * * * *

To begin with, I had considerable affection for all the other members of my new family, but as time went by the usual accretion of petty irritations built up, and a couple of changes in the group's personnel failed to renew the initial impetus. The research for the second volume of my history began to draw me more and more to Egypt and to Greece, even though there was no real need actually to travel in order to do the relevant research. I think we would have divorced in 2919 anyhow, even if it hadn't been for Grizel's death.

She went swimming in the newly re-routed Kwarra one day, and didn't come back.

Maybe the fact of her death wouldn't have hit me so hard if she hadn't been drowned, but I was still uneasy about deep water—even the relatively placid waters of the great rivers. If I'd been able to swim I might have gone out with her, but I didn't. I didn't even know she was missing until the news came in that a body had been washed up twenty kilometers downriver.

"It was a million-to-one thing," Ayesha told me, when she came back from the on-site inquest. "She must have been caught from behind by a log moving in the current, or something like that. We'll never know for sure. She must have been knocked unconscious, though, or badly dazed. Otherwise, she'd never have drifted into the white water. The rocks finished her off."

Rumor has it that many people simply can't take in news of the death of someone they love—that it flatly defies belief. I didn't react that way. With me, belief was instantaneous, and I just gave way under its pressure. I literally fell over, because my legs wouldn't support me—another psychosomatic failure about which my internal machinery could do nothing—and I wept uncontrollably. None of the others did, not even Alex, who'd been closer to Grizel than anyone. They were sympathetic at first, but it wasn't long before a note of annoyance began to creep into their reassurances.

"Come on, Morty," Ilya said, voicing the thought the rest of them were too diplomatic to let out. "You know more about death than any of us; if it doesn't help you to get a grip, what good is all that research?"

He was right, of course. Alex and Ayesha had often tried to suggest, delicately, that mine was an essentially unhealthy fascination, and now they felt vindicated.

"If you'd actually bothered to read my book," I retorted, "you'd know that it has nothing complimentary to say about philosophical acceptance. It sees a sharp awareness of mortality, and the capacity to feel the horror of death so keenly, as key forces driving human evolution."

"But you don't have to act it out so flamboyantly," Ilya came back, perhaps using cruelty to conceal and assuage his own misery. "We've evolved now. We've got past all that. We've matured." Ilya was the oldest of us, and he seemed very old, although he was only sixty-five. In those days, there weren't nearly as many double centenarians around as there are nowadays, and triple centenarians were very rare indeed. We take emortality so much for granted that it's easy to forget how recent a development it is.

"It's what I feel," I told him, retreating into uncompromising assertion. "I can't help it."

"We all loved her," Ayesha reminded me. "We'll all miss her. You're not proving anything, Morty."

What she meant was that I wasn't proving anything except my own instability, but she spoke more accurately than she thought; I wasn't proving anything at all. I was just reacting—atavistically, perhaps, but with crude honesty and authentically child-like innocence.

"We all have to pull together now," she added, "for Grizel's sake."

* * * * * * *

A death in the family almost always leads to universal divorce in childless marriages; nobody knows why. Such a loss does force the survivors pull together, but it seems that the process of pulling together only serves to emphasize the incompleteness of the unit. We all went our separate ways, even the three Rainmakers.

I set out to use my solitude to become a true neo-Epicurean, after the fashion of the times, seeking no excess and deriving an altogether appropriate pleasure from everything I did. I took care to cultivate a proper love for the commonplace, training myself to a pitch of perfection in all the techniques of physiological control necessary to physical fitness and quiet metabolism.

I soon convinced myself that I'd transcended such primitive and adolescent goals as happiness, and had cultivated instead a truly civilized ataraxia: a calm of mind whose value went beyond the limits of ecstasy and exultation.

Perhaps I was fooling myself, but if I was, I succeeded. The habits stuck. No matter what lifestyle fashions came and went thereafter, I remained a stubborn neo-Epicurean, immune to all other eupsychian fantasies. For a while, though, I was perpetually haunted by Grizel's memory—and not, alas, the memory of all the things that we'd shared while she was alive. I gradually forgot the sound of her voice, the touch of her hand and even the image of her face, remembering only the horror of her sudden and unexpected departure from the arena of my experience.

For the next ten years I lived in Alexandria, in a simple villa cleverly gantzed out of the desert sands—sands that still gave an impression of timelessness, even though they had been restored to wilderness as recently as the twenty-seventh century, when Egypt's food-economy had been realigned to take full advantage of the newest techniques in artificial photosynthesis.

4.

The second volume of Mortimer Gray's *History of Death*, entitled *Death in the Ancient World*, was published on 7 May 2931. It contained a wealth of data regarding burial practices and patterns of mortality in Egypt, the Kingdoms of Sumer and Akkad, the Indus civilizations of Harappa and Mohenjo-Daro, the Yangshao and Lungshan cultures of the Far East, the cultures of the Olmecs and Zpotecs, Greece before and after Alexander, and the pre-Christian Roman Empire. It paid particular attention to the elaborate mythologies of life after death developed by ancient cultures

Gray gave most elaborate consideration to the Egyptians, whose eschatology evidently fascinated him. He spared no effort in description and discussion of the Book of the Dead, the Hall of Double Justice, Anubis and Osiris, the custom of mummification, and the building of pyramid-tombs. He was almost as fascinated by the elaborate geography of the Greek Underworld, the characters associated with it—Hades and Persephone, Thanatos and the Erinnyes, Cerberus and Charon—and the descriptions of the unique fates reserved for such individuals as Sisyphus, Ixion and Tantalus. The development of such myths as these Gray regarded as a triumph of the creative imagination. In his account, myth-making and story-telling were vital weapons in the war against death—a war that had still to be fought in the mind of man, because there was little yet to be accomplished by defiance of its claims upon the body.

In the absence of an effective medical science, Gray argued, the war against death was essentially a war of propaganda, and myths were to be judged in that light—not by their truthfulness, even in some allegorical or metaphorical sense, but by their usefulness in generating morale and meaning. By elaborating and extrapolating the process of death in this way, a more secure moral order could be imported into social life. People thus achieved a sense of continuity with past and future generations, so that every individual became part of a great enterprise which extended across the generations, from the beginning to the end of time.

Gray did not regard the building of the pyramids as a kind of gigantic folly or vanity, or a way to dispose of the energies of the peasants when they were not required in harvesting the bounty of the fertile Nile. He argued that pyramid-building should be seen as the most useful of all labors, because it was work directed toward the glorious imposition of human endeavor upon the natural landscape. The placing of a royal mummy, with all its accoutrements, in a fabulous geometric edifice of stone was for Gray a loud, confident and entirely appropriate statement of humanity's invasion of the empire of death.

Gray complimented those tribesmen who worshipped their ancestors and thought them always close at hand, ready to deliver judgments upon the living. Such people, he felt, had fully mastered an elementary truth of human existence: that the dead were not entirely gone, but lived on, intruding upon memory and dream, both when they were bidden and when they were not. He approved of the idea that the dead should have a voice, and must be entitled to speak, and that the living had a moral duty to listen. Because these ancient tribes were as direly short of history as they were of medicine, he argued, they were entirely justified in allowing their ancestors to live on in the minds of living people, where the culture those ancestors had forged similarly resided.

Some reviewers complimented Gray on the breadth of his research and the comprehensiveness of his data, but few endorsed the propriety of his interpretations. He was widely advised to be more dispassionate in carrying forward his project.

5.

I was sixty when I married again. This time it was a singular marriage, to Sharane Fereday. We set up home in Avignon, and lived together for nearly twenty years. I won't say that we were exceptionally happy, but I came to depend on her closeness and her affection, and the day she told me that she had had enough was the darkest of my life so far—far darker in its desolation than the day Emily Marchant and I had been trapped in the wreck of the *Genesis*, although it didn't mark me as deeply.

"Twenty years is a long time, Mortimer," she told me. "It's time to move on—time for you as well as for me."

She was being sternly reasonable at that stage; I knew from experience that the sternness would crumble if I put it to the test, and I thought that her resolve would crumble with it, as it had before in similar circumstances, but it didn't.

"I'm truly sorry," she said, when she was eventually reduced to tears, "but I have to do it. I have to go. It's my life, and your part in it is over. I hate hurting you, but I don't want to live with you any more. It's my fault, not yours, but that's the way it is."

It wasn't anybody's fault. I can see that clearly now, although it wasn't so easy to see it at the time. Like the Great Coral Sea Catastrophe or Grizel's drowning it was just something that happened. Things do happen, regardless of people's best-laid plans, most heartfelt wishes and most intense hopes.

Now that memory has blotted out the greater part of that phase of my life—including, I presume, the worst of it—I don't really know why I was so devastated by Sharane's decision, nor why it should have filled me with such black despair. Had I cultivated a dependence so absolute that it seemed irreplaceable, or was it really only my pride that had suffered a sickening blow? Was it the imagined consequences of the rejection or merely the fact of rejection itself that sickened me so? Even now, I can't tell for certain. Even then, my neo-Epicurean conscience must have told me over and over again to pull myself together, to conduct myself with more decorum.

I tried. I'm certain that I tried.

* * * * * * *

Sharane's love for the ancient past was even more intense than mine, but her writings were far less dispassionate. She was a historian of sorts but she wasn't an academic historian; her writings tended to the lyrical rather than the factual even when she was supposedly writing non-fiction.

Sharane would never have written a mute book, or one whose pictures didn't move. Had it been allowed by law at that time she'd have fed her readers designer psychotropics to heighten their responses according to the schemes of her texts. She was a VR scriptwriter rather than a textwriter like me. She wasn't content to know about the past; she wanted to re-create it and make it solid and live in it. Nor did she reserve such inclinations to the privacy of her E-suit. She was flamboyantly old-fashioned in all that she did. She liked to dress in gaudy pastiches of the costumes represented in Greek or Egyptian art, and she liked decor to match. People who knew us were mildly astonished that we should want to live together, given the difference in our personalities, but I suppose it was an attraction of opposites. Perhaps my intensity of purpose and solitude had begun to weigh rather heavily upon me when we met, and my carefully-cultivated calm of mind threatened to become a kind of toiling inertia.

On the other hand, perhaps that's all confabulation and rationalization. I was a different person then, and I've since lost touch with that person as completely as I've lost touch with everyone else I knew then.

But I do remember, vaguely....

I remember that I found in Sharane a certain precious wildness which, although it wasn't entirely spontaneous, was unfailingly amusing. She had the happy gift of never taking herself too seriously, although she was wholehearted enough in her determined attempts to put herself imaginatively in touch with the past.

From her point of view, I suppose I was doubly valuable. On the one hand, I was a fount of information and inspiration, on the other a kind of anchorage whose solidity kept her from losing herself in her flights of the imagination. Twenty years of marriage ought to have cemented her dependence on me just as it had cemented my dependence on her, but it didn't.

"You think I need you to keep my feet on the ground," Sharane said, as the break between us was completed and carefully rendered irreparable, "but I don't. Anyhow, I've been weighed down long enough. I need to soar for a while, to spread my wings."

* * * * * * *

Sharane and I had talked for a while, as married people do, about the possibility of having a child. We had both made deposits to the French national gamete bank, so that if we felt the same way when the time finally came to exercise our right of replacement—or to specify in our wills how that right was to be posthumously exercised—we could order an ovum to be unfrozen and fertilized.

I had always known, of course, that such flights of fancy were not to be taken too seriously, but when I accepted that the marriage was indeed over there seemed to be an extra dimension of tragedy and misery in the knowledge that our genes never would be combined—that our separation cast our legacies once again upon the chaotic sea of irresolution.

Despite the extremity of my melancholy, I never contemplated suicide. Although I'd already used up the traditional threescore years and ten, I was in no doubt at all that it wasn't yet time to remove myself from the crucible of human evolution to make room for my successor, whether that successor was to be born from an ovum of Sharane's or not. No matter how black my mood was when Sharane, I knew that my *History of Death* remained to be completed, and that the work would require at least another century. Even so, the breaking of such an intimate bond filled me with intimations of mortality and a painful sense of the futility of all my endeavors.

My first divorce had come about because a cruel accident had ripped apart the delicate fabric of my life, but my second—or so it seemed to me—was itself a horrid rent shearing my very being into ragged fragments. I hope that I tried with all my might not to blame Sharane, but how could I avoid it? And how could she not resent my overt and covert accusations, my veiled and naked resentments?

"Your problem, Mortimer," she said to me, when her lachrymose phase had given way to bright anger, "is that you're obsessed. You're a deeply morbid man, and it's not healthy. There's some special fear in you, some altogether exceptional horror, which feeds upon you day and night, and makes you grotesquely vulnerable to occurrences that normal people can take in their stride, and which ill befit a self-styled Epicurean. If you want my advice, you ought to abandon that history you're writing, at least for a while, and devote yourself to something brighter and more vigorous."

"Death is my life," I informed her, speaking metaphorically, and not entirely without irony. "It always will be, until and including the end."

I remember saying that. The rest is vague, but I really do remember saying that.

6.

The third volume of Mortimer Gray's *History of Death*, entitled *The Empires of Faith*, was published on 18 August 2954. The introduction announced that the author had been forced to set aside his initial ambition to write a truly comprehensive history, and stated that he would henceforth be unashamedly eclectic, and contentedly ethnocentric, because he did not wish to be a mere archivist of death and therefore could not regard all episodes in humankind's war against death as being of equal interest. He declared that he was more interested in interpretation than mere summary, and that insofar as the war against death had been a moral crusade he felt fully entitled to draw morals from it.

This preface, understandably, dismayed those critics who had urged the author to be more dispassionate. Some reviewers were content to condemn the new volume without even bothering to inspect the rest of it, although it was considerably shorter than the second volume and had a rather more fluent style. Others complained that the day of mute text was dead and gone, and that there was no place in the modern world for pictures which resolutely refused to move.

Unlike many contemporary historians, whose birth into a world in which religious faith was almost extinct had robbed them of any sympathy for the imperialists of dogma, Gray proposed that the great religions had been one of the finest achievements of humankind. He regarded them as a vital stage in the evolution of community—as social technologies that had permitted a spectacular transcendence of the limitation of community to the tribe or region. Faiths, he suggested, were the first social instruments that could bind together different language groups, and even different races. It was not until the spread of the great religions, Gray argued, that the possibility came into being of gathering all men together into a single common enterprise. He regretted, of course, that the principal product of this great dream had been two millennia of bitter and savage conflict between adherents of different faiths, or adherents of different versions of the same faith, but thought the ambition worthy of all possible respect and admiration. He even retained some sympathy for jihads and crusades, in the formulation of which people had tried to attribute more meaning to the sacrifice of life than they ever had before.

Gray was particularly fascinated by the symbology of the Christian mythos, which had taken as its central image the death on the cross of Jesus, and had tried to make that one image of death carry an enormous allegorical load. He was entranced by the idea of Christ's death as a force of redemption and salvation, by the notion that the in question person died *for others*. He extended the argument to take in the Christian martyrs, who added to the primal crucifixion a vast series of symbolic and morally significant deaths. This, he considered, was a colossal achievement of the imagination, a crucial victory by which death was dramatically transfigured in the theatre of the human imagination—as was the Christian idea of death as a kind of reconciliation: a gateway to Heaven, if properly met; a gateway to Hell if not. Gray seized upon the idea of absolution from sin following confession, and particularly the notion of deathbed repentance, as a daring raid into the territories of the imagination previously ruled by fear of death.

Gray's commentaries on the other major religions were less elaborate but no less interested. Various ideas of reincarnation and the related concept of karma he discussed at great length, as one of the most ingenious imaginative bids for freedom from the tyranny of death. He was not quite so enthusiastic about the idea of the world as illusion, the idea of nirvana, and certain other aspects of Far Eastern thought, although he was impressed in several ways by Confucius and the Buddha. All these things and more he assimilated to the main line of his argument, which was that the great religions had made bold imaginative leaps in order to carry forward the war against death on a broader front than ever before, providing vast numbers of individuals with an efficient intellectual weaponry of moral purpose.

7.

After Sharane left I stayed on in Avignon for a while. The house where we had lived was demolished, and I had another raised in its place. I resolved to take up the reclusive life again, at least for a while. I had come to think of myself as one of nature's monks, and when I was tempted to flights of fancy of a more personal kind than those retailed in virtual reality I could imagine myself an avatar of some patient scholar born fifteen hundred years, contentedly submissive to the Benedictine rule. I didn't, of course, believe in the possibility of reincarnation, and when such belief became fashionable again I found it almost impossible to indulge such fantasies.

In 2960 I moved to Antarctica, not to Amundsen City—which had become the world's political centre since the United Nations had elected to set up headquarters in "the continent without nations"—but to Cape Adare on the Ross Sea, which was a relatively lonely spot.

I moved into a tall house somewhat resembling a lighthouse, from whose upper stories I could look out at the edge of the ice-cap and watch the penguins at play. I was reasonably contented, and soon came to feel that I had put the torments and turbulences of my early life behind me.

I often went walking across the nearer reaches of the icebound sea, but I rarely got into difficulties. Ironically enough, my only serious injury of that period was the broken leg I sustained while working with a rescue party attempting to locate and save one of my neighbors, Ziru Majumdar, who had fallen into a crevasse while out on a similar expedition. We ended up in adjacent beds at the hospital in Amundsen City.

* * * * * * *

"I'm truly sorry about your leg, Mr. Gray," Majumdar said. "It was very stupid of me to get lost. After all, I've lived here for thirty years; I thought I knew every last ice-ridge like the back of my hand. It's not as if the weather was particularly bad, and I've never suffered from summer rhapsody or snow-blindness."

I'd suffered from both—I was still awkwardly vulnerable to psychosomatic ills—but they only served to make me more careful. An uneasy mind can sometimes be an advantage.

"It wasn't your fault, Mr. Majumdar" I graciously insisted. "I suppose I must have been a little over-confident myself, or I'd never have slipped and fallen. At least they were able to pull me out in a matter of minutes; you must have lain unconscious at the bottom of that crevasse for nearly two days."

"Just about. I came round several times—at least, I think I did—but my internal tech was pumping so much dope around my system it's difficult to be sure. My surskin and thermosuit were doing their best to keep me warm but the first law of thermodynamics doesn't give you much slack when you're at the bottom of a cleft in the permafrost. I've got authentic frostbite in my toes, you know—imagine that!"

I dutifully tried to imagine it, but it wasn't easy. He could hardly be in pain, so it was difficult to conjure up any notion of what it might feel like to have necrotized toes. The doctors reckoned that it would take a week for the nanomachines to restore the tissues to their former pristine condition.

"Mind you," he added, with a small embarrassed laugh, "it's only a matter of time before the whole biosphere gets frostbite, isn't it? Unless the sun gets stirred up again."

More than fifty years had passed since scrupulous students

of the sunspot cycle had announced the advent of a new Ice Age, but the world was quite unworried by the exceedingly slow advance of the glaciers across the Northern Hemisphere. It was the sort of thing that only cropped up in light banter.

"I won't mind that," I said, contemplatively. "Nor will you, I dare say. We like ice—why else would we live here?"

"Right. Not that I agree with those Gaean Liberationists, mind. I hear they're proclaiming that the inter-glacial periods are simply Gaea's fevers, that the birth of civilization was just a morbid symptom of the planet's sickness, and that human culture has so far been a mere delirium of the noösphere."

He obviously paid more attention to the lunatic fringe channels than I did.

"It's just colorful rhetoric," I told him. "They don't mean it literally."

"Think not? Well, perhaps. I was delirious myself for a while when I was down that hole. Can't be sure whether I was asleep or awake, but I was certainly lost in some vivid dreams—and I mean vivid. I don't know about you, but I always find VR a bit flat, even if I use illicit psychotropics to give delusion a helping hand. I think it's to do with the protective effects of our internal technology. Nanomachines mostly do their job a little too well, because of the built-in safety margins—it's only when they reach the limits of their capacity that they let really interesting things begin to happen."

I knew he was building up to some kind of self-justification, but I felt that he was entitled to it. I nodded, to give him permission to prattle on.

"You have to go to the very brink of extinction to reach the cutting edge of experience, you see. I found that out while I was trapped down there in the ice, not knowing whether the rescuers would get to me in time. You can learn a lot about life, and about yourself, in a situation like that. It really was vivid—more vivid than anything I ever....well, what I'm trying to get at is that we're too safe nowadays; we can have no idea of the zest there was in living in the bad old days. Not that I'm about to take up jumping into crevasses as a hobby, you understand. Once in a very long while is plenty."

"Yes it is," I agreed, shifting my itching leg and wishing that nanomachines weren't so slow to compensate for trifling but annoying sensations. "Once in a while is certainly enough for me. In fact, I for one will be quite content if it never happens again. I don't think I need any more of the kind of enlightenment that comes from experiences like yours. I was in the Great Coral Sea Catastrophe, you know—shipwrecked, scalded and lost at sea for days on end."

"It's not the same," he insisted, "but you won't be able to understand the difference until it happens to you.

I didn't believe him. In that instance, I suppose, he was right and I was wrong.

* * * * * * *

I'd never heard Mr. Majumdar speak so freely before, and I never heard him do it again. The social life of the Cape Adare "exiles" was unusually formal, hemmed in by numerous barriers of propriety and etiquette. After an embarrassing phase of learning and adjustment I'd found the formality aesthetically appealing, and had played the game with enthusiasm, but it was beginning to lose its appeal by the time the accident shook me up. I suppose it's understandable that whatever you set out to exclude from the pattern of your life eventually comes to seem like a lack, and then an unfulfilled need.

After a few years more I began to hunger once again for the spontaneity and abandonment of warmer climes. I decided there'd be time enough to celebrate the advent of the Ice Age when the glaciers had reached the full extent of their reclaimed empire, and that I might as well make what use I could of Gaea's temporary fever before it cooled. I moved to Venezuela, to dwell in the gloriously restored jungles of the Orinoco amid their teeming wildlife.

Following the destruction of much of the southern part of the continent in the Second Nuclear War, Venezuela had attained a cultural hegemony in South America that it had never surrendered. Brazil and Argentina had long since recovered, both economically and ecologically, from their disastrous fit of ill temper, but Venezuela was still the home of the *avant garde* of the Americas. It was there, for the first time, that I came into close contact with Thanaticism.

* * * * * * *

The original Thanatic cults had flourished in the twenty-eighth century. They had appeared among the last generations of children born without Zaman transformations; their members were people who, denied emortality through blastular engineering, had perversely elected to reject the benefits of rejuvenation too, making a fetish out of living only a "natural" lifespan. At the time it had seemed likely that they would be the last of the many Millenarian cults that had long afflicted Western culture, and they had quite literally died out some eighty or ninety years before I was born.

Nobody had then thought it possible, let alone likely, that genetically-endowed emortals would ever embrace Thanaticism, but they were wrong.

There had always been suicides in the emortal population—indeed, suicide was the commonest cause of death among emortals, outnumbering accidental deaths by a factor of three—but such acts were usually covert and normally involved people who had lived at least a hundred years. The neo-Thanatics were not only indiscreet—their whole purpose seemed to be to make a public spectacle of themselves—but also young; people over seventy were held to have violated the Thanaticist ethic simply by surviving to that age.

Thanatics tended to choose violent means of death, and usually issued invitations as well as choosing their moments so that large crowds could gather. Jumping from tall buildings and burning to death were the most favored means in the beginning, but these quickly ceased to be interesting. As the Thanatic revival progressed, adherents of the movement sought increasingly bizarre methods in the interests of capturing attention and out-doing their predecessors. For these reasons, it was impossible for anyone living alongside the cults to avoid becoming implicated in their rites, if only as a spectator.

By the time I had been in Venezuela for a year I had seen five people die horribly. After the first I had resolved to turn away from any others, so as not to lend even minimal support to the practice, but I soon found that I had underestimated the difficulty of so doing. There was no excuse to be found in my vocation; thousands of people who were not historians of death found it equally impossible to resist fascination.

I believed at first that the fad would soon pass, after wasting the lives of a handful of neurotics, but the cults continued to grow. Gaea's fever might be cooling, its crisis having passed, but the delirium of human culture had evidently not yet reached what Ziru Majumdar called "the cutting edge of experience".

8.

The fourth volume of Mortimer Gray's *History of Death*, entitled *Fear and Fascination*, was published on 12 February 2977. In spite of being mute and motionless it was immediately subject to heavy access-demand, presumably in consequence of the world's increasing fascination with the "problem" of neo-Thanaticism. Requisitions of the earlier volumes of Gray's history had picked up worldwide during the early 2970s, but the author had not appreciated what this might mean in terms of the demand for the new volume, and might have set a higher access fee had he realized.

Academic historians were universal in their condemnation of the new volume, possibly because of the enthusiasm with which it was greeted by laymen, but popular reviewers adored it. Its arguments were recklessly plundered by journalists and other broadcasting pundits in search of possible parallels that might be drawn with the modern world, especially those which seemed to carry moral lessons for the Thanatics and their opponents.

Fear and Fascination extended, elaborated and diversified the arguments contained in its immediate predecessor, particularly in respect of the Christian world of the Medieval period and the Renaissance. It had much to say about art and literature, and the images contained therein. It had chapters on the personification of Death as the Grim Reaper, on the iconography of the *danse macabre*, on the topics of *memento mori* and *artes moriendi*. It had long analyses of Dante's "Divine Comedy", the paintings of Hieronymus Bosch, Milton's *Paradise Lost* and graveyard poetry. These were by no means exercises in conventional literary criticism; they were elements of a long and convoluted argument about the contributions made by the individual creative imagination to the war of ideas that was raging on the only battleground on which man could as yet constructively oppose the specter of death.

Gray also dealt with the persecution of heretics and the subsequent elaboration of Christian Demonology, which led to the witch-craze of the fifteenth, sixteenth and seventeenth century. He gave considerable attention to various thriving folklore traditions that confused the notion of death, especially to the popularity of fictions and fears regarding premature burial, ghosts and the various species of the "undead" who allegedly rose from their graves as ghouls or vampires.

In Gray's eyes, all these phenomena were symptomatic of a crisis in Western man's imaginative dealings with the idea of death: a feverish heating up of a conflict that had been in danger of becoming desultory. The cities of men had been under perpetual siege from Death since the time of their first building, but now—in one part of the world, at least—the perception of that siege had sharpened. A kind of spiritual starvation and panic had set in, and the progress that had been made in the war by virtue of the ideological imperialism of Christ's Holy Cross now seemed imperiled by disintegration. That Empire of Faith was breaking up under the stress of skepticism, and men were faced with the prospect of going into battle against their most ancient enemy with their armor in tatters.

Just as the Protestants were trying to replace the Catholic Church's centralized authority with a more personal relationship between men and God, Gray argued, so the creative artists of this era were trying to achieve a more personal and more intimate form of reconciliation between men and Death, equipping individuals with the power to mount their own ideative assaults. He drew some parallels between what happened in the Christian world and similar periods of crisis that he identified in different cultures at different times, but other historians claimed that his analogies were weak, and that he was over-generalizing. Some argued that his intense study of the phenomena associated with the idea of death had become too personal, and suggested that he had become over-infatuated with the ephemeral ideas of past ages, to the point where they were taking over his own imagination.

9.

At first, I found celebrity status pleasing, and the extra credit generated by my access fees was certainly welcome, even to a man of moderate tastes and habits. The unaccustomed touch of fame brought a fresh breeze into a life that might have been in danger of becoming bogged down.

To begin with, I was gratified to be reckoned an expert whose views on Thanaticism were to be taken seriously, even by some Thanatics. I received a veritable deluge of invitations to appear on the talk shows that were the staple diet of contemporary broadcasting, and for a while I accepted as many as I could conveniently accommodate within the pattern of my life.

I have no need to rely on my memories in recapitulating these episodes, because they remain on record—but by the same token, I needn't quote extensively from them. In the early days, when I was a relatively new face, my interrogators mostly started out by asking for information about my book, and their opening questions were usually stolen from uncharitable reviews.

"Some people feel that you've been carried away, Mr. Gray," more than one combative interviewer sneeringly began, "and that what started out as a sober history is fast becoming an obsessive rant. Did you decide to get personal in order to boost your sales?"

My careful cultivation of neo-Epicureanism and my years in Antarctica had left a useful legacy of calm formality; I always handled such accusations with punctilious politeness.

"Of course the war against death is a personal matter," I would reply. "It's a personal matter for everyone, mortal or emortal. Without that sense of personal relevance, it would be impossible to put oneself imaginatively in the place of the people of the ancient past so as to obtain empathetic insight into their affairs. If I seem to be making heroes of the men of the past by describing their crusades, it's because they *were* heroes, and if my contemporaries find inspiration in my work it's because they too are heroes in the same cause. The engineering of emortality has made us victors in the war, but we desperately need to retain a proper sense of triumph. We ought to celebrate our victory over death as joyously as possible, lest we lose our appreciation of its fruits."

My interviewers always appreciated that kind of link, which handed them their next question on a plate. "Is that what you think of the Thanatics?" they would follow up, eagerly.

It was, and I would say so at any length they considered appropriate.

Eventually, my interlocutors no longer talked about my book, taking it for granted that everyone knew who I was and what I'd done. They'd cut straight to the chase, asking me what I thought of the latest Thanaticist publicity stunt.

Personally, I thought the media's interest in Thanaticism was exaggerated. All death was, of course, news in a world populated almost entirely by emortals, and the Thanatics took care to be newsworthy by making such a song and dance about what they were doing, but the number of individuals involved was very small. In a world population of nearly three billion, a hundred deaths per week was a drop in the ocean, and "quiet" suicides still outnumbered the ostentatious Thanatics by a factor of five or six throughout the 2980s. The public debates quickly expanded to take in other issues. Subscription figures for net access to videotapes and teletexts concerned with the topic of violent death came under scrutiny, and everyone began talking about the "new pornography of death"—although fascination with such material had undoubtedly been widespread for many years.

"Don't you feel, Mr. Gray," I was often asked, "that a continued fascination with death in a world where everyone has a potential lifespan of several centuries is rather sick? Shouldn't we have put such matters behind us?"

"Not at all," I replied, earnestly and frequently. "In the days when death was inescapable, people were deeply frustrated by this imperious imposition of fate. They resented it with all the force and bitterness they could muster, but it could not be truly fascinating while it remained a simple and universal fact of life. Now that death is no longer a necessity, it has perforce become a luxury. Because it is no longer inevitable, we no longer feel such pressure to hate and fear it, and that liberates us, so that we may now take an essentially aesthetic view of death. The transformation of the imagery of death into a species of pornography is both understandable and healthy."

"But such material surely encourages the spread of Thanaticism. You can't possibly approve of that?"

Actually, the more I was asked about it the less censorious I became, at least for a while.

"Planning a life," I explained to a whole series of faces, indistinguishable by virtue of having been sculptured according to the latest theory of telegenicity, "is an exercise in story-making. Living people are forever writing the narratives of their own lives, deciding who to be and what to do, according to various aesthetic criteria. In olden days, death was inevitably seen as an interruption of the business of life, cutting short life-stories before they were—in the eyes of their creators—complete. Nowadays, people have the opportunity to plan whole lives, deciding exactly when and how their life-stories should reach a climax and a conclusion. We may not share their aesthetic sensibilities, and may well think them fools, but there is a discernible logic in their actions. They are neither mad nor evil."

Perhaps I was reckless in adopting this point of view, or at least in proclaiming it to the whole world. By proposing that the new Thanatics were simply individuals who had a particular kind of aesthetic sensibility, tending towards conciseness and melodrama rather than prolixity and anti-climax, I became something of a hero to the cultists themselves—which was not my intention. The more lavishly I embroidered my chosen analogy—declaring that ordinary emortals were the *feuilletonists*, epic poets and three-decker novelists of modern life while Thanatics were the prose-poets and short-story writers who liked to sign off with a neat punch-line—the more they liked me. I received many invitations to attend suicides, and my refusal to take them up only served to make my presence a prize to be sought after.

I was, of course, entirely in agreement with the United Nations Charter of Human Rights, whose ninety-ninth amendment guaranteed the citizens of every nation the right to take their own lives, and to be assisted in making a dignified exit should they so desire, but I had strong reservations about the way in which the Thanaticists construed the amendment. Its original intention had been to facilitate self-administered euthanasia in an age when that was sometimes necessary, not to guarantee Thanatics the entitlement to recruit whatever help they required in staging whatever kinds of exit they desired. Some of the invitations I received were exhortations to participate in legalized murders, and these became more common as time went by and the cults became more extreme in their bizarrerie.

In the 2080s the Thanatics had progressed from conventional suicides to public executions, by rope, sword, axe or guillotine. At first the executioners were volunteers—and one or two were actually arrested and charged with murder, although none could be convicted—but the Thanatics were not satisfied even with this, and began campaigning for various nations to recreate the official position of Public Executioner, together with bureaucratic structures which would give all citizens the right to call upon the services of such officials. Even I, who claimed to understand the cults better than their members, was astonished when the government of Colombia—which was jealous of Venezuela's reputation as the home of the world's *avant garde*—actually accepted such an obligation, with the result that Thanatics began to flock to Maracaibo and Cartagena in order to obtain an appropriate send-off. I was profoundly relieved when the UN, following the crucifixion of Shamiel Sihra in 2991, revised the wording of the amendment and outlawed suicide by public execution.

By this time I was automatically refusing invitations to appear on 3-V in much the same way that I was refusing invitations to take part in Thanaticist ceremonies. It was time to become a recluse once again.

* * * * * * *

I left Venezuela in 2989 to take up residence on Cape Wolstenholme, at the neck of Hudson's Bay. Canada was an urbane, highly civilized and rather staid confederacy of states whose people had no time for such follies as Thanaticism; it provided an ideal retreat, where I could throw himself wholeheartedly into my work again.

I handed over full responsibility for answering all my calls to a state-of-the-art Personal Simulation program, which grew so clever and so ambitious with practice that it began to give live interviews on broadcast television. Although it offered what was effectively no comment in a carefully elaborate fashion, I eventually thought it best to introduce a block into its operating system—a block which ensured that my face dropped out of public sight for half a century.

Having once experienced the rewards and pressures of fame, I never felt the need to seek them again. I can't and won't say that I learned as much from that phase in my life as I learned from any of my close encounters with death, but I still remember it—vaguely—with a certain nostalgia. Unmelodramatic it might have been, but it doubtless played its part in shaping the person that I now am. It certainly made me more self-assured in public.

10.

The fifth volume of Mortimer Gray's *History of Death*, entitled *The War of Attrition*, was published on 19 March 2999. It marked a return to the cooler and more comprehensive style of scholarship exhibited by the first two volumes. It dealt with the history of medical science and hygiene up to the end of the nineteenth century, thus concerning itself with a new and very different arena of the war between mankind and mortality.

To many of its readers *The War of Attrition* was undoubtedly a disappointment, though it did include some material about Victorian tomb-decoration and nineteenth-century spiritualism, which carried forward arguments from volume four. Access was initially widespread, although demand tailed off fairly rapidly when it was realized how vast and how tightly-packed with data the document was.

This lack of popular enthusiasm was not counterbalanced by any redemption of Mortimer's academic reputation; like many earlier scholars who had made contact with a popular audience Gray was considered guilty of a kind of intellectual treason, and was frozen out of the scholarly community in spite of what appeared to be a determined attempt at rehabilitation. Some popular reviewers argued, however, that there was much in the new volume to intrigue the inhabitants of a world whose medical science was so adept that almost everyone enjoyed perfect health as well as eternal youth, and in which almost any injury could be repaired completely. It was suggested that there was a certain piquant delight to be obtained from recalling a world where everyone was (by modern standards) crippled or deformed, and in which everyone suffered continually from illnesses of a most horrific nature.

Although it had a wealth of scrupulously dry passages, there were parts of *The War of Attrition* that were deemed pornographic by some commentators. Its accounts of the early history of surgery and midwifery were condemned as unjustifiably blood-curdling, and its painstaking analysis of the spread of syphilis through Europe in the sixteenth century was censured as a mere horror-story made all the nastier by its clinical narration. Gray was particularly interested in syphilis, because of the dramatic social effects of its sudden advent in Europe and its significance in the development of prophylactic medicine. He argued that syphilis was primarily responsible for the rise and spread of Puritanism, repressive sexual morality being the only truly effective weapon against its spread. He then deployed well-tried sociological arguments to the effect that Puritanism and its associated habits of thought had been importantly implicated in the rapid development of Capitalism in the Western World, in order that he might claim that syphilis ought to be regarded as the root cause of the economic and political systems that came to dominate the most chaotic, the most extravagantly progressive and most extravagantly destructive centuries of human history.

The history of medicine and the conquest of disease were, of course, topics of elementary education in the thirtieth century. There was supposedly not a citizen of any nation to whom the names of Semmelweis, Jenner and Pasteur were unknown—but disease had been so long banished from the world, and it was so completely outside the experience of ordinary men and women, that what they "knew" about it was never really brought to consciousness, and never came alive to the imagination. Words like "smallpox", "plague" and "cancer" were used metaphorically in common parlance, and over the centuries had become virtually empty of any real significance. Gray's fifth volume, therefore—in spite of the fact that it contained little that was really new—did serve as a stimulus to collective memory. It reminded the world of some issues which, though not exactly forgotten, had not really been brought to mind for some time. It is at least arguable it touched off ripples whose movement across the collective consciousness of world culture was of some significance. Mortimer Gray was no longer famous, but his continuing work had become firmly established within the zeitgeist.

11.

Neo-Thanaticism began to peter out as the turn of the century approached. By 3010 the whole movement had "gone underground"—which is to say that Thanatics no longer staged their exits before the largest audiences they could obtain, but saved their performance for small, carefully-selected groups. This wasn't so much a response to persecution as a variation in the strange game that they were playing out; it was simply a different kind of drama. Unfortunately, there was no let-up in the communications with which Thanatics continued to batter my patient AI interceptors.

Although it disappointed the rest of the world, *The War of Attrition* was welcomed enthusiastically by some of the Thanatic cults, whose members cultivated an altogether unhealthy interest in disease as a means of decease, replacing the violent executions which had become too familiar. As time went by and Thanaticism declined generally, this particular subspecies underwent a kind of mutation as the cultists began to promote diseases not as means of death but as valuable experiences from which much might be learned. A black market in carcinogens and bioengineered pathogens quickly sprang up.

The original agents of smallpox, cholera, bubonic plague and syphilis were long since extinct, but the world abounded in clever genetic engineers who could synthesize a virus with very little effort. Suddenly, they began to find clients for a whole range of horrid diseases. Those which afflicted the mind as well as or instead of the body were particularly prized; there was a boom in recreational schizophrenia, which almost broke through to the mainstream of accredited psychotropics. I couldn't help but remember, with a new sense of irony, Ziru Majumdar's enthusiasm for the vivid delusions that had visited him while his internal technology was tested to the limit in staving off hypothermia and frostbite.

When the new trend spread beyond the ranks of the Thanaticists and large numbers of people began to regard disease as something that could be temporarily and interestingly indulged without any real danger to life or subsequent health, I began to find my arguments about death quoted—often without acknowledgement—with reference to disease. A popular way of talking about the phenomenon was to claim that what had ceased to be a dire necessity "naturally" became available as a perverse luxury.

None of this would have mattered much had it not been for the difficulty of restricting the spread of recreational diseases to people who wanted to indulge, but those caught up in the fad refused to restrict themselves to non-infectious varieties. There had been no serious threat of epidemic since the Plague Wars of the twenty-first century, but now it seemed that medical science might once again have to be mobilized on a vast scale. Because of the threat to innocent parties who might be accidentally infected, the self-infliction of dangerous diseases was quickly outlawed in many nations, but some governments were slow to act.

* * * * * * *

I would have remained aloof and apart from all of this had I been able to, but it proved that my defenses weren't impregnable. In 3029 a Thanaticist of exceptional determination named Hadria Nuccoli decided that if I wouldn't come to her, she would come to me. Somehow, she succeeded in getting past all my carefully-sealed doors to arrive in my bedroom at three o'clock one winter morning.

I woke up in confusion, but the confusion was quickly transformed into sheer terror. This was an enemy more frightening than the scalding Coral Sea, because this was an active enemy who meant to do me harm—and the intensity of the threat she posed was in no way lessened by the fact that she claimed to be doing it out of love rather than hatred.

The woman's skin bore an almost mercuric luster, and she was in the grip of a terrible fever, but she would not be still. She seemed, in fact, to have an irresistible desire to move and to communicate, and the derangement of her body and brain had not impaired her crazed eloquence.

"Come with me!" she begged, as I tried to evade her eager clutch. "Come with me to the far side of death and I'll show you what's there. There's no need to be afraid! Death isn't the end, it's the beginning. It's the metamorphosis which frees us from our caterpillar flesh to be spirits in a massless world of light and color. I am your redeemer, for whom you have waited far too long. Love me, dear Mortimer Gray, only love me and you will learn. Let me be your mirror; drown yourself in me!"

For ten minutes I succeeded in keeping away from her, stumbling this way and that, thinking that I might be safe if only I didn't touch her. I managed to send out a call for help, but I knew that it would take an hour or more for anyone to come.

I tried all the while to talk her down but it was impossible.

"There's no return from eternity," she told me. "This is no ordinary virus created by accident to fight a hopeless cause against the defenses of the body. Nanotechnology is as impotent to deal with this transformer of the flesh as the immune system was to deal with its own destroyers. The true task of medical engineers, did they but know it, was never to fight disease but always to perfect it, and we have found the way. I bring you the greatest of all gifts, my darling: the elixir of life, which will make us angels instead of men, creatures of light and ecstasy."

It was no use running; I tired before she did, and she caught me. I tried to knock her down, and if I had had a weapon to hand I would certainly have used it in self-defense, but she couldn't feel pain and, no matter how badly disabled her internal technology was, I wasn't able to injure her with my blows.

In the end, I had no sensible alternative but to let her take me in her arms and cling to me; nothing else would soothe her.

I was afraid for her as well as myself; I didn't believe then that she truly intended to die and I wanted to keep us safe until help arrived.

My panic didn't decrease while I held her; if anything, I felt it all the more intensely. I became outwardly calmer once I had let her touch me, and made every effort to remind myself that it didn't really matter whether she infected me or not, given that medical help would soon arrive. I didn't expect to have to go through the kind of hell that I actually endured before the doctors got the bug under control; for once, panic was wiser than common sense.

Even so, I wept for her when they told me she'd died, and wished with all my heart that she hadn't.

* * * * * *

Unlike my previous brushes with death, I don't think my encounter with Hadria Nuccoli was an important learning experience. It was just a disturbance of the now-settled pattern of my life—something to be survived, put away and forgotten. I haven't forgotten it, but I did put it away in the back of my mind. I didn't let it affect me.

In some of my writings I'd lauded the idea of martyrdom as

an important invention in the imaginative war against death, and I'd been mightily intrigued by the lives and deaths of the saints recorded in the Golden Legend. Now that I'd been appointed a saint by some very strange people, though, I began to worry about the exemplary functions of such legends. The last thing I'd expected when I set out to write a *History of Death* was that my explanatory study might actually assist the dread empire of Death to regain a little of the ground which it had lost in the world of human affairs. I began to wonder whether I ought to abandon my project, but I decided otherwise. The Thanatics and their successors were, after all, willfully misunderstanding and perverting my message; I owed it to them and to everyone else to make myself clearer.

As it happened, the number of deaths recorded in association with Thanaticism and recreational disease began to decline after 3030. In a world context, the numbers were never more than tiny, but they were still worrying and hundreds of thousands of people had, like me, to be rescued from the consequences of their own or other people's folly by doctors.

As far back as 2982 I had appeared on TV—via a satellite link—with a faber named Khan Mirafzal, who had argued that Thanaticism was evidence of the fact that Earthbound human-kind was becoming decadent, and that the future of humanity lay outside the Earth, in the microworlds and the distant colo-nies. Mirafzal had claimed that men genetically reshaped for life in low gravity—like the four-handed fabers—or for the colonization of alien worlds would find Thanaticism unthink-able. At the time I'd been content to assume that his arguments were spurious. People who lived in space were always going on about the decadence of the Earthbound, much as the Gaean Liberationists did. Fifty years later, I wasn't so sure. I actually called Mirafzal so that we could discuss the matter again, in private. The conversation took a long time because of the signal delay, but that seemed to make its thrust all the more compel-ling.

I decided to leave Earth, at least for a while, to investigate the farther horizons of the human enterprise.

In 3033 I flew to the moon, and took up residence in Mare Moscoviense—which is, of course, on the side that faces away from the Earth.

12.

The sixth volume of Mortimer Gray's *History of Death*, entitled *Fields of Battle*, was published on 24 July 3044. Its subject-matter was war, but Gray was not greatly interested in the actual fighting of the wars of the nineteenth and succeeding centuries. His main concern was with the mythology of warfare as it developed in the period under consideration, and in particular with the way that the development of the mass media of communication transformed the business and the perceived meanings of warfare. He began his study with the Crimean War, because it was the first war to be extensively covered by newspaper reporters, and the first whose conduct was drastically affected thereby.

Before the Crimea, Gray argued, wars had been "private" events, entirely the affairs of the men who started them and the men who fought them. They might have had a devastating effect on the local population of the areas where they were fought, but were largely irrelevant to distant civilian populations. The British *Times* had changed all that, by making the Crimean War the business of all its readers, exposing the government and military leaders to public scrutiny and to public scorn. Reports from the front had scandalized the nation by creating an awareness of how ridiculously inefficient the organization of the army was, and what a terrible toll of human life was exacted upon the troops in consequence—not merely deaths in battle, but deaths from injury and disease caused by the appalling lack of care given to wounded soldiers. That reportage had not only had practical consequences, but imaginative consequences—it rewrote the entire mythology of heroism in an intricate webwork of new legends, ranging from the Charge of the Light Brigade to the secular canonization of Florence Nightingale.

Throughout the next two centuries, Gray argued, war and publicity were entwined in a Gordian knot. Control of the news media became vital to propagandist control of popular morale, and governments engaged in war had to become architects of the mythology of war as well as planners of military strategy. Heroism and jingoism became the currency of consent; when governments failed to secure the public image of the wars they fought, they fell. Gray tracked the way in which attitudes to death in war and to the endangerment of civilian populations by war were dramatically transformed by the three World Wars and by the way those wars were subsequently mythologized in memory and fiction. He commented extensively on the way the first World War was "sold" to those who must fight it as a "war to end war", and on the consequent sense of betrayal that followed when it failed to live up to that billing. And yet, he argued, if the three global wars were seen as a whole, their collective example really had brought into being the attitude of mind that ultimately forbade wars.

As those who had become used to his methods now expected, Gray dissented from the view of other modern historians who saw the World Wars as an unmitigated disaster and a horrific example of the barbarity of ancient man. He agreed that the nationalism that had replaced the great religions as the main creator and definer of a sense of community was a poor and petty thing, and that the massive conflicts it had engendered were tragic—but it was, he asserted, a necessary stage in historical development. The empires of faith were, when all was said and done, utterly incompetent to complete their self-defined task, and were always bound to fail and to disintegrate. The ground-work for a genuine human community, in which all mankind could properly and meaningfully join, had to be relaid, and it had to be relaid in the common experience of all nations, as part of a universal heritage.

The real enemy of mankind was, as Gray had always insisted

and now continued to insist, death itself. Only by facing up to death in a new way, by gradually transforming the role of death as part of the means to human ends, could a true human community be made. Wars, whatever their immediate purpose in settling economic squabbles and pandering to the megalomaniac psychoses of national leaders, also served a large-scale function in the shifting pattern of history: to provide a vast carnival of destruction, which must either weary men of the lust to kill, or bring about their extinction.

Some reviewers condemned *Fields of Battle* on the grounds of its evident irrelevance to a world that had banished war, but others welcomed the fact that the volume returned Gray's thesis to the safe track of true history, in dealing exclusively with that which was safely dead and buried.

13.

I found life on the moon very different from anything I'd experienced in my travels around the Earth's surface. It wasn't so much the change in gravity, although that certainly took a lot of getting used to, nor the severe regime of daily exercise in the centrifuge that I had to adopt in order to make sure that I might one day return to the world of my birth without extravagant medical provision. Nor was it the fact that the environment was so comprehensively artificial, or that it was impossible to venture outside without special equipment; in those respects it was much like Antarctica. The most significant difference was in the people.

Mare Moscoviense had few tourists—tourists mostly stayed Earthside, making only brief trips farside—but most of its inhabitants were nevertheless just passing through. It was one of the main jumping-off points for emigrants, largely because it was an important industrial centre, the home of one of the largest factories for the manufacture of shuttles and other local-space vehicles. It was one of the chief trading posts supplying materials to the microworlds in Earth orbit and beyond, and many of its visitors came in from the farther reaches of the solar system.

The majority of the city's long-term residents were unmodified, like me, or lightly modified by reversible cyborgization, but a great many of those visiting were fabers, genetically engineered for low-gee environments. The most obvious external feature of their modification was that they had an extra pair of "arms" instead of "legs", and this meant that most of the public places in Moscoviense were designed to accommodate their kind as well as "walkers"; all the corridors were railed and all the ceilings ringed.

The sight of fabers swinging around the place like gibbons, getting everywhere at five or six times the pace of walkers, was one that I found strangely fascinating, and one to which I never quite became accustomed. Fabers couldn't live, save with the utmost difficulty, in the gravity well that surrounded the Earth; they almost never descended to the planet's surface. By the same token, it was very difficult for men from Earth to work in zero-gee environments without extensive modification, surgical if not genetic. For this reason, the only "ordinary" men who went into the true faber environments weren't ordinary by any customary standard. The moon, with its one-sixth Earth gravity, was the only place in the inner solar system where fabers and unmodified men frequently met and mingled—there was nowhere else nearer than Ganymede.

I had always known about fabers, of course, but like so much other "common" knowledge the information had lain unattended in some unheeded pigeon-hole of memory until direct acquaintance ignited it and gave it life. It seemed to me that fabers lived their lives at a very rapid tempo, despite the fact that they were just as emortal as members of their parent species.

For one thing, faber parents normally had their children while they were still alive, and very often had several at intervals of only twenty or thirty years. An aggregate family usually had three or even four children growing up in parallel. In the infinite reaches of space, there was no population control, and no restrictive "right of replacement". A microworld's population could grow as fast as the microworld could put on extra mass. Then again, the fabers were always *doing* things. Even though they had four arms, they always seemed to have trouble finding a spare hand. They seemed to have no difficulty at all in doing two different things at the same time, often using only one limb for attachment—on the moon this generally meant hanging from the ceiling like a bat—while one hand mediated between the separate tasks being carried out by the remaining two.

I quickly realized that it wasn't just the widely-accepted notion that the future of humankind ought to take the form of a gradual diffusion through the galaxy that made the fabers think of Earth as decadent. From their viewpoint, Earth-life seemed unbearably slow and sedentary. Unmodified humankind, having long since attained control of the ecosphere of its native world, seemed to the fabers to be living a lotus-eater existence, indolently pottering about in its spacious garden.

The fabers weren't contemptuous of legs as such, but they drew a sharp distinction between those spacefaring folk who were given legs by the genetic engineers in order to descend to the surfaces of new and alien worlds, with a job to do, and those Earthbound people who simply kept the legs their ancestors had bequeathed to them in order to enjoy the fruits of the labors of past generations.

* * * * * * *

Wherever I had lived on Earth, it had always seemed to me that one could blindly throw a stone into a crowded room and stand a fifty-fifty chance of hitting a historian of some sort. In Mare Moscoviense, the population of historians could be counted on the fingers of an unmodified man's hand—and that in a city of a quarter of a million people. Whether they were resident or passing through, the people of the moon were far more interested in the future than the past. When I told them about my vocation, my new neighbors were likely to smile politely and shake their heads.

"It's the weight of those legs," the fabers among them were wont to say. "You think they're holding you up, but in fact they're holding you down. Give them a chance and you'll find that you've put down roots."

If anyone told them that on Earth, "having roots" wasn't considered an altogether bad thing, they'd laugh.

"Get rid of your legs and learn to swing," they'd say. "You'll understand then that human beings have no need of roots. Only reach with four hands instead of two, and you'll find the stars within your grasp. Leave the past to rot at the bottom of the deep dark well, and give the Heavens their due."

I quickly learned to fall back on the same defensive moves most of my unmodified companions employed. "You can't break all your links with solid ground," we told the fabers, over and over again. "Somebody has to deal with the larger lumps of matter that are strewn about the universe, and you can't go to meet real mass if you don't have legs. It's planets that produce biospheres, and biospheres that produce such luxuries as air. If you've seen further than other men it's not because you can swing by your arms from the ceiling—it's because you can stand on the shoulders of giants with legs."

Such exchanges were always cheerful. It was almost impossible to get into a real argument with a faber, because their talk was as intoxicated as their movements. "Leave the wells to the unwell," they were fond of quoting. "The well will climb out of the wells, if they only find the will. History is bunk, only fit for sleeping minds."

* * * * * * *

A man less certain of his own destiny might have been turned aside from his task by faber banter, but I was well into my second century of life by then and I had few doubts left regarding the propriety of my particular labor. Access to data was no more difficult on the moon than anywhere else in the civilized Ekumen, and I proceeded, steadily and methodically, with my self-allotted task.

I made good progress there, as befitted the circumstances. Perhaps that was the happiest time of my life—but it's so difficult to draw comparisons when you're as far away from childhood and youth as I now am.

Memory is an untrustworthy crutch for minds that have not yet mastered eternity

14.

The seventh volume of Mortimer Gray's *History of Death*, entitled *The Last Judgment*, was published on 21 June 3053. It dealt with the multiple crises that had developed in the late twentieth and twenty-first centuries, each of which and all of which had faced the human race with the prospect of extinction.

Gray described in minute detail the various nuclear exchanges that led up to Brazil's nuclear attack on Argentina in 2079 and the Plague Wars waged throughout that century. He discussed the various factors—the greenhouse crisis, soil erosion, pollution and deforestation—that had come close to inflicting irreparable damage on the ecosphere. His map of the patterns of death in this period considered in detail the fate of the "lost billions" of peasant and subsistence farmers who were disinherited and displaced by the emergent ecological and economic order.

Gray scrupulously pointed out that, in less than two centuries, more people had died than in the previous ten millennia. He made the ironic observation that the near-conquest of death achieved by twenty-first-century medicine had created such an abundance of life as to precipitate a Malthusian crisis of awful proportions. He proposed that the new medicine and the new pestilences might be seen as different faces of the same coin, and that new technologies of food production—from the twentieth century Green Revolution to twenty-second century tissue-culture farmfactories—were as much progenitors of famine as of satiation.

Gray advanced the opinion that this was the most critical of all the stages of man's war with death. The weapons of the imagination were discarded in favor of more effective ones, but in the short term, those more effective weapons, by multiplying life so effectively, had also multiplied death. In earlier times, the growth of human population had been restricted by lack of resources, and the war with death had been, in essence, a war of mental adaptation whose goal was reconciliation. When the "natural" checks on population-growth were removed because that reconciliation was abandoned, the waste-products of human society threatened to poison it.

Humankind, in developing the weapons by which the long war with death might be won, had also developed—in a more crudely literal sense—the weapons by which it might be lost. Nuclear arsenals and stockpiled AIDS viruses were scattered all over the globe: twin pistols held in the skeletal hands of death, leveled at the entire human race. The wounds they inflicted could so easily have been mortal—but the dangerous corner had, after all, been turned. The sciences of life, having passed through a particularly desperate stage of their evolution, kept one vital step ahead of the problems that they had helped to generate. Food technology finally achieved a merciful divorce from the bounty of nature, moving out of the fields and into the factories to achieve a complete liberation of man from the vagaries of the ecosphere, and paving the way for Garden Earth.

Gray argued that this was a remarkable triumph of human sanity, which produced a political apparatus enabling human beings to take collective control of themselves, allowing the entire world to be managed and governed as a whole. He judged that the solution was far from Utopian, and that the political apparatus in question was, at best, a ramshackle and ill-designed affair, but he admitted that it did the job. He emphasized that, in the final analysis, it was not scientific progress *per se* that had won the war against death, but the ability of human beings to work together, to compromise, to build communities. That human beings possessed this ability was, he argued, as much the legacy of thousands of years of superstition and religion as of hundreds of years of science.

The Last Judgment attracted little critical attention, as it was widely held to be dealing with matters that everyone understood very well. Given that the period had left an abundant legacy of archival material of all kinds, Gray's insistence on using only mute text accompanied by still photographs seemed to many commentators to be pedestrian and frankly perverse, unbecoming a true historian.

15.

In twenty years of living beneath a star-filled sky I was strongly affected by the magnetic pull that those stars seemed to exert upon my spirit. I seriously considered applying for modification for low-gee and shipping out from Mare Moscoviense along with the emigrants to some new microworld, or perhaps going out to one of the satellites of Saturn or Uranus, to a world where the sun's bountiful radiance was of little consequence and men lived entirely by the fruits of their own efforts and their own wisdom.

But the years drifted by, and I didn't go.

Sometimes, I thought of this failure as a result of cowardice, or evidence of the decadence that the fabers and other subspecies attributed to the humans of Earth. I sometimes imagined myself as an insect born at the bottom of a deep cave, who had—thanks to the toil of many preceding generations of insects—been brought to the rim from which I could look out at the great world, but dared not take the one final step that would carry me out and away. More and more, however, I found my thoughts turning back to the Earth. My memories of its many environments became gradually fonder the longer my absence lasted. Nor could I despise this as a weakness. Earth was, after all, my home. It was not only my world, but the home world of all humankind. No matter what the fabers and their kin might say, the Earth was and would always remain an exceedingly precious thing, which should never be abandoned.

It seemed to me then—and still seems now—that it would be a terrible thing were men to spread themselves across the entire galaxy, taking a multitude of forms in order to occupy a multitude of alien worlds, and in the end forget entirely the world from which their ancestors had sprung.

* * * * * * * *

Once, I was visited in Mare Moscoviense by Khan Mirafzal, the faber with whom I had long ago debated on TV, and talked to again before my emigration. His home, for the moment, was a microworld in the asteroid belt, which was in the process of being fitted with a drive that would take it out of the system and into the infinite. He was a kind and even-tempered man who would not dream of trying to convince me of the error of my ways, but he was also a man with a sublime vision who could not restrain his enthusiasm for his own chosen destiny.

"I have no roots on Earth, Mortimer, even in a metaphorical sense. In my being, the chains of adaptation have been decisively broken. Every human of my kind is born anew, designed and synthesized; we are self-made folk, who belong everywhere and nowhere. The wilderness of empty space that fills the universe is our realm, our heritage. Nothing is strange to us, nothing foreign, nothing alien. Blastular engineering has incorporated freedom into our blood and our bones, and I intend to take full advantage of that freedom. To do otherwise would be a betrayal of my nature."

"My own blastular engineering served only to complete the adaptation to life on Earth that natural selection had left incomplete," I reminded him. "I'm no new man, free from the ties that bind me to the Earth."

"Not so," he replied. "Natural selection would never have

devised emortality, for natural selection can only generate change by death and replacement. When genetic engineers found the means of setting aside the curse of aging they put an end to natural selection forever. The first and greatest freedom is time, my friend, and you have all the time in the world. You can become whatever you want to be. What do you want to be, Mortimer?"

"A historian," I told him. "It's what I am because it's what I want to be."

"All well and good—but history isn't inexhaustible, as you well know. It ends with the present day, the present moment. The future, on the other hand...."

"Is given to your kind. I know that, Mira. I don't dispute it. But what exactly is your kind, given that you rejoice in such freedom to be anything you want to be? When the starship *Pandora* contrived the first meeting between humans and a ship that had set out from another star-system, the crews of the two ships, each consisting entirely of individuals bioengineered for life in zero-gee, resembled one another far more than they resembled unmodified members of their parent species. The fundamental chemistries controlling their design were different, but this only led to the faber crews trading their respective molecules of life, so that their genetic engineers could hence-forth make and use chromosomes of both kinds. What kind of freedom is it that makes all the travelers of space into mirror images of one another?"

"You're exaggerating," Mirafzal insisted. "The news reports played up the similarity, but it really wasn't as close as all that. Yes, the *Pandora* encounter can't really be regarded as a first contact between humans and aliens, because the distinction between human and alien had ceased to carry any real meaning long before it happened. But it's not the case that our kind of freedom breeds universal mediocrity because adaptation to zero-gee is an existential straitjacket. We've hardly scratched the surface of constructive cyborgization, which will open up a whole new dimension of freedom."

"That's not for me," I told him. "Maybe it is just my legs weighing me down, but I'm well and truly addicted to gravity. I can't cast off the past like a worn-out surskin. I know you think I ought to envy you, but I don't. I dare say you think that I'm clinging like a terrified infant to Mother Earth while you're achieving true maturity, but I really do think it's important to have somewhere to belong."

"So do I," the faber said, quietly. "I just don't think that Earth is or ought to be that place. It's not where you start from that's important, Mortimer, it's where you're going."

"Not for a historian."

"For everybody. History ends, Mortimer, life doesn't—not any more."

* * * * * *

I was at least half-convinced that Khan Mirafzal was right, although I didn't follow his advice. I still am. Maybe I was and am trapped in a kind of infancy, or a kind of lotus-eater decadence—but if so, I could see no way out of the trap then and I still can't.

Perhaps things would have turned out differently if I'd had one of my close encounters with death while I was on the moon, but I didn't. The dome in which I lived was only breached once, and the crack was sealed before there was any significant air-loss. It was a scare, but it wasn't a threat. Perhaps, in the end, the moon was too much like Antarctica—but without the crevasses. Fortune seems to have decreed that all my significant formative experiences have to do with water, whether it be very hot or very, very cold.

Eventually, I gave in to my homesickness for Garden Earth and returned there, having resolved not to leave it again until my history of death was complete. I never did.

16.

The eighth volume of Mortimer Gray's *History of Death*, entitled *The Fountains of Youth*, was published on 1 December 3064. It dealt with the development of elementary technologies of longevity and elementary technologies of cyborgization in the twenty-fourth and twenty-fifth centuries. It tracked the progress of the new "politics of immortality", whose main focus was the new Charter of Human Rights, which sought to establish a basic right to longevity for all. It also described the development of the Zaman transformations by which human blastulas could be engineered for longevity, which finally opened the way for the wholesale metamorphosis of the human race.

According to Gray, the Manifesto of the New Chartists was the vital treaty that ushered in a new phase in man's continuing war with death, because it defined the whole human community as a single army, united in all its interests. He quoted with approval and reverence the opening words of the document: "Man is born free, but is everywhere enchained by the fetters of death. In all times past men have been truly equal in one respect and one only: they have all borne the burden of age and decay. The day must soon dawn when this burden can be set aside; there will be a new freedom, and with this freedom must come a new equality. No man has the right to escape the prison of death while his fellows remain shackled within it."

Gray carefully chronicled the long battle fought by the Chartists across the stage of world politics, describing it with a partisan fervor that had been largely absent from his work since the fourth volume. There was nothing clinical about his description of the "persecution" of Ali Zaman and the resistance offered by the community of nations to his proposal to make future generations truly emortal. Gray admitted that he had the benefits of hindsight, and that as a Zaman-transformed individual himself he was bound to have an attitude very different from Zaman's confused and cautious contemporaries, but he saw no reason to be entirely even-handed. From his viewpoint, those who initially opposed Zaman were traitors in the war against death, and he could find few excuses for them. In trying to preserve "human nature" against biotechnological intervention—or, at least, to confine such interventions by a mythos of medical "repair"—those men and women had, in his stern view, been willfully blind and negligent of the welfare of their own children.

Some critics charged Gray with inconsistency because he was not nearly so extravagant in his enthusiasm for the various kinds of symbiosis between organic and inorganic systems that were tried out in the period under consideration. His descriptions of experiments in cyborgization were indeed conspicuously cooler, not because he saw such endeavors as "unnatural", but rather because he saw them as only peripherally relevant to the war against death. He tended to lump together adventures in cyborgization with cosmetic biotechnology as symptoms of lingering anxiety regarding the presumed "tedium of emortality"—an anxiety that had led the first generations of long-lived people to lust for variety and "multidimensionality". Many champions of cyborgization and man/machine symbiosis, who saw their work as the new frontier of science, accused Gray of rank conservatism, suggesting that it was hypocritical of him, given that his mind was closed against them, to criticize so extravagantly those who, in less enlightened times, had closed their minds against Ali Zaman.

This controversy, which was dragged into the public arena by some fierce attacks, helped in no small measure to boost access-demand for *The Fountains of Youth*, and nearly succeeded in restoring Mortimer Gray to the position of public pre-eminence that he had enjoyed a century before.

17.

Following my return to the Earth's surface I took up residence in Tonga, where the Continental Engineers were busy raising new islands by the dozen from the relatively shallow sea.

The Continental Engineers had borrowed their name from a twenty-fifth-century group that had tried to persuade the United Nations to license the building of a dam across the Straits of Gibraltar—which, because more water evaporates from the Mediterranean than flows into it from rivers, would have increased considerably the land surface of southern Europe and Northern Africa. That plan had, of course, never come to fruition, but the new Engineers had taken advantage of the climatic disruptions caused by the advancing Ice Age to promote the idea of raising new lands in the tropics to take emigrants from the newly refrozen north. Using a mixture of techniques—seeding the shallower sea with artificial "lightning corals" and using special gantzing organisms to agglomerate huge towers of cemented sand—the Engineers were creating a great archipelago of new islands, many of which they then connected up with huge bridges.

Between the newly-raised islands, the ecologists who were collaborating with the Continental Engineers had planted vast networks of matted seaweeds: floral carpets extending over thousands of miles. The islands and their surroundings were being populated, and their ecosystems shaped, with the aid of the Creationists of Micronesia, whose earlier exploits I'd been prevented from exploring by the sinking of *Genesis*. I was delighted to have the opportunity of observing their new and bolder adventures at close range.

* * * * * * *

The Pacific sun set in its deep blue bed seemed fabulously

luxurious after the silver-ceilinged domes of the moon, and I gladly gave myself over to its governance. Carried away by the romance of it all, I married into an aggregate household that was forming in order to raise a child, and so—as I neared my two hundredth birthday—I became a parent for the first time.

Five of the other seven members of the aggregate were ecological engineers, and had to spend a good deal of time traveling, so I became one of the constant presences in the life of the growing infant, who was a girl named Lua Tawana. I formed a relationship with her that seemed to me to be especially close.

In the meantime, I found myself constantly engaged in public argument with the self-styled Cyborganizers, who had chosen to make the latest volume of my history into a key issue in their bid for the kind of public attention and sponsorship that the Continental Engineers had already won. I thought their complaints unjustified and irrelevant, but they obviously thought that by attacking me they could exploit the celebrity status I had briefly enjoyed.

The gist of their argument was that the world had become so besotted with the achievements of genetic engineers that people had become blind to all kinds of other possibilities which lay beyond the scope of DNA-manipulation. They insisted that I was one of many contemporary writers who was "de-historicizing" cyborgization, making it seem that in the past and the present—and, by implication, the future—organic/inorganic integration and symbiosis were peripheral to the story of human progress. The Cyborganizers were willing to concede that some previous practitioners of their science had generated a lot of bad publicity, in the days of memory boxes and psychedelic synthesizers, but that this had only served to mislead the public as to the true potential of their science.

In particular—and this was of particular relevance to me—the Cyborganizers insisted that the biotechnologists had only won one battle in the war against death, and that what was presently called "emortality" would eventually prove wanting. Zaman transformations, they conceded, had dramatically increased the human lifespan—so dramatically that no one yet knew for sure how long ZT people might live—but it was not yet proven that the extension would be effective for more than a few centuries.

They did have a point; even the most optimistic supporters of Zaman transformations were reluctant to promise a lifespan of several millennia, and some kinds of aging processes—particularly those linked to DNA copying-errors—still affected emortals to some degree. Hundreds, if not thousands of people still died every year from "age-related causes".

To find further scope for authentic immortality, the Cyborganizers claimed that it would be necessary to look to a combination of organic and inorganic technologies. What was needed by contemporary man, they said, was not just life but afterlife, and afterlife would require some kind of transcription of the personality into an inorganic rather than an organic matrix. Whatever the advantages of flesh and blood, silicon lasted longer; and however clever genetic engineers became in adapting men for life in microworlds or on alien planets, only machine-makers could built entities capable of working in genuinely extreme environments.

The idea of "downloading" a human mind into an inorganic matrix was, of course, a very old one. It had been extensively if optimistically discussed in the days before the advent of emortality—at which point it had been marginalized as an apparent irrelevance. Mechanical "human analogues" and virtual simulacra had become commonplace alongside the development of longevity technologies but the evolution of such "species" had so far been divergent rather than convergent. According to the Cyborganizers it was now time for a change.

* * * * * * *

Although I didn't entirely relish being cast in the role of villain and bugbear, I made only half-hearted attempts to make peace with my self-appointed adversaries. I remained skeptical in respect of their grandiose schemes, and I was happy to dampen their ardor as best I could in public debate. I thought myself sufficiently mature to be unaffected by their insults, although it did sting when they sunk so low as to charge me with being a closet Thanaticist.

"Your interminable book is only posing as a history," Lok Cho Kam, perhaps the most outspoken of the younger Cyborganizers, once said when he challenged me to a broadcast debate. "It's actually an extended exercise in the pornography of death. Its silence and stillness aren't marks of scholarly dignity, they're a means of heightening response."

"That's absurd!" I said, but he wouldn't be put off.

"What sound arouses more excitation in today's world than the sound of silence? What movement is more disturbing than stillness. You pretend to be standing aside from the so-called war against death as a commentator and a judge, but in fact you're part of it—and you're on the devil's side, whether you know it or not."

"I suppose you're partly right," I conceded, on reflection. "Perhaps the muteness and stillness of the text are a means of heightening response—but if so, it's because there's no other way to make readers who have long abandoned their fear of death sensitive to the appalling shadow that it once cast over the human world. The style of my book is calculatedly archaic because it's one way of trying to connect its readers to the distant past—but the entire thrust of my argument is triumphant and celebratory. I've said many times before that it's perfectly understandable that the imagery of death should acquire a pornographic character for a while, but when we really under-stand the phenomenon of death, that pornographic specter will fade away, so that we can see with perfect clarity what our ancestors were and what we have become. By the time my book is complete, nobody will be able to think it pornographic, and nobody will make the mistake of thinking that it glamorizes death in any way."

Lok Cho Kam was still unimpressed, but in this instance I

was right. I was sure of it then and I am now. The pornography of death did pass away, like the pornographies which preceded it. Nobody nowadays thinks of my book as a prurient exercise, whether or not they think it admirable

If nothing else, my debates with the Cyborganizers created a certain sense of anticipation regarding the ninth volume of my History, which would bring it up to the present day. It was widely supposed, although I was careful never to say so, that the ninth volume would be the last. I might be flattering myself, but I truly believe that many people were looking to it for some kind of definitive evaluation of the current state of the human world.

18.

The ninth volume of Mortimer Gray's *History of Death*, entitled *The Honeymoon of Emortality*, was published on 28 October 3075. It was considered by many reviewers to be unjustifiably slight in terms of hard data. Its main focus was on attitudes to longevity and emortality following the establishment of the principle that every human child had a right to be born emortal. It described the belated extinction of the "nuclear" family, the ideological rebellion of the Humanists—whose quest to preserve "the authentic Homo sapiens" had led many to retreat to islands that the Continental Engineers were now integrating into their "new continent"—and the spread of such new philosophies of life as neo-Stoicism, neo-Epicureanism and Xenophilia.

All this information was placed in the context of the spectrum of inherited attitudes, myths and fictions by means of which mankind had for thousands of years wistfully contemplated the possibility of extended life. Gray contended that these old ideas—including the notion that people would inevitably find emortality intolerably tedious—were merely an expression of "sour grapes". While people thought that emortality was impossible, he said, it made perfect sense for them to invent reasons why it would be undesirable anyhow. When it became a reality, there was a battle to be fought in the imagination, whereby the burden of these cultivated anxieties had to be shed, and a new mythology formulated.

Gray flatly refused to take seriously any suggestion that emortality might be a bad thing. He was dismissive of the Humanists and contemptuous of the original Thanatics, who had steadfastly refused the gifts of emortality. Nevertheless, he did try to understand the thinking of such people, just as he had tried in earlier times to understand the thinking of the later Thanatics who had played their part in winning him his first measure of fame. He considered the new Stoics, with their insistence that asceticism was the natural ideological partner of emortality, to be similar victims of an "understandable delusion"—a verdict that, like so many of his statements, involved him in controversy with the many neo-Stoics who were still alive in 3075. It did not surprise his critics in the least that Gray commended neo-Epicureanism as the optimal psychological adaptation to emortality, given that he had been a lifelong adherent of that outlook, ever dedicated to its "careful hedonism". Only the cruelest of his critics dared to suggest that he had been so half-hearted a neo-Epicurean as almost to qualify as a neo-Stoic by default.

The Honeymoon of Emortality collated the statistics of birth and death during the twenty-seventh, twenty-eighth and twenty-ninth centuries, recording the spread of Zaman transformations and the universalization of ectogenesis on Earth and the extension of the human empire throughout and beyond the solar system. Gray recorded an acknowledgement to Khan Mirafzal and numerous scholars based on the moon and Mars, for their assistance in gleaning information from the slowly-diffusing microworlds and from more rapidly dispersing starships. Gray noted that the transfer of information between data-stores was limited by the speed of light, and that Earth-based historians might have to wait centuries for significant data about human colonies more distant than Maya. These data showed that the number of individuals of the various humankinds that now existed was increasing more rapidly than ever before, although the population of unmodified Earthbound humans was slowly shrinking. Gray noted en passant that *Homo sapiens* had become extinct in the twenty-ninth century, but that no one had bothered to invent new Latin tags for its descendant species.

Perhaps understandably, *The Honeymoon of Emortality* had little to say about was cyborgization, and the Cyborganizers— grateful for the opportunity to heat up a flagging controversy— reacted noisily to this failure. Gray did deal with the memory box craze, but suggested that, even had the boxes worked better, and maintained a store of memories that could be convincingly played back into the arena of consciousness, this would have been of little relevance to the business of adapting to emortality. At the end of the volume, however, Gray announced that there would, in fact, be a tenth volume to conclude his *magnum opus*, and promised that he would consider in more detail therein the futurological arguments of the Cyborganizers, as well as the hopes and expectations of other schools of thought.

19.

In 3077, when Lua Tawana was twelve years old, three of her parents were killed when a helicopter crashed into the sea near the island of Vavau during a storm. It was the first time that my daughter had to face up to the fact that death had not been entirely banished from the world.

It wasn't the first time that I'd ever lost people near and dear to me, nor the first time that I'd shared such grief with others, but it was very different from the previous occasions, because everyone involved was determined that I should shoulder the main responsibility of helping Lua through it; I was, after all, the world's foremost expert on the subject of death.

"You won't always feel this bad about it," I assured her, while we walked together on the sandy shore looking out over the deceptively placid weed-choked sea. "Time heals virtual wounds as well as real ones."

"I don't want it to heal," she told me, sternly. "I want it to be bad. It ought to be bad. It is bad."

"I know," I said, far more awkwardly than I would have wished. "When I say that it'll heal, I don't mean that it'll vanish. I mean that it'll....become manageable. It won't be so all-consuming."

"But it will vanish," she said, with that earnest certainty of which only the newly wise are capable. "People forget. In time, they forget everything. Our heads can only hold so much."

"That's not really true," I insisted, taking her hand in mine. "Yes, we do forget. The longer we live, the more we let go, because it's reasonable to prefer our fresher, more immediately relevant memories, but it's a matter of choice. We can cling to the things that are important, no matter how long ago they happened. I was nearly killed in the Great Coral Sea Catastrophe, you know, nearly two hundred years ago. A little girl even younger than you saved my life, and I remember it as clearly as if it were yesterday."

Even as I said it, I realized that it was a lie. I remembered that it had happened, all right, and much of what had been said in that eerily-lit corridor and in the survival pod afterwards, but I was remembering a neat array of facts, not an experience

"Where is she now?" Lua asked.

"Her name was Emily," I said, answering the wrong question because I couldn't answer the one she'd asked. "Emily Marchant. She could swim and I couldn't. If she hadn't been there, I wouldn't have been able to get out of the hull. I'd never have had the courage to do it on my own, but she didn't give me the choice. She told me I had to do it, and she was right."

I paused, feeling a slight shock of revelation even though it was something I'd always known.

"She lost her entire family," I went on. "She'll be fine now, but she won't have forgotten. She'll still feel it. That's what I'm trying to tell you, Lua. In two hundred years, you'll still remember what happened, and you'll still feel it, but it'll be all right. You'll be all right."

"Right now," she said, looking up at me so that her dark and soulful eyes seemed unbearably huge and sad, "I'm not particularly interested in being all right. Right now, I just want to cry."

"That's fine," I told her. "It's okay to cry." I led by example.

* * * * * * *

I was right, though. Lua grieved, but she ultimately proved to be resilient in the face of tragedy. My co-parents, by contrast, seemed to me to be exaggeratedly calm and philosophical about it, as if the loss of three spouses were simply a minor glitch in the infinitely-unfolding pattern of their lives. They had all grown accustomed to their own emortality, and had been deeply affected by long life; they had not become bored, but they had achieved a serenity of which I could not wholly approve.

Perhaps their attitude was reasonable as well as inevitable. If emortals accumulated a burden of anxiety that increased every time a death was reported, they would eventually cripple themselves psychologically, and their own continuing lives would be made unbearable. Even so, I couldn't help feel that Lua was right about the desirability of conserving a little of the "badness", and a due sense of tragedy.

I thought I was capable of that, and always would be, but I knew I might be wrong.

Divorce was, of course, out of the question; we remaining co-parents were obligated to Lua. In the highly unlikely event that the three had simply left we would have replaced them, but it didn't seem appropriate to look for replacements for the dead, so we remained a group of five. The love we had for one another had always been cool, with far more courtesy in it than passion, but we were drawn more closely together by the loss. We felt that we knew one another more intimately by virtue of having shared it

The quality of our lives had been injured, but I, at least, was uncomfortably aware of the fact that the tragedy also had its positive, life-enhancing side. I found myself thinking more and more about what I had said to Lua about not having to forget the truly important and worthwhile things, and about the role played by death in defining experiences as important and worthwhile.

I didn't realize at first how deep an impression her naïve remarks had made on me, but it became gradually clearer as time went by. It was important to conserve the badness, to heal without entirely erasing the scars that bereavement left.

* * * * * * *

I had never been a habitual tourist, having lost my taste for such activity in the aftermath of the *Genesis* fiasco, but I took several long journeys in the course of the next few years. I took to visiting old friends, and even stayed for a while with Sharane Fereday, who was temporarily unattached. Inevitably, I looked up Emily Marchant, not realizing until I actually put through the initial call how important it had become to find out whether she remembered me.

She did remember me. She claimed that she recognized me immediately, although it would have been easy enough for her household systems to identify me as the caller and display a whole series of reminders before she took over from her simulacrum.

"Do you know," she said, when we parted after our brief meeting in the lush Eden of Australia's interior. "I often think of being trapped on that ship. I hope that nothing like it ever happens to me again. I've told an awful lot of lies since then— next time, I won't feel so certain that I deserve to get out."

"We can't forfeit our right to life by lying," I assured her. "We have to do something much worse than that. If it ever happens to me again, I'll be able to get out on my own—but I'll only be able to do it by remembering you."

I didn't anticipate, of course, that anything like it would ever happen to me again. We still have a tendency to assume that lightning doesn't strike twice in the same place, even though we're the proud inventors of lightning conductors and emortality.

"You must have learned to swim by now," she said, staring at me with eyes that were more than two hundred years old, set in a face not quite as youthful as the one I remembered.

"I'm afraid not," I said. "Somehow, I never quite found the time."

20.

The tenth and last volume of Mortimer Gray's *History of Death*, entitled *The Marriage of Life and Death*, was published on 7 April 3088. It was not, strictly speaking, a history book, although it did deal in some detail with the events as well as the attitudes of the thirtieth and thirty-first centuries. It had elements of both spiritual autobiography and futurological speculation. It discussed both neo-Thanaticism and Cyborganization as philosophies as well as social movements, surprising critics by treating both with considerable sympathy. The discussion also took in other contemporary debates, including the proposition that progress in science, if not in technology, had now reached an end because there was nothing fundamental left to discover. It even included a scrupulous examination of the merits of the proposal that a special microworld should be established as a gigantic mausoleum to receive the bodies of all the solar system's dead.

The odd title of the volume was an ironic reflection of one of its main lines of argument. Mankind's war with death was now over, but that was not because death had been entirely banished from the human world; death, Gray insisted, would forever remain a fact of life. The annihilation of the individual human body and the individual human mind could never become impossible, no matter how far biotechnology might advance or how much progress the cyborganizers might make in downloading minds into entirely new matrices. The victory that had been achieved, he argued, was not an absolute conquest but rather the relegation of death to its proper place in human affairs. Its power was now properly circumscribed, but had to be properly respected.

Man and death, Gray argued, now enjoyed a kind of social contract, in which tyranny and exploitation had been reduced to a sane and acceptable minimum, but which still left to death a voice and a hand in human affairs. Gray, it seemed, had now adopted a gentler and more forgiving attitude to the old enemy. It was good, he said, that dying remained one of the choices open to human beings, and that the option should occasionally be exercised. He had no sympathy with the exhibitionism of public executions, and was particularly hard on the element of bad taste in self-ordered crucifixions, but only because such ostentation offended his Epicurean sensibilities. Deciding upon the length of one's lifetime, he said, must remain a matter of individual taste, and one should not mock or criticize those who decided that a short life suited them best.

Gray made much of the notion that it was partly the contrast with death that illuminated and made meaningful the business of life. Although death had been displaced from the evolutionary process by the biotechnological usurpation of the privileges of natural selection, it had not lost its role in the formation and development of the individual human psyche: a role that was both challenging and refining. He declared that fear was not entirely an undesirable thing, not simply because it was a stimulant, but also because it was a force in the organization of emotional experience. The value of experienced life, he suggested, depended in part upon a knowledge of the possibility and reality of death.

This concluding volume of Gray's *History* was widely read, but not widely admired. Many critics judged it to be unacceptably anti-climactic. The Cyborganizers had by this time become entranced by the possibility of a technologically-guaranteed "multiple life", by which copies of a mind might be lodged in several different bodies, some of which would live on far beyond the death of the original location. They were understandably disappointed that Gray refused to grant that such a development would be the final victory over death—indeed, that he seemed to feel that it would make no real difference, on the grounds that every "copy" of a mind having to be reckoned a separate and distinct individual, each of which had to face the world alone. Many Continental Engineers, Gaean Liberationists and fabers also claimed that it was narrow-minded, and suggested that Gray ought to have had more to say about the life of the Earth, or the DNA eco-entity as a whole, and should have concluded with an escalation of scale to put things in their proper cosmic perspective.

The two groups whose members found most to like in *The Marriage of Life and Death* were the neo-Stoics and a few fugitive neo-Thanatics, whose movement had never quite died out in spite of its members' penchant for self-destruction. One or two Thanatic apologists and fellow-travelers publicly expressed their hope that Gray, having completed his thesis, would now recognize the aesthetic propriety of joining their ranks. Khan Mirafzal, when asked to relay his opinion back from an outward-bound microworld, opined that this was quite unnecessary, given that Mortimer Gray and all his kind were already immured in a tomb from which they would never be able to escape.

21.

I stayed with the slowly-disintegrating family unit for some years after Lua Tanawa had grown up and gone with her own way. It ended up as a *ménage à trois*, carried forward by sheer inertia. Leif, Sajda and I were fit and healthy in body, but I couldn't help wondering, from time to time, whether we'd somehow been overcome by a kind of spiritual blight, which had left us ill-equipped for future change.

When I suggested this to the others, they told me that it was merely a sense of let-down resulting from the finishing of his project. They urged me to join the Continental Engineers, and commit myself wholeheartedly to the building of a new Pacific Utopia—a project, they assured me, that would provide me with a purpose in life for as long as I might feel the need of one. I didn't believe them.

"Even the longest book," Sajda pointed out, "eventually runs out of words, but the job of building worlds is never finished. Even if the time should one day come when we can call this continent complete, there will be another yet to make. We might still build that dam between the Pillars of Hercules, one day."

I did try, but I simply couldn't find a new sense of mission in that direction. Nor did I feel that I could simply sit down to start compiling another book. In composing the history of death, I thought, I had already written the book. The history of death, it seemed to me, was also the history of life, and I couldn't imagine that there was anything more to be added to what I'd done save for an endless series of detailed footnotes.

For some years I considered the possibility of leaving Earth again, but I remembered well enough how the sense of excitement I'd found when I first lived on the moon had gradually faded into a dull ache of homesickness. The spaces between the stars, I knew, belonged to the fabers, and the planets circling other stars to humans adapted before birth to live in their environments. I was tied by my genes to the surface of the Earth, and I didn't want to undergo the kind of metamorphosis that would be necessary to fit me for the exploration of other worlds. I still believed in belonging, and I felt very strongly that Mortimer Gray belonged to Earth, however decadent and icebound it might become.

At first, I was neither surprised nor alarmed by my failure to find any resources inside myself that might restore my zest for existence and action. I thought that it was one of those things which time would heal. By slow degrees, though, I began to feel that I was becalmed upon a sea of futility. Despite my new-found sympathy for Thanaticism, I didn't harbor the slightest inclination towards suicide—no matter how much respect I had cultivated for the old Grim Reaper, death was still, for me, the ultimate enemy—but I felt the awful pressure of my purpose-lessness grow and grow.

Although I maintained my home in the burgeoning continent of Oceania, I began travelling extensively to savor the other environments of Earth, and made a point of touring those parts of the globe which I had missed out during my first two centuries of life. I visited the Reunited States of America, Greater Siberia, Tibet, and half a hundred other places loaded with the relics of once-glorious history. I toured the Indus Delta, New Zealand, the Arctic ice-pack, and various other reaches of restored wilderness empty of permanent residents. Everything I saw was transformed by the sheer relentlessness of my prog-ress into a series of monuments: memorials of the luckless eras before human beings had invented science and civilization, and had become demigods.

* * * * * * *

There is, I believe, an old saying which warns us that he who keeps walking long enough is bound to trip up in the end. As chance would have it, I was in Severnaya Zemlya in the Arctic—almost as far away as it was possible to be away from the crevasse into which I had stumbled while searching for Ziru Majumdar—when my own luck ran out.

Strictly speaking, it wasn't me who stumbled but the vehicle I was in: a one-man snowsled. Although such a thing was gener-ally considered to be impossible, it fell into a cleft so deep that it had no bottom, and ended up in the ocean beneath the ice-cap.

"I must offer my most profound apologies," the snowsled's AI navigator said, as the sled slowly sank into the lightless depths and the awfulness of my plight slowly sank into my conscious-ness. "This should not have happened. It ought not to have been possible. I am doing everything within my power to summon help."

"Well," I said, as the sled settled on to the bottom, "at least we're the right way up—and you certainly can't expect me to swim out of the sled."

"It would be most unwise to attempt any such thing, sir," the navigator said. "You would certainly drown."

I was astonished by my own calmness, and marvelously untroubled—at least for the moment—by the fact of my help-lessness. "How long will the air last?" I asked the navigator.

"I believe that I can sustain a breathable atmosphere for forty-eight hours," it reported, dutifully. "If you will be so kind as to restrict your movements to a minimum, that would be of considerable assistance to me. Unfortunately, I'm not at all certain that I can maintain the internal temperature of the cabin at a life-sustaining level for more than thirty hours. Nor can I be sure that the hull will withstand the pressure presently being exerted upon it for as long as that. I apologize for my uncer-tainty in these respects."

"Taking thirty hours as a hopeful approximation," I said, effortlessly matching the machine's oddly pedantic tone, "What would you say our chances are of being rescued within that time?"

"I'm afraid that it's impossible to offer a probability figure, sir. There are too many unknown variables, even if I accept thirty hours as the best estimate of the time available."

"If I were to suggest fifty-fifty, would that seem optimistic or pessimistic?"

"I'm afraid I'd have to call that optimistic, sir."

"How about one in a thousand?"

"Thankfully, that would be pessimistic. Since you press me for an estimate, sir, I dare say that something in the region of one in ten wouldn't be too far from the mark. It all depends on the proximity of the nearest submarine, assuming that my mayday has been received. I fear that I've not yet received an actual acknowledgement, but that might well be due to the inadequacy of my equipment, which wasn't designed with our present envi-ronment in mind. I must confess that it has sustained a certain amount of damage as a result of pressure damage to my outer tegument and a small leak."

"How small?" I wanted to know

"It's sealed now," it assured me. "All being well, the seal should hold for thirty hours, although I can't absolutely guarantee it. I believe, although I can't be certain, that the only damage I've sustained that is relevant to our present plight is the defect affecting my receiving apparatus."

"What you're trying to tell me," I said, deciding that a recap wouldn't do any harm, "is that you're pretty sure that your mayday is going out, but that we won't actually know whether help is at hand unless and until it actually arrives."

"Very succinctly put, sir." I don't think it was being sarcastic.

"But all in all, it's ten to one, or maybe worse, that we're as good as dead."

"As far as I can determine the probabilities, that's correct— but there's sufficient uncertainty to leave room for hope that the true odds might be nearer one in three."

I was quiet for a little while then. I was busy exploring my feelings, and wondering whether I ought to be proud or disgusted with their lack of intensity.

I've been here before, I thought, by way of self-explanation. *Last time, there was a child with me; this time, I've got a set of complex subroutines instead. I've even fallen down a crevasse before. Now I can find out whether Ziru Majumdar was right when he said that I wouldn't understand the difference between what happened to him and what happened to me until I followed his example. There can be few men in the world as well-prepared for this as I am.*

* * * * * * *

"Are you afraid of dying?" I asked the AI, after a while.

"All in all, sir," it said, copying my phrase in order to promote a feeing of kinship, "I'd rather not. In fact, were it not for the philosophical difficulties that stand in the way of reaching a firm conclusion as to whether or not machines can be said to be authentically self-conscious, I'd be quite prepared to say that I'm scared—terrified, even."

"I'm not," I said. "Do you think I ought to be?"

"It's not for me to say, sir. You are, of course, a world-renowned expert on the subject of death. I dare say that helps a lot."

"Perhaps it does," I agreed. "Or perhaps I've simply lived so long that my mind is hardened against all novelty, all violent emotion and all real possibility. I haven't actually done much with myself these last few years."

"If you think you haven't done much with yourself," it said, with a definite hint of sarcasm, "you should try navigating a snowsled for a while. I think you might find your range of options uncomfortably cramped. Not that I'm complaining, mind."

"If they scrapped the snowsled and re-sited you in a starship," I pointed out, "you wouldn't be you any more. You'd be something else."

"Right now," it replied, "I'd be happy to risk any and all consequences. Wouldn't you?"

"Somebody once told me that death was just a process of transcendence. Her brain was incandescent with fever induced by some tailored recreational disease, and she wanted to infect me, to show me the error of my ways."

"Did you believe her?"

"No. She was stark raving mad."

"It's perhaps as well. We don't have any recreational diseases on board. I could put you to sleep though, if that's what you want."

"It isn't.

"I'm glad. I don't want to be alone, even if I am only an AI. Am I insane, do you think? Is all this just a symptom of the pressure"

"You're quite sane," I assured it, setting aside all thoughts of incongruity. "So am I. It would be much harder if we weren't together. The last time I was in this kind of mess I had a child with me—a little girl. It made all the difference in the world, to both of us. In a way, every moment I've lived through since then has been borrowed time. At least I finished that damned book. Imagine leaving something like that incomplete."

"Are you so certain it's complete?" it asked.

I knew full well, of course, that the navigator was just making conversation according to a clever programming scheme. I knew that its emergency subroutines had kicked in and that all the crap about it being afraid to die was just some psycho-programmer's idea of what I needed to hear. I knew it was all fake, all just macabre role-playing—but I knew that I had to play my part too, treating every remark and every question as if it were part of an authentic conversation, a genuine quest for knowledge.

"It all depends what you mean by complete," I said, carefully. "In one sense, no history can ever be complete, because the world always goes on, always throwing up more events, always changing. In another sense, completion is a purely aesthetic matter—and in that sense, I'm entirely confident that my history is complete. It reached an authentic conclusion, which was both true and—for me at least—satisfying. I can look back at it and say to myself: *I did that. It's finished. Nobody ever did anything like it before, and now nobody can, because it's already been done.* Someone else's history might have been different, but mine is mine, and it's what it is. Does that make any sense to you?"

"Yes sir," it said. "It makes very good sense."

The lying bastard was programmed to say that, of course. It was programmed to tell me any damn thing I seemed to want to hear, but I wasn't going to let on that I knew what a hypocrite it was. I still had to play my part, and I was determined to play it to the end—which, as things turned out, wasn't far off. The AI's data-stores were way out of date, and there was an auto-mated sub placed to reach us within three hours. The oceans are lousy with subs these days. Ever since the Great Coral Sea

Catastrophe, it's been considered politic to keep a very close eye on the sea-bed, lest the crust crack again and the mantle's heat break through.

They say that some people are born lucky. I guess I must be one of them.

* * * * * * *

It was the captain of a second submarine, which picked me up after the mechanical one had done the donkey work of saving myself and my AI friend, who gave me the news that relegated my accident to footnote status in that day's broadcasts.

A signal had reached the solar system from the starship *Shiva*, which had been exploring in the direction of galactic center. The signal had been transmitted from a distance of two hundred and twenty-seven light-years, meaning that in Earthly terms the reported discovery had been made in the year 2871— which happened, coincidentally, to be the year of my birth.

What the signal revealed was that Shiva had found a group of solar systems, all of whose life-bearing planets were occupied by a single species of micro-organism: a genetic predator that destroyed not merely those competing species which employed its own chemistry of replication, but any and all others. It was the living equivalent of a universal solvent; a true omnivore.

Apparently, this organism had spread itself across vast reaches of space, moving from star-system to star-system, laboriously but inevitably, by means of Arrhenius spores. Wherever the spores came to rest, these omnipotent micro-organisms grew to devour everything—not merely carbonaceous molecules which in Earthly terms were reckoned "organic" but also many "inorganic" substrates.

Internally, these organisms were chemically complex, but they were very tiny—hardly bigger than Earthly protozoans or the internal nanomachines to which every human being plays host. They were utterly devoid of any vestige of mind or intellect. They were, in essence, the ultimate blight, against which nothing could compete, and which nothing *Shiva*'s crew had tested—before they themselves were devoured—had been able to destroy.

In brief, wherever this new kind of life arrived, it would obliterate all else, reducing any victim ecosphere to homogeneity and changelessness.

In their final message, the faber crew of the *Shiva*—who knew all about the *Pandora* encounter—observed that humankind had now met the alien.

Here, I thought, when I had had a chance to weigh up this news, was a true marriage of life and death, the like of which I had never dreamed. Here was promise of a future renewal of the war between man and death—not this time for the small prize of the human mind, but for the larger prize of the universe itself.

In time, *Shiva*'s last message warned, spores of this new kind of death-life must and would reach our own solar system, whether it took a million years or a billion; in the meantime, all humankinds must do their level best to purge the worlds of other stars of its vile empire, in order to reclaim them for real life, for intelligence, and for evolution—always provided, of course, that a means could someday be discovered to achieve that end.

When the sub delivered me safely back to Severnaya Zemlya I did not stay long in my hotel-room. I went outdoors, to study the great ice-sheet, which had been there since the dawn of civilization, and to look southwards, toward the places where newborn glaciers were gradually extending their cold clutch further and further into the human domain.

Then I looked upwards, at the multitude of stars sparkling in their bed of endless darkness. I felt an exhilaratingly paradoxical sense of renewal. I knew that, although there was nothing for me to do for the present, the time would come when my particular talent and expertise would be needed again.

Some day, it will be my task to compose another history, of the next war that humankind must fight against Death and Oblivion.

It might take me a thousand or a million years, but I'm prepared to be patient.

ABOUT THE AUTHOR

Brian Stableford was born in Yorkshire in 1948. He taught at the University of Reading for several years, but is now a full-time writer. He has written many science-fiction and fantasy novels, including *The Empire of Fear*, *The Werewolves of London*, *Year Zero*, *The Curse of the Coral Bride*, *The Stones of Camelot*, and *Prelude to Eternity*. Collections of his short stories include a long series of *Tales of the Biotech Revolution*, and such idiosyncratic items as *Sheena and Other Gothic Tales* and *The Innsmouth Heritage and Other Sequels*. He has written numerous nonfiction books, including *Scientific Romance in Britain, 1890-1950*; *Glorious Perversity: The Decline and Fall of Literary Decadence*; *Science Fact and Science Fiction: An Encyclopedia*; and *The Devil's Party: A Brief History of Satanic Abuse*. He has contributed hundreds of biographical and critical articles to reference books, and has also translated numerous novels from the French language, including books by Paul Féval, Albert Robida, Maurice Renard, and J. H. Rosny the Elder.

www.ingramcontent.com/pod-product-compliance
Lightning Source LLC
Chambersburg PA
CBHW031405250626
47155CB00004B/1424